# JIMMY MACK

*Strong Love (Side A)*

# John Knight

Published in 2018 by FeedARead.com Publishing

First Edition

Book and cover design by John Knight. Final interior by the author.

A CIP catalogue record for this title is available from the British
Library.

This is a work of fiction. Names, characters, businesses, places,
events, locales, and incidents are either the products of the author's
imagination or used in a **fictitious** manner. Any resemblance to actual
persons, living or dead, or actual events is purely **coincidental.**
Celebrities, singers, bands, groups are mentioned in their historic real
time appearances.

*To Mack, Effy and Angie.*
*May you live long and prosper in readers minds.*
*It's my great pleasure to know you as I do.*
*Without you this novel could not exist.*

*"Love is worth whatever the cost"*
**Françoise Sagan**

# CHAPTER 1

Something About You – The Four Tops (Tamla Motown TMG 542 – 1965)

*Wednesday 21 December 1966*

Mack was not impressed with the reception at the breakfast table. Jane MacKinnon stared at her son's face, covered in tiny pieces of blood-soaked tissue paper. Effy and Grace sat open-mouthed. Even Mack's father, usually hidden behind The Daily Telegraph, stopped reading.

"I thought I'd shown you how to shave?"

"You did. That so-called new Gillette blade you gave me is as blunt as hell. I used it this morning for the second time and look at me! I've shredded my face. Are you sure it was new? When I took it out and had a look, the blade edges were jagged. You'd think I'd used it for sharpening pencils."

"Yes, I'm sure it was new and unused." Robert MacKinnon folded the newspaper, sounding indignant. "It came from a brand-new sealed packet."

Effy and Grace exchanged glances.

Mack's mind drifted into a detached musing as he buttered a slice of toast. Since Effy and Grace had moved in the predominantly masculine character of the household had changed. The bathroom was where he noticed it most. The cabinet shelves bulged with creams, lotions, shampoos, conditioners and sundry products. The attic bedroom where the two girls slept had been transformed into a true boudoir. Even the washing line was a disturbing sign of the times.

The realities of Effy's presence made her more desirable than ever. The sight of her underwear on the washing line billowing in the breeze kept his mind in sharp focus. Would those be the briefs he peeled from her body the next time they made love? Nor was this desire one-sided: Effy wanted him as much as he wanted her. Even in the few moments alone together, her hands always sought to touch him. But opportunities for intimacy were few and, when they did arise, were often frustrated.

1

Jane MacKinnon had always maintained a woman's touch in an otherwise masculine household. When there had been three males living here this had seemed a near-impossible task. Now that Adam had married and moved out the arrival of the sisters signalled change. Mack's mother used her surrogate daughters as the ideal excuse to unleash her transformation. Mack and his father had watched on, startled and bemused at its speed.

Mack was ensconced in what had been Adam's room but he missed his old one. It had been there that Effy had presented him with her virginity. The loss of his old room was not the only change. Now his parents had revamped it in readiness for the new arrival. He was still coming to terms with his mother's pregnancy. The idea of a baby brother or sister seventeen going on eighteen years his junior was bizarre and disconcerting. Knowing that he could be a parent himself by now was disconcerting too. Weirder still was the thought that his niece would be older than his new brother or sister. How embarrassing could it get? The thought of his mum asking him and Effy to take the baby out in the pram brought on a wry smile.

Mack could envisage the scene as some stranger cooed over the newborn. "You two don't look old enough to be parents."

Better still, he imagined his mum and dad hearing, "Oh, what a lovely grandchild you have there."

The fine cuts and scratches on his face were irritating. Chewing on toast exacerbated the irritation. At least he'd managed to get through puberty without the indignities of greasy skin and teen acne. Blackheads could still appear but Clearasil sorted the problem. Effy's skin was unbelievable and the source of a lot of envy. Other girls, including Grace and Ellen, struggled with blemishes, greasy skin, and unruly hair though not this miraculous female. Blissfully unaffected, to the annoyance of her sisters and the girls at school, she had blossomed into a beauty.

"We've got a confession to make." Effy gave Grace a swift look before turning, blushing, to Mack. "We may be responsible for your razor cuts."

He looked at his girlfriend. She had tied up her strawberry blonde hair this morning. Usually those shining green eyes were capable of making him melt every time she smiled. But she wasn't smiling now. At that moment he knew something was wrong by the upset written in her face.

"Don't tell me, you borrowed the blade to do some Art homework?"

"No. Actually we – that is Grace and myself – had to use your razor to shave."

"Shave? *You* needed to shave? Girls don't shave."

"Yes, we do." His mum smiled at her seventeen-year-old son's ignorance. "Little girls don't, but young women like Effy and Grace do. So do older women, like myself."

"Really?"

"Yes. We do."

"Well, you don't shave your faces or I would have noticed by now."

"They shave their legs and underarms." His father tapped him on the head with the newspaper. "Sometimes your ignorance astounds me. Did you think their legs were hairless?"

Mack looked at Effy. "Why?"

Her imploring glance begged Jane MacKinnon to provide the explanation. Mack's mother smiled back, indicating it was up to Effy to do the explaining. Robert MacKinnon, reading the signal, intervened.

"James, during the war women's stockings became difficult to come by. Many women dyed their legs with cold tea to give the impression of wearing stockings. They even drew seams down the back of their legs. To make the illusion realistic they shaved their legs smooth. These days they shave them so the fine hairs don't poke through the stockings. Goes to show. All those books you read don't include information like this. You know a lot for a seventeen-year-old but there's lots more you still have to learn – much of which is not in books."

It made sense. When he'd been in bed with Effy, her legs had always been smooth as silk. Nor did she have any underarm hair now he thought about it. The only hair he could recollect was her small pubic triangle. What would it be like if she shaved there too?

"Jane, buy the girls a couple of safety razors today. And some blades before our son disfigures himself further." Robert MacKinnon grinned. "We don't want him falling out with Effy and Grace over their female beauty regimes, do we? Oh, and women like to shave their underarms when wearing a sleeveless dress or blouse. Well, son, I hope that contributes to your further education about the ways of the opposite sex."

"Gee, thanks, Dad. I see they didn't use your razor."

"That's because I wised up years ago, making sure I kept mine safe from your mother." He winked at his wife. "Especially after the same thing happened to me. Now, girls, we need to be setting off if I'm to get you to school on time. So grab your school things and let's go before 'Scarface' MacKinnon gets annoyed with you for using his razor."

3

Effy came round from her side of the table to give him a kiss on the cheek. "I'm so sorry," she whispered. "I'll make it up to you later. You know how, don't you?"

He had a good idea, feeling himself hardening. Effy had a way of doing this to him.

# CHAPTER 2

## Determination – The Contours (Tamla Motown TMG 564 – 1966)

*Wednesday 21 December 1966*

"Love was a far more complicated matter in Jane Austen's time. Romantic love may be desirable but for most not a practical reality. The women in *Emma* face stark and often limited choices. Marry for money and domestic security in the shape of a wealthy husband. Or choose the insecurity of marrying some impoverished man for romantic love. All, that is, except Emma Woodhouse. She alone is in the fortunate position of being able to marry who she wants, be it for love or for money."

Effy was taking notes, only half-listening to Miss Thorpe. Lost in erotic imaginings, she was on automatic pilot. In a semi-dreamlike state, she was caressing Mack's testicles. Anticipating how he would react was making her aroused. So much so she found herself crossing her legs. It was dreadful. She couldn't stop thinking about their next sexual encounter. It was as if she was becoming addicted to the pleasures his body gave her.

As much as she enjoyed studying Jane Austen, it was the last day of term before the Christmas holiday. Sex was foremost on her mind.

"… So the question I pose is this: if Emma Woodhouse was in the same position as someone like Miss Taylor, would she still put romantic love before material security? Would she, for example, marry a Mr Weston? Or even an Elton? What are your thoughts, Fiona?"

Effy groaned inwardly at the interruption. In her sexual fantasising she was massaging Mack to a frenzied climax. Putting her pen down, she was back in the real world, her mind focused on answering.

"Women of gentility in reduced circumstances would have little choice. They would have to be practical where marriage was concerned. Romantic love would be desirable but poverty would not. A financially secure marriage was a priority. Our circumstances today are different. Times have changed. We can choose to marry for love. It's our choice."

"I take it, Fiona, that in Jane Austen's time, you would have done the same?" There was mischief in her teacher's words. It wasn't the first time, either. Rumours of Effy's relationship with Mack had, it seemed, become

5

common staffroom gossip. It was inevitable, she supposed, following her recent semantic game-playing with some of the teachers.

Effy determined on some mischief of her own. She laid it on mustard thick. "I would still marry for love, Miss Thorpe, and I would be prepared to live in sin and poverty. I wouldn't hesitate as long as I was with my one true love. I'd want a life of passion and ecstasy, not empty emotional coldness and dissatisfaction."

Effy's response created a flicker in her teacher's face. Quite what the reaction to her response would be, she was unsure. The other girls in the group were open-mouthed on hearing her words.

"I'm certain you would have been completely ostracised by society as a consequence." Miss Thorpe chose her words with care but her disapproval over Effy's comment about living in sin was clear. "This is a Catholic girls' grammar with high moral and spiritual aspiration for its young charges."

Turning to Chloe Johnson, who was sitting next to Effy, she asked, "And what about you, Chloe? Would you marry for love or for convenience?"

Chloe, a small dark-haired girl, stopped tapping her lip with the end of her biro. "I'd do the same as Fiona. Like her, I'd choose to live in sin and poverty if faced with such restricted choice. We're fortunate we don't live in those times, so it's pure conjecture isn't it, Miss Thorpe?"

Effy gave her classmate a broad grin. Bravo, Chloe! She was delighted they were on the same wavelength. They had always been in different groups before the Lower Sixth. She'd only known Chloe by sight until they ended up in the same A Level English group. Of the twelve girls in the group, Chloe was by far the friendliest. Effy had taken to her, liking what she found in this pleasant unassuming girl.

Miss Thorpe was relentless in her questioning. "Tell me, Chloe, how would you know love in Jane Austen's time? There were no opportunities for dating. Interaction between the sexes had to conform to accepted rules of propriety. At your age you would 'come out' onto the marriage market, so to speak. You couldn't be alone with a young man without a chaperone. Members of the opposite sex couldn't touch. A kiss sealed an intention to marry. In those circumstances love would be problematic, would it not?"

Chloe looked lost.

Effy picked up for her. "Well, there's always love at first sight.

Having said that, isn't Emma infatuated with Frank Churchill? She has a kind of initial crush on him. George Knightley's hardly love at first sight. There's a seventeen-year age gap. He's known her from being an infant, which strikes me as a bit dodgy. In the end Knightley is the safe bet. Frank Churchill was never going to be in the running. It's a case of better the devil you know. Then again, there don't appear to be any other eligible young men on the horizon for Emma. Chloe, like every girl here, would only have a limited market of men to choose or be chosen from. Given limited perceptions, even intuition, how else could she decide if a man was suitable husband material?"

"Fiona's right, Miss Thorpe," Chloe agreed. "To get to know a person in such restricted circumstances would make choosing a lifelong partner difficult. Emma is fortunate in that she's known George Knightley all her life. At least she knows what she's getting."

"So is there any romantic love involved at all in her choice of husband?"

"Depends on how we understand romantic love," Chloe responded.

"We should ask our *resident expert*. Fiona, what is your understanding of romantic love?"

That was uncalled for. Mack had once said to her, when verbal sparring fails verbal bare knuckles come next. The imaginary gloves came off.

"Romance comes from the medieval idea of chivalry. Since then it has come to mean love as in Eros or eroticism. Romantic love implies a strong sexual attraction where lovers are driven by sexual desire." Effy paused long enough to ensure her next outrageous comment would have maximum effect. There was a stirring amongst the other girls. "I emphasise desire as meaning *needing fulfilment*. In blunt terms, it's when a woman feels the need to spread her legs for the love of the man in her life. She does so irrespective of her marital status and the possibility of an unwanted pregnancy."

Stunned expressions were always fascinating. This was something Mack had told her and he was right. It was a gem of a moment and she enjoyed savouring it. Gasps and titters from the girls in the group were audible as they realised what Effy had said. Mack had once told her he believed boundaries existed for pushing. To Effy, this was a boundary worth pushing. She believed, as he did, that their generation was not going to accept how things were just because the older generation said so. They were

7

here to challenge the established order of things.

Miss Thorpe looked as though she could scarcely believe what she'd heard. It was worth the inevitable telling-off Effy was likely to receive. Chloe was blushing while trying to stop laughing. But Effy wasn't done; now came her verbal *coup de grace*.

"After all, it's what Lydia Bennett does with Wickham in *Pride and Prejudice*, and Maria Bertram with Henry Crawford in *Mansfield Park*. As for Marianne Dashwood with Willoughby in *Sense and Sensibility*, it has to make you wonder? What *did* they get up to gallivanting round the countryside without a chaperone? Even if they didn't have sex I suspect she broke all the other rules about kissing and inappropriate touching. That's pure guesswork, because Austen doesn't actually say so. She infers it, whereas she implies Willoughby is already guilty of fathering a child by Eliza. He's nothing but a Regency playboy who uses women. Why should he stop at seducing one girl when he can carry on doing it to others? Oh, and Harriet Smith! I'd almost forgotten her. She's someone's illegitimate child. It seems to me that romantic love was Austen's shorthand for steamy sex, either in or out of marriage. She was aware that some women of her time were satisfying their natural urges out of marriage. Settling for financial security or convenience was settling for a great deal less."

"That was somewhat indelicate, Fiona. It's not how young ladies in this Sixth Form should express themselves." Miss Thorpe managed to find her voice. "Though at least it does appear you've read some of Austen's other works. I have to say you do show a deeper understanding than I would expect from someone in the Lower Sixth."

"Actually, Miss Thorpe, I've read all her novels, even *Northanger Abbey*." A further spicy retaliatory comment felt necessary. "I may be seventeen but give me romantic love and passion every time – although I would use a little more common sense and contraception. Firsthand experience has to be better than reading about it. If that qualifies me as a resident expert I don't mind. Incidentally, Miss Thorpe, I have Irish ancestry but I was born and raised in Yorkshire. One of the virtues of Yorkshire people is plain speaking. So I won't refrain from calling a spade a spade. I refuse to use alternatives. Sex is what it is. Sex. We should not be coy about calling it sex."

Miss Thorpe found herself astonished, yet in a strange way marvelling at Fiona Halloran's sermonising. This young woman was nothing like the shy little girl she had first encountered. In the lower school Fiona

8

Halloran had sought mouse-like invisibility. But she had matured into an interesting young woman who was confident, decisive, strongminded and prepared to show it. None of the teachers had ever suspected her cleverness until her outstanding exam results at the end of the Fifth Form. This young Miss was no dumb blonde. On the contrary she was intelligent, quick-witted and sharp. In the past few minutes she had demonstrated her independent thinking and a resolute strong personality. In the shadows of her elder sister Deidre, little of her potential had surfaced. Now it burned bright like a beacon. What was the truth of the staffroom gossip and innuendo surrounding her?

As she contemplated Fiona Halloran, Miss Thorpe realised where she had failed in her own life. At forty-one, the same age as Austen had been when she'd died, Miss Thorpe was experiencing a different kind of death. This was in contrast to the spirited young woman referred to as Effy by her contemporaries.

"Homework, ladies."

"Miss Thorpe, do we have to? It's Christmas," came a plaintive plea from someone.

Miss Thorpe continued, inured to the begging. "Explain what advice Jane Austen might have to offer a young woman today about love and marriage. On a single side of foolscap make a list of points. Write a concise explanation for each point in no more than a couple of sentences."

Chloe rolled her eyes at the prospect. "Oh, well. It could be worse. It could have been another essay. I suppose we ought to thank our lucky stars for small mercies."

Effy's smile said it all.

# CHAPTER 3

**He's a Rebel – The Crystals (London 45-HLU 9611 – 1962)**

*Wednesday 21 December 1966 – Afternoon*

"So, MacKinnon?" Mack found his daydreaming disturbed. "Rationalist, pragmatist or empiricist. Which one are you?"

It was the last General Studies tutorial before the end of the day and the term. Philosophy was not on his mind or on the minds of anyone in the group; they were all contenting themselves with counting down the minutes in mindless inactivity. Preoccupied by reliving sex with Effy, Mack found his daydream dissolved in an instant. He'd known Effy for two years but with every passing day he was more and more captivated by the intense passion they felt for one another. It was annoying being distracted from thinking about her breasts.

"As an existentialist, sir, I don't think these labels are relevant."

"An existentialist, eh?" Mack had sparked Bentham's interest. With a surname like Bentham, how could he not qualify to teach the philosophy component? "And what exactly does an existentialist like yourself believe? Enlighten us, *Mister* MacKinnon."

There was an uncomfortable stirring amongst his fellow inmates. No one felt inclined to get dragged into an insufferable brain-shaking discussion. Neither was Mack, with his thoughts focused on kissing Effy's breasts. But why not play the game to pass some time?

"Well, it's like this, Mr Bentham. We're born into this world without a say. It's not as if we're given the choice. Once we're aware that we're in it we're faced with a choice. To be or not to be, as the Bard wrote. If we choose *to be* we have to find our purpose for living. Life needs a meaning or it's pointless. It's up to us to find meaning in life. If life's only purpose is the perpetuation of the species, then life is pointless and ridiculous. So we're faced with two choices. We can choose to end existence because we find it's absurd. Or we can choose to find meaning in existence."

"You do surprise, MacKinnon. I was not aware that they taught philosophy and Shakespeare at secondary moderns?"

Of course he had to expect yet another supercilious dig from yet

10

another grammar school teacher with a superiority complex.

"It wasn't, but I note it's not taught here either. No Philosophy O Level on offer as an option." It was not the counter Bentham was expecting as Mack delivered his retaliatory swipe. He followed it up with a further barbed dig. "I'm here to learn *what has been decided for me to learn*. But *I choose to learn that which isn't.*"

They eyed one another in silence for a couple of seconds, both weighing up Mack's words.

"So tell me, Mr MacKinnon, where does religious belief feature? Does it have a place?"

"If you want it as your *raison d'etre* then it's your choice. The Abrahamic religions leave me cold. In fact all religions leave me cold. I have neither the time for nor interest in any of them. In accepting religious dogma people allow themselves to become enslaved by it. It's an act of intellectual bankruptcy surrendering yourself to the thoughts of others. It's intellectual laziness. As individuals it's up to each one of us to think for ourselves and challenge accepted beliefs."

Unprepared for those words, Bentham wondered how to react. His students rarely posited such forceful ideas in such a clear way. "So do you believe in anything at all?"

"Ethical hedonism."

Mack relished these moments. His tutor seemed taken aback, dredging memory to recall what ethical hedonism was and meant.

"So you are an Epicurean?"

Game over; close but no cigar.

"No. Not at all. A true Epicurean wouldn't indulge in the pleasures of the flesh like sex. That wouldn't do for me. No. I'm resolute in believing in the greatest amount of happiness and pleasure with the least pain for everyone."

Mack had read that Jeremy Bentham the philosopher was a utilitarian who believed in the idea of the greatest happiness for the greatest number. It was another barbed comment – and so appropriate for his namesake teacher.

Mack heard guffawing in the group. On hearing the word "sex" a rapid upsurge of interest by the group followed. His swipe had gone unnoticed by his classmates but not by the tutor. Bentham thought it wiser not to pursue his namesake's ideas. MacKinnon was a wily hunter. He would not become his victim.

"Back to the perpetuation of the species, eh, Mr MacKinnon?"

"Not at all. Contraception now makes sex a hedonistic pursuit." Mack enjoyed rattling his tutor's cage. "Sex is no longer only for procreation."

"I find this line of thinking interesting and refreshing. A young man with such decided ideas and knowledge of philosophy."

"Not everyone from a secondary modern is a semi-literate oik, sir. Failing the Eleven Plus may be no guide to what happens later in life."

"It appears not," Bentham replied. "I dare say we'll have to see, won't we? Enlighten me further. I'm sure we're all intrigued. How did you become so knowledgeable about philosophy and with such certainties?"

It was irresistible. On reflection, he could have avoided smirking.

"There are these places called libraries. They contain objects called books. I like to read the odd one now and again." Laughter echoed around the room. Knowing Bentham taught Classics, Mack couldn't resist a further comment. "Having stated this, I don't have time to waste on Latin classics, although I did once read *Julius Caesar*. Sun Tzu's *Art of War* and Machiavelli's *The Prince* meet today's needs better. Saying this, I still have plenty to learn. My father reminded me only this morning there are some things you can't learn from books."

Bentham's amused curiosity led him to ask. "Do tell."

"I've yet to read a book that tells me women shave their legs and underarms."

Clearly Bentham found this comment entertaining; he gave a broad grin. When Mack looked around the group, however, it was obvious that this was news to some.

"Indeed," said Bentham. "As you rightly say. Some things you cannot learn from books. And what are you currently reading?"

"I finished reading Jane Austen's *Emma* late last night."

"A strange choice. You're not studying English Literature, are you?"

"No, sir. Austen broadens my horizons, enabling me to share my girlfriend's interests."

"You should see his choice bird, Mr Bentham. She's a stunning looker," chipped in a youth by the name of Dzerzhinsky. Then, lowering his voice, he added, "I bet she broadens his horizons too."

"I'll see you outside," Mack responded. "Then we can discuss how I limit yours."

12

Bentham curbed yet another smile. Dzerzhinsky appeared stricken at MacKinnon's words. According to his registration tutor this newcomer kept himself to himself. He sought minimal involvement in the life of the Sixth Form. It appeared that he inspired genuine fear among some students, as Bentham had now witnessed with Dzerzhinsky. MacKinnon looked harmless enough. Impeccable dress sense, polite, handsome and well-spoken, he was anything but harmless. At least according to classroom rumours he'd overheard. Bentham liked this young man's acerbic wit and intelligence.

"Since the season of goodwill is upon us I implore you to forgive poor Dzerzhinsky his transgression. I'm sure whatever nerve he touched would not be worth appearing before the headmaster. The Monsignor does not take kindly to violence in the Sixth Form. Perhaps a little charity towards Dzerzhinsky is called for? To err is human, after all."

Turning to Dzerzhinsky, Mack made a papal-style sign of the cross and uttered in Church Latin, "*Ego te absolvo*, Dzerzhinsky. *Ite in pace.*"

Dzerzhinsky looked relieved. Bentham found Mack's liturgical forgiving droll.

"Nice one. Looks like you're off the hook, Jersey. Mack's absolved you of your sin and you can go in peace," jeered Smith. Still grinning, he made a point of asking, "Does that make MacKinnon divine? What do you think, sir? Given that forgiveness is supposed to be divine?"

Bentham cleared his throat. "The original quote is from Seneca the Younger rather than Alexander Pope the poet. As I recall it was *errare humanum est perseverare diabolicum* or *to err is human, to persist is diabolical.*"

"So, MacKinnon's more divine than diabolical in that case?"

Mack turned to Smith and mouthed, albeit with good humour, "Piss off."

"Can an atheistic existential hedonist even relate to the divine as a reality?" the tutor responded to Tim.

"One moment please, Mr Bentham," Mack interrupted. "I never said I was an atheist. It's a matter of semantics. I am an existentialist agnostic who is ethically hedonistic. I may have no interest in organised religions, true enough. But it doesn't mean that I dismiss the possible existence of a deity."

"Mmmh, interesting. Is it possible for a deity to exist in a universe without purpose?"

"Why assume a deity even has a purpose? Creating the universe may have been nothing more than a moment of whimsy or madness. Let's face it,

13

the human race is like an uncaring parent's abandoned children. If this deity were a human parent, social workers would have put his family into care long ago."

"Mack has a point," Smith waded in. "We only have to look at Vietnam today. Or go back in the past and take Hitler, Stalin, Genghis Khan and history in general to see that the human race is delinquent."

"Which brings us to the core question. *If God created everything then he must have created evil too?*" Mack posed.

"That is a question best answered by a theologian. I'm sure the school chaplain would be better qualified to answer that one," Bentham responded.

The long-awaited bell finally rang, ending the day.

"It seems we shall have much to discuss in the New Year. May I wish you the usual seasonal best with the hope that Santa brings you big boys whatever it is you big boys want. You may go."

Some wit responded with the words, "*Deo Gratias.*"

Mack and Smith were the last to leave the room. Dzerzhinsky was waiting outside, looking nervous. "I'm sorry, I didn't mean to upset you."

"I was messing with you," Mack replied, "but someone else might not be. In future take care what you say and to whom. You never know how they'll take it. See you in the New Year and have a good Christmas."

"Same to you." Dzerzhinsky disappeared through the heaving mass of bodies dashing to leave.

"Take no notice of Jersey. He's harmless. Actually, he's a decent chap. He wouldn't mean any harm. He was trying to be clever. You certainly scared the shit out of him. Tales travel fast. He must have heard how you decked three Upper Six guys behind the common room. They didn't look too happy afterwards. That bunch of bozos had it coming. Can't say I liked their bullying. Came a cropper with you, didn't they?"

"I seem to attract troublemakers."

"That's the problem you've got being a Mod. Dressing flash and riding in every day on that Lambretta. It makes you stand out, and a target for arseholes like them."

"Being a Mod's not a problem – only for those who aren't. Where do they get this idea that Mods are a bunch of effeminate softies?"

"Is that what caused it?"

"I took no notice when they started calling me a 'woofta'. I gave them the two-finger salute and told them to stop scraping their knuckles on the ground. They didn't like what I'd said and that's when they thought they could rough me up. They shouldn't have started pushing me about. So I did unto them, as they believed they could do unto me. Amen."

"There was a rumour a while back that you'd twatted four or five blokes one night down in the city centre. Is it true?"

"It's been somewhat exaggerated." Mack recalled the incident where he'd played football kicking Osborn and his accomplice down the end of Godwin Street to Thornton Road. "You shouldn't believe everything you hear."

"How's the photography coming along? Got the darkroom up and running yet?" Smith changed the conversation.

"Going to set it up tonight. Thanks for lending me the books and mags. All I need now is a better camera than the old Brownie. My Dad got me some of the chemicals I'll need and something that'll act as a developing tank. At least it should keep costs down by making my own prints. My Dad's even showing me the ropes round his Leica and how to use all the settings and light meter. I'm hoping he might buy me a decent camera for Christmas."

"Changing the subject, did you know you've met my girlfriend?"

"No. When?"

"Chloe Johnson. Down at St. Jo's one morning. She took you to the office? She knows Fiona. They do English Lit together."

Mack remembered his visit when he'd taken absence notes into the College for Effy and her sisters. He recollected a petite dark-haired girl who'd helped him find the office. So that was Tim Smith's girlfriend? He hadn't paid her much attention at the time.

"We should meet up as a foursome in the new year," said Smith. "You and Fiona have a good Christmas."

# CHAPTER 4

## He's a Lover – Mary Wells (Stateside SS 439 – 1965)

*Wednesday 21 December 1966 – Evening*

Effy recounted the events of the English Lit lesson at length. Her annoyance verged on fiery anger but soon faded to dying embers. Mack didn't interrupt as she covered all the implications and intricacies of the English Lit class; he'd learned that Effy and her sister Grace needed to talk through their worries when they came home. It was a waste of time offering answers. Neither seemed to want these. He'd found this difficult to grasp. Once again his father had enlightened him after hearing him venting his frustration. Mack's suggested solutions were obvious but the girls never listened or took any notice. It was as if they didn't want the solutions. Wasn't this illogical? His father's patient explanation enlightened him.

What women wanted was for someone to listen. Talking seemed to be a way of clean sweeping their worries. This was how they let off steam. It was the same when his mother demanded his father's attention. According to his father this was a unique female trait. The important thing was sympathetic listening. It had taken his father years to grasp. So he was pleased to pass on this piece of wisdom to his son. Listening was something men didn't usually do well. His dad's advice made sense. Robert MacKinnon then qualified what he'd said. He admitted he was guilty of not always listening, as he should. So Mack did the logical thing. He began taking his father's advice, making an effort to become more attentive.

Once again his father's advice proved sound. He was going to have to have more long chats with him to pick up more tips.

The relationship between father and son had deepened over the last two years. It had begun to change on the day when his parents had caught Adam in bed with Caitlin. Since then Mack had learned to respect his father as more than a parent. His dad had this uncanny ability of making him realise he didn't know it all. This was why he found it easy to talk to him about all sorts. Robert MacKinnon was nothing like his friend's fathers. He was exceptional, in his son's eyes at least, treating him man to man whenever they talked. They had a father and son relationship many of his friends would

16

envy. Mutual antagonism seemed a common complaint with too many of his friends. Even his cousin Tom had regular flare-ups with his dad and Uncle Phil was such an easy-going bloke.

Mack listened to Effy whenever she needed to work through anything preying on her mind. She appreciated Mack's empathetic willingness to listen. Her feelings for him had deepened as their mutual trust grew. She felt secure knowing she could always unburden herself to him.

If he were honest, Mack was not a natural listener. Listening to Grace, he sometimes switched off until she ran out of steam. But with Effy it was different. It didn't matter how trivial or how deep the topic. Mack loved her for the way she shared everything about her daily life. Her willingness to be so completely open made Mack open up to her, too. He'd found it easy and natural to confide in her after a while. It had felt unnatural at first and not very masculine. Both began to know one another's vulnerabilities. This made the bond between them closer and stronger. Given what they had gone through over the past two years it was not surprising. Yet there were things that had happened he could not and would not share.

"Now she'll think I'm some kind of loose woman."

"Why should she think that? It's not like you gave anything away."

"I may have implied it when I talked about first-hand experience."

"But you know you're not a loose woman, that's what's important." Mack took her hand to reassure her. "And sticking with the words you used you never implied you were sexually experienced."

"That's true. I don't think I did, did I? You haven't forgotten what we have to do tomorrow, have you?" she whispered.

"No. Like I would."

Mack knew exactly. He had to whisk her to Halifax on the scooter to the Family Planning Clinic. She had an appointment with Angie Thornton's sister. Some presents and cards also needed dropping off. This was a good excuse for making the journey to cover up the real reason. They thought they might also do some last-minute Christmas present shopping. At least these were the excuses to conceal the journey's real purpose.

"What's Grace doing?"

"Watching television with your dad. When your mum's ready she's going down with her to our house to help Deidre do some sprucing if it's needed. Your dad and Adam are taking their cars to help Bridget and Ellen get their things to move back in."

Mack felt mild annoyance. "Nobody tells me anything. Or was I not listening at the time?"

"Don't fret." Effy nuzzled his ear. "Because you know what happens when the cats are away? This little mouse likes to play."

"It's not as if we can do anything until you've restocked tomorrow," he whispered.

"That shouldn't stop us from having some fun. There's something I want to try."

"What are you two whispering about?" Grace came into the front room. "Oh, let me guess. Sweet nothings?"

Effy tapped the side of her nose with her finger. "Don't be nosey, sis."

An hour later, alone in the house, they were in Mack's room taking advantage of the opportunity.

"I've no spermicidal cream left and no Durex. So we can't go all the way. That is, until after tomorrow. But there's something I've wanted to do to you. It's been preying on my mind all day." Effy had a little bottle of Johnson's Baby Oil with a small flannel in one hand. In the other hand was a silk scarf.

"What have you got in mind?" Mack asked, noting her nervousness and viewing the objects with suspicion.

"Do you trust me?"

"Of course I do. You know I do. What are those for?"

"Don't ask. I'd rather not say. If I told you I wouldn't be able go ahead. You'd laugh and spoil it. I wouldn't know where to put myself."

"Okay. I won't ask. What do you want me to do?"

"Lie on the bed. Let me blindfold you with this scarf. Do whatever I want without asking why. Better still, don't say anything at all."

So he did as she'd asked. Effy checked the blindfold twice to ensure he couldn't see any anything. She noticed he was tensing. It was peculiar finding himself deprived of sight. Her lips touched his but did not linger for a kiss. Then, breathing into his ear, she uttered the word, "Relax." A gentle nibble of his earlobe followed. Taking a deep breath to steady her nervousness, she hoped she was not doing something foolish.

With deliberate slowness she undid his trouser belt before unzipping the fly on his trousers.

Mack felt her tugging his trousers and underpants down together in one motion. Raising his buttocks he helped, easing her efforts. She took them

18

down as far his knees, leaving him exposed and hardening. His shirt and pullover were next, drawn to below his ribs. As much as he wanted to ask what was going to happen next, he refrained. He'd passed control over his body to her. This physical surrender wasn't easy. He experienced some embarrassment but his trust in her was implicit.

He heard the baby-oil top click open. Seconds later cool drops of oil fell on his already hard member and testicles. There was no way he could control the quivering anticipation of what she was about to do next. He felt her straddle him, the texture of her stockings rubbing against his outer thighs. Like a trained masseuse she began to work the oil all over his genitals. She took and held each testicle, cupping them in the palms of her small hands. This strange embrace made him judder with pleasure. Her gentle thumb pressed on the base of his penis, making it rise. With deliberate slowness she moved along the shaft, reaching the uncircumcised foreskin. He felt her draw it back and touch the top with a gentle fingertip. Compensating for the lack of sight, his body's reaction to touch was now his sensitive primary sense. He felt a fingernail moving around the exposed rim of the foreskin. The sensuousness was unbelievable. Her hand began the masturbatory movement in slow caressing strokes. The tempo increased in steady increments. He could not stop himself uttering pleasurable moans as she began working him to an inevitable climax. He enjoyed the strange sensation of surrendering control of himself to her. While she had him in her hands he was her property and she could do what she liked with him.

"Warn me when you're ready to come." She spoke for the first time since beginning his sexual arousal, her voice husky and nervous. It wasn't easy for her to tell when he was ready to explode until almost the last moment. Then it was too late.

"Any moment now."

He felt her press his penis flat to his abdomen, continuing to excite the eruption. Try as hard as he could to delay the climax he couldn't prevent it. The firm but gentle pressure made him give up the struggle. He felt the released warm semen splash against his naked stomach. The sheer sensuousness of the experience under her ministration was beyond describing. Her fingers were still busy squeezing the last of the fluid from the end as the last pulsing ebbed away and he felt himself softening.

Effy removed the blindfold and Mack had to adjust his eyesight to light once again. She was still straddling him. Using the flannel she began to clean him, mopping up the semen.

"Was that okay?" Flushed and coy, she sounded almost breathless.

"No." He paused. "It was beyond okay. As Stevie Wonder would say, it was 'uptight outta sight'. Any time you want to do that to me again, you can. Don't hesitate to ask. There's only one thing I need to know. What made you want to do that to me?"

"Well, for a start I have to keep the man in my life happy. It was my way of saying sorry for using your razor to shave my legs. I had my own reasons, too."

"Oh, yeah?"

"Oh, yeah." Effy mimicked him.

"Like what other reasons?"

She blushed. "Well, you know when we've gone all the way?"

"Yes?"

"I was curious to see what happened when you ejaculated."

"You're kidding! And?"

"Not so much a spurt as a gunshot. I couldn't believe how much of it there was. You know that final time we did it when I lost my virginity? When I'd run out of Durex?"

"What about it?"

"You must have flooded me."

What surprised him most was that she wasn't too embarrassed to tell him.

"Now," she purred as he pulled up his underpants, "would you like to return the favour? You need to flick my switch because I'm in serious – but serious – need of being turned on."

How could he say no to her? He watched her slipping her briefs off. After the incredible pleasure she'd given him, there was no way he was going to refuse. Hitching her skirt up to her waist she lay down beside him, her pubic triangle enticing him. Slipping his hand between her thighs he found she was already aroused, wetter than he expected. Their lips met and their eyes closed. No sooner had his finger entered her opening touching her clitoris than she began having an orgasmic spasm. He felt her vagina spurting its own fluid with surprising force. Her hips rose and fell as she cried out in frenzied uncontrolled passion. At other times when he'd done the same it could take a minute or so to turn her on. This evening it was instant. Turning him on had also proved a massive turn-on for her. Heart pounding, she gasped with each breath. Clinging to him she found his lips kissing her again. As she subsided, her grip on him gradually slackened.

"Don't dare ask if I got turned on," she said, breathing hard. "You know I did."

"So was it like 240 volts when I flicked the switch?" he quipped.

"More like 5000 volts." She giggled. As they lay arm in arm, relaxing, she asked, "Is there anything you're curious about me when it comes to sex?"

"Only one thing. If you shave your legs and underarms do you ever do the same there?"

Effy blushed and giggled some more. "No. I've never shaved down there. But I have to admit when I've gone swimming I've had to give myself a trim so no hairs peeked out from the bottom of my cossy. Why do you ask?"

"I was curious. I did wonder what you would look like if you shaved down there."

"Well, you can keep on wondering." She climbed off his bed and he watched her slip into her briefs.

"I'm a bit worried." She looked concerned, adjusting her suspender belt and stockings. "I can't help thinking I'm becoming sex mad. I can't stop myself daydreaming about having sex with you. It's on my mind all the time. Thinking about it and having sex… it's becoming a craving."

"And here's me thinking it was only me."

"I'm serious! It's becoming an obsession. Sometimes in lessons I can't stop thinking about what you do to me. I get turned on thinking about you pulling my pants down. It's all I can do to stay focused on whatever's going on in lessons. The other day in Art we were studying how to draw the human body. I found myself doing a nude study of you."

"That's very flattering. Believe me, I don't think it's only you. It's me as well. I've never told you this before, and I'm uncomfortable admitting it, but I get hard three or four times in a day for much the same reasons. Sometimes I think my concentration's completely shot."

"Really?"

"Yes, honest." Mack looked as serious as he could. "I don't think it's anything unusual. I think it's what's happening to us because we're so in love. And yes, I do love you, Effy Halloran. You're everything to me. One day I'm going to propose to you. I hope you'll say yes and marry me."

"I will. I want to be all yours. I'm already all yours."

"Was it a good likeness of me?"

She began to giggle again. "Well, one part of it was. My teacher told me it looked true to life and he would know, being a man! Anyway, we'd better get back downstairs. I don't want your mum banning me from living here. Remember the promise we made to her about no hanky panky?"

"I also remember her telling my Dad to fit a lock on your bedroom door so you could keep me out at night. I notice he never did."

"We've both kept that side of the bargain. The only lock on the door now is Grace. No chance with her here of anything happening."

"True. But there's been plenty of hanky panky on the quiet. Anyway, I don't believe my mum would send you packing to Bridget's now. You're not only like an adopted daughter, you're like my mum's newest best friend and confidante. She'll try holding on to you after your mum and dad return from Ireland in summer. I suspect she has plans for you to be an extra pair of hands when the baby arrives."

"I must admit she's like another mum to me and to Grace, too. And I do think you're right. And I do hope I can stay. Not only because of the baby. I'd like to be around to help out, but it would also mean I could stay close to you."

# CHAPTER 5

**Nothing's Too Good for My Baby – Stevie Wonder**
**(Tamla Motown TMG 558 – 1966)**

*Thursday 22 December 1966*

"Was everything all right?" Mack asked as Effy came out of the Family Clinic doors.

"Yes and no. I've a fresh supply of things and Angie's sister was great, but there's something we need to have a chat about. Can we go to The Beefeater for a coffee before Angie meets us there?"

George's Square was busy. Mack noticed a couple of scooters parked belonging to some of the guys he knew but their riders were nowhere around. The shops had a festive air, festooned with Christmas decorations and artificial snow. The coffee bar was busy as it was coming up to midday. Instead of using the cellar part, which was the usual hangout, they settled for sitting upstairs overlooking the Square.

Effy seemed unusually preoccupied and quiet, which was never good. "Angie's sister thinks I ought to consider going on the Pill."

"Why?"

"There are a couple of problems."

"Okay. Tell me what they are."

"Well, first of all she asked how often we were having sex. When I told her, she was concerned. There's a greater chance of getting pregnant especially if I rush and don't fit the diaphragm properly. To be honest it's a bit of a faff using it. Sometimes, when I've rushed, I've wondered if I've fitted it right. Then there's the possibility that the condom may split. And if the diaphragm's not right, you know what that could mean? This is why she's suggesting I go on the Pill. Anyway, I'm certain you don't like using condoms."

"If I'm honest, I don't. But we can't take risks. We're much too young to start a family. The last thing I want to do is get you in the family way before either of us is ready. Why is she suggesting you go on the Pill?"

"It's safer, as long as I don't forget to take it."

"You don't sound too happy about that."

23

"When I asked Caitlin why she wasn't on the Pill, she said she wasn't happy about the risks. Also, at the moment they only prescribe the Pill to married women."

"Well, that settles it. If you're not married you can't go on the Pill. There's nothing much you can do about it, is there? End of problem."

"Let me tell you about the second thing. It's kind of relevant. Gillian could be in trouble if she continues to help Ellen and myself."

"Why?" Clearly there was something she'd not told him.

"Gillian isn't supposed to help unmarried girls get contraception. Angie asked her to help Ellen and myself as a favour, because we're Angie's friends. Now we have to see a doctor so we can get the Pill prescribed. She can't do it."

"So, what you're saying, Eff, is this. Unless all three of you are married there's no more contraceptives. Have I got that about right?"

"Yes. That's about it."

"That's not good."

"There is a possible way round this." Effy looked uncomfortable.

"And what's that?"

She gave him a wistful, rather embarrassed look. "If I come back as a married woman in the New Year, then I can go on the Pill."

"Oh, great!" Mack exclaimed. "As much as I want to marry you when we're old enough, it's not possible right now, is it? For a start we're seventeen and studying for A Levels. Aside from which, can you imagine our parents' reactions? Somehow, I don't think we'd get their approval. Or maybe we should elope to Scotland?"

"No, I don't think we could or should." Effy became exasperated. "I'm not making myself clear, am I? What I meant to say was would you mind if, for the purposes of the Family Planning clinic, I called myself Mrs James MacKinnon?"

"Don't you mean Mrs Fiona MacKinnon?" Mack sounded puzzled.

"If you like. Well?"

"Effy, make it a little clearer for me, please. Why will calling yourself Mrs MacKinnon help get you on the Pill?"

"If I pretend I'm married I can go on the Pill."

"Won't they check to see if you're married?"

"According to Gillian, the doctor doesn't check. All you have to do is to wear a wedding ring and an engagement ring and they assume you're married."

24

"You're kidding."

"Apparently not."

"Well, Mrs Fiona MacKinnon, looks like we'll have to find you some convincing jewellery. But they must check surely?" He remained unconvinced.

Thirty minutes later, dashing to meet Mack and Effy, Angie Thornton left work. Working in a town centre's chemist's was convenient for meeting friends. It was also convenient for lunch-hour shopping. Today would involve both.

The secret Angie shared with Mack had become an unspoken bond between them. That one night they had shared was a night of regret for them both. It had to remain their secret. Mack feared losing Effy. Angie feared the loss of Effy's friendship. Though she dared not admit it to herself, she also feared losing Mack. He had a place in her heart that felt like a helpless hopeless aching. She knew she was in denial over him. Somehow there was nothing she felt she could do about it. One thing she was conscious of was weighing her words with care before giving them breath. No matter what her feelings were, nothing could come between the three of them.

Plonking herself down in front of the pair, she took them by surprise. Their coffee cups were empty and it was evident they had been waiting quite a while. "Treat's on me. Tea or coffee, you two? And don't say no or else! We haven't got long. We're going to Woollies to do some shopping."

"Are we? Why?" Effy was surprised.

"Mack can help you pick out an engagement and a wedding ring from their finest selection of cheapo jewellery. I take it Gillian explained the problem?"

"She did. When did you find out?"

"Gillian came home to let me know. She's worried in case her boss finds out she's been helping us single girls. Oh, you'd better warn your sister too. I'd hate to see TC having a heart attack."

"Will faking that you're married work?" queried Mack, his disbelief still clear.

"Yes." Angie looked at Mack. "They don't check. All you have to do is flash the third finger of the left hand and use a married name. Bingo. That's it. All Effy needs to say is she's Mrs MacKinnon or Mrs Halloran."

"So what are you going to call yourself?"

"Ah, now that's a bit tricky. I'm going to have to invent a married name. What with Gillian working there it might be a bit risky, seeing as there's a strong family resemblance."

"How about something like Smith?" Mack offered.

"Oh, no!" Effy protested. "It sounds so fake."

"Yeah." Angie giggled. "Sounds like a dirty weekend name."

"How about Marsden? You look a bit like Beryl Marsden's younger sister," Mack suggested.

"Mmmh." Angie seemed to mull it over for a few seconds before trying it out. "Mrs Angela Marsden. Hey, that sounds okay. Nice one, Mack. I used to go to school with an Annie Marsden. Round here it sounds genuine enough."

"So how much is it going to cost going on the Pill?" Curiosity prompted him to ask.

Effy and Angie gave each other a long look as though messaging with their eyes.

"It's not cheap," Angie began, giving Effy a gentle tap with her foot under the table. "You may have to help her with the cost."

How much could it cost? He would have to help her bear some of the cost, if not all of it. He hazarded a guess. "About ten bob?"

Angie made a noise more typical of a tradesman, implying it was going to cost lots more. Effy played along, looking mortified. "These things don't come cheap!"

"With the pleasure comes the pain. Good girls are bad girls who never get caught. You wouldn't want Effy to get caught out, would you?" Angie tried to look appalled. "Is that what you think these pills cost?"

"I've no idea what they cost. How am I supposed to know what they cost?" He was getting exasperated. "Go on, tell me the worst."

"Promise you won't be cross when we tell you." Effy did her best to act frightened.

"You have to promise." Angie sounded serious.

"Okay. Promise." There was a pause. The two girls exchanged glances. "Go on, then. Spill."

Effy lowered her eyes, doing her best to look upset. "It's two bob."

"What?" Mack exclaimed. "Two shillings a pill?"

Both girls burst out laughing so loudly that other customers began looking round at them. His expression was unforgettable.

"No. For a month's supply, you dope. You've just been had!" Angie ribbed him, her dark eyes sparkling. Winding him up had been fun.

"Oh, very amusing, you two. Don't forget what goes around comes around." Mack buried his annoyance and resentment. Turning to Effy, he added, "I'm surprised at you winding me up. Knowing what Angie's like I should have guessed I was being had."

It may only have been cheap cosmetic jewellery but the girls took their time. They made their choice of rings with serious deliberation. It was as though they were doing it for real and it made him smile. They picked matching yellow Lucite rings that could pass for wedding bands. Mack bought one too, for a laugh. Later these rings would come to have a greater significance. As Angie's lunch hour came to an end, they walked her back to the chemist's. On the way they made detailed arrangements to meet up on Friday evening and also over Christmas.

# CHAPTER 6

**Said I Wasn't Gonna Tell Nobody – Sam & Dave (Atlantic 484047 – 1965)**

*Christmas Eve, Thursday 24 December 1966*

"Grace, are you happy living with us?" Jane MacKinnon asked as she peeled the potatoes for the evening meal.

Grace took a break from peeling the carrots. "I love living here so much. I'm so grateful that you took me and Effy in. It's always so calm, peaceful and relaxed here."

"Don't you miss home and your mother and sisters?"

"Sometimes. I miss seeing my sisters every day. But I suppose that's what happens when they begin to leave home and lead their own lives. At least Effy is here, which doesn't make it feel so bad. And Ellen's never far away now that Bridget's moved back into our house. I can always nip down the road to see them both. Caitlin's not far away so that helps but it's not the same. I don't suppose it can be."

Jane MacKinnon allowed herself a gentle smile, listening to the youngster's words. "What about your mother?"

Grace paused to clear the carrot tops and skins to one side and let out a sigh. "Yes, I do. I only wish she had been more open with us. Now I know what the problems were, I feel terrible about how we treated her and my da at the time. I can't help wonder how she's coping with him. It won't be easy for her. I never realised how hard it must have been. It was awful."

"You mustn't feel upset, Grace. Nor should your sisters. Your mother was trying to protect you all as best she knew how."

"I'm so glad you are such a good friend to my ma. I don't know how she could have carried on all those years without your support. You arranged for Father Jumeaux's help, didn't you?"

Jane MacKinnon gave a silent nod.

"I thought so."

"What do you think of Effy's friend, Angie?" It was a calculated change of topic.

"I like her," Grace responded without hesitation. "I've done the carrots. Do you want me to do anything else?"

28

"No, dear. Thanks for helping." Jane paused. "Angie and Effy seem so different, almost like opposites. You don't think Angie has taken a fancy to James, do you?"

For a moment Grace found herself disconcerted. She had to admit that the thought had occurred to her several times. It wasn't implausible. She'd always dismissed the idea but now Jane MacKinnon had raised the question, it was uncomfortable. Yes, Angie could have feelings for Mack. It was possible. After all, she had confessed her own born-too-late feelings to him two weeks ago. It had almost felt like betraying her sister by doing it. So why shouldn't Angie have feelings for him? The question was, should she mention this to her sister? Grace dismissed the idea again.

"I don't think she does. Well, if she has it's pointless. Mack and Eff only have eyes for each other. Angie's genuinely just his friend. I can understand why Angie and Effy get on. She's Effy's best friend, that's certain. It's nice for her to have a friend that's not one of us sisters but on the outside so to speak. She was never one for making close friends in school."

"Surely your sisters are your friends too?"

"I'm lucky, mine are. We do get on well. Mostly. But my friends are different. They let me see what life's like outside our family." Grace noted Jane's sympathetic demeanour before continuing. "Angie and Effy have become very close. I suppose being the same age they have lots in common. Sometimes I miss the relationship we used to have. It's like Effy's different. She's so much more grown up. She and Ellen seem closer than they've ever been. I feel a bit left out."

"Don't worry yourself about that, dear. As you both get older you'll grow close again. Knowing Effy, I can't imagine it would be otherwise. Right now, she's finding out who she is as well as wondering what her future holds. It's called becoming a grown up."

# CHAPTER 7

**Jingle Bells – Booker T & The MG's (Atlantic 584060 – 1966)**

*Sunday 25 December 1966*

"Wow, Dad." Mack was overcome as he unwrapped his Christmas present. It was not what he had expected from his father. "This is your Leica and light meter!"

"They were mine, but they're yours now. Don't you like them, James?"

"Yes. Of course I do! But the camera's your pride and joy. It's a Leica IIIf. I thought you might get me a cheap Kodak to replace the old Brownie."

"If you're going to put photography as a hobby on your CV then you'd better do it right. Especially after telling me what you had planned."

"Is it expensive?" queried Effy.

"Just a bit." Mack sighed, delighted.

"I've got you six rolls of thirty-five millimetre film, three colour, and three black and white. After that you buy your own."

"Do Effy and Grace know what you planned?"

Grace and Effy looked at each other, puzzled.

"What are you up to?" asked Grace.

"You mean you're going to do it?" Effy looked delighted. "You're going to help me with my fashion portfolio?"

"That's exactly what I'm going to do. Kill two birds with one photo shoot."

"What photo shoot?" Grace was a picture of bewilderment.

"Effy wants you and her to model all the dresses you've made. She wants me to photograph them so she can show how they've gone from sketched designs to finished items."

"You do realise fashion photography is very specialised, don't you? It's all about the lighting. Most of the shoots take place under strong studio lights," advised Robert MacKinnon. "Well, girls, come along. Open your presents. We can talk about photo shoots later."

30

Jane and Granny MacKinnon came into the lounge from the kitchen. "We've got the dinner underway. Do your sisters know what time to come up for the meal today?"

"Yes, I told Bridget. She's less likely to forget than Ellen," answered Effy.

"I'm somewhat surprised at Deidre. You'd think she'd want to spend Christmas with her sisters. Instead she's off to her boyfriend's family in Kent."

"Not as surprised as we are," stressed Grace. "Didn't take her long to find herself a boyfriend. You won't believe how she met him!"

"Do tell." Granny MacKinnon looked at Mack and Effy. "I'm always curious about how young people get together."

"They were dissecting a dead body!" Grace shuddered. "Can you imagine that? That's how they first met. That is *so* disturbing."

"Well, it's certainly unusual!" responded Jane, trying not to laugh. "What's he like?"

"Effy didn't meet him but I did. He's got a mop of curly black hair and a beard and he wears Buddy Holly-style glasses. Looks a bit like that keyboard player in Manfred Mann. Got a beatnik look about him."

Mack, having heard all this from Grace earlier, began singing Manfred Mann's *Just Like a Woman* in a quiet voice. Grinning, Effy gave him a gentle tap with her foot.

"Yes, Grace, but what's he like as a person?" Granny MacKinnon asked.

"A bit on the serious side, doesn't say much, and it's always serious when he does, so he's well matched with our Deidre."

"Call me Mary, girls. Show me what you've got for Christmas." Granny MacKinnon changed the topic. Like her daughter-in-law she, too, had to contain her laughter after hearing about Deidre's ghoulish romance.

"Jane and Rob have spoiled Grace and myself. We've got two pairs of tights…"

"I thought you'd need them, seeing how short your skirts and dresses are getting," Jane added. "Somewhat safer than stockings."

"…Underwear," continued Effy, "and make-up and a make-up bag, a small eau de cologne and a blouse. From Mack, two book tokens."

Effy then listed what she and Grace had received from her sisters and her parents.

"As I hadn't met you two young ladies I didn't know what to get you. Jane and Robert had told me a little about Effy but precious little about you, Grace. I hope you don't mind me giving you a little something instead that you might find helpful.' She handed each of the sisters an envelope. Inside a Christmas card each of the girls found ten pounds as two five-pound notes.

"We can't accept this, Mrs MacKinnon." Effy sounded shocked. "It's far too much."

"Nonsense, Effy. I'm certain both you and Grace can use it to buy materials to make smarter fashionable dresses. So let me hear no more of it."

In a quiet moment after Christmas dinner Effy spoke to Mack as they took an all-too-brief refuge in the new nursery. "I can't believe how much money your Gran gave me. I feel awful taking that much from a pensioner."

Mack smiled. "You only got a tenner because she's never met you. Wait till your birthday and next Christmas when she does know you better."

"Why?"

"Wait and see."

"So what did she get you?"

"A clan MacKinnon tie… and fifty pounds."

"How much?" Effy's face made Mack burst out laughing.

"She may be a pensioner but she's not exactly poor. You should see her house in Edinburgh. She owns a lot of commercial property in the city and is quite a wealthy woman. When Granddad passed away he left her a merry widow. With my uncles killed in the war, Dad and my Aunt Ellen will inherit it some day."

"Goodness."

"Under the circumstances, as she'd never met you or Grace, a tenner each isn't surprising."

"Then why are Adam and Caitlin so poor? Doesn't she like them?"

"Gran, like Granddad, and my parents, believe their children should go out into the world and make their own way. Be self-reliant. Having said that, Mum's father was much the same. He wasn't exactly poor, either, but she didn't get any help. That wasn't his way. As for Adam and Caitlin I overheard Gran telling Dad she was giving them a hundred pounds. She's giving another twenty quid for the little girl to be put into her savings account. I know my Dad's different. He helps my brother and Caitlin on the quiet."

"Goodness me," Effy repeated.

32

"But," Mack paused, "please don't say anything to Grace or to your sisters about any of this. I suspect Tom will have got the same as she gave me, with Ellen getting the same as you and Grace. And don't you dare say 'goodness' again."

Effy closed her mouth and smiled at him. Then after a few seconds she added, "I can't get over your gran's generosity. Nor your mum and dad's. I didn't say anything but both Grace and I each had five one-pound notes in with our presents. So how much did you get?"

"Nothing except the camera, light meter and rolls of film. Oh, and I can get a roll of wool and mohair mix from the mill for a new suit. They'll pay for it and go halves over the tailoring costs."

"You got no money at all from them?"

"No. Mind you, I wasn't expecting any. I'm still glad Dad's giving me a pound pocket money each week. With what I earn at Benny's I get by for the time being."

"I feel upset having heard that."

"Don't, Effy. You and Grace are in a difficult situation. I'm not. I know your mum and dad offered some money towards your keep here. My parents refused to accept it. The pocket money you've received each week, that's from your parents. Again, don't say anything about this to Grace or Ellen. Bridget is receiving some money to look after Ellen."

"I didn't know any of this. I'm staggered at how generous your family has been towards Grace and myself."

"We'd better get back downstairs. I know they'll be missing us. Anyway, I happen to know Gran wants to chat to you and Grace alone."

"What about?" Effy sounded concerned.

"Don't worry. She told me she wanted to get to get to know you both and take a look at all those frocks you've been knocking out between you."

"They're not frocks. They're dresses!"

# CHAPTER 8

**Who Could Ever Doubt My Love – The Isley Brothers
(Tamla Motown TMG 566 – 1966)**

*Christmas Day, Sunday 25 December 1966*

"These are so gorgeous." Mary MacKinnon's delight was clear as she looked through the girls' selection of dresses. "So well-made I can't believe they're not shop-bought! And you designed these yourselves?"

"We made them but Effy did most of the designs," Grace answered.

"You didn't copy the designs, did you, Effy?"

"Only these." Effy indicated some of their early efforts. "The rest were our designs."

"Where did you get your fabrics?"

Grace looked at Effy. "We get what we can from wherever we can. We've even recut clothes from jumble sales."

"Lately we've been lucky. Grace's friend Jean has found a place that sells inexpensive materials. We tried nylon but found it has too many drawbacks. Polyester wasn't much better."

"So what's the drawback with nylon?"

"It clings to the body too much and can cause minor static discharges which are not very pleasant. Also, it causes you to perspire and to be honest it's not comfortable to wear. Crimplene's a decent fabric. At least it doesn't crease so we we'll try using it a bit more. I'll try poplin, too, if we can find some going cheap. Most of our dresses are cotton, although we've tried damask linen. That can look stylish and is comfortable. The trouble with damask is it creases and it's expensive."

"And if it's patterned," interjected Grace with enthusiasm, "you have to check the pattern weave on a bolt first before you buy it to make sure it will all match up."

"Rayon is a better material, we like working with it," Effy added, sounding professional.

There was a knock on the door. "Is it alright for me to come in?" It was Jane MacKinnon.

"Of course it is," replied Grace.

34

"Well, Jane. These young women have impressed me. So much talent and skill."

"I wish I had half their skills when it comes to sewing and dress-making, Mary. I was taught the bare rudiments as a girl."

"Yes, I suppose it was the same for me. We were never expected to make our own clothes. I know for a fact my father would have frowned on it. He said it was no activity for a middle-class girl. My parents expected me to learn other accomplishments."

Effy wondered what those other accomplishments could be.

"You don't appear to have a seamstress's mannequin. How do you manage without one?"

"With some difficulty," conceded Effy. "My mother has an ancient rickety one that about does the job but it's not level or in good condition. It's well past its best."

"The girls need a dressmaker's mannequin, Mary. We should try to find one for them."

Mary MacKinnon smiled and gave a knowing glance at her daughter-in-law. "Yes. I believe we should, Jane, I believe we should."

"Oh, please don't go to any trouble." Effy experienced a sharp pain as Grace kicked her ankle.

"Oh, it won't be any trouble, Effy. We'll see what we can do, won't we, Jane?"

Jane smiled. "I'll find them one."

"Jane has told me that you have quite a few designs in readiness. Would you like to show me what you have planned?"

Over the next half hour Effy showed them her design sketches. The two older women looked bemused but the drawings impressed them. They were even more impressed when comparing the original sketches with the dresses. Effy explained she had designed them for herself and Grace although they had made one before for Angie as well as another for her eighteenth birthday. Mary and Jane were insistent on seeing this latest creation. Grace brought it out, making mention of how they had selected the colours to match Angie's skin tone. The dress was a straight line cut made from sparkling indigo Lurex material with a minute pale blue dot print. It was sleeveless and had a mandarin collar. When asked how they knew Angie's measurements, Grace explained that Effy was the exact same build and height. Both were petite with straight figures. Effy found herself having to model the dress; the hem was six inches above the knee. The real surprise came when she heard Mary MacKinnon's comment on the length of the hemline.

"Do you know, Effy, I wish I were young again. I would wear that dress without a moment's hesitation." On seeing her daughter-in-law's amazed expression, she continued, "Don't look so shocked, Jane. On someone Effy's age this looks breathtaking. It's what the young should be wearing. It's 'trendy', as they say these days. There's nothing wrong with showing some leg. Remind me to show you photographs of myself as a 'flapper'. My family considered me a scandalous young thing. Hemlines were short then, though not as short as now. I suppose not having tights back then didn't allow for shorter hems. Admit it, Jane. If you were Effy and Grace's age you'd love to wear a dress this daring."

"I'm not their age. Besides we're only as young as our knees and mine wouldn't look good in something so short. I'm in my forties and pregnant. And don't you think these mini skirts and dresses are too provocative? They can only encourage the wrong kind of male attention."

Mary turned to Effy. "What do you think? Does it encourage the wrong kind of attention?"

"Maybe... but I do think we have the right to wear what we want. It's time women had a better deal in society, and more freedom, Mack... James says the same."

"Seems that your son supports the feminine cause, Jane."

"That should come as no surprise to an old suffragette like yourself," replied Jane. "No wonder my husband has always expressed such pro-feminist sympathies. Well, it's no terrible thing to have enlightened men in the family. Unfortunately they're not typical of the average man today. As for myself fashion was not on my list of priorities at their age. There was a war on. My place at university went on hold and then ended when the war was over. I became a Wren to serve my country. Soon after that a mother, then a working mother, and finally a housewife – only to become a mother once more. Most of those years of post-war austerity and rationing ended my dream of dreaming spires."

The regret tinged with bitterness was not lost on Effy. She knew from Mack that his mother had served in the Royal Navy. He had shown her photographs of his parents in their naval uniforms. But she couldn't remember any mention of his mother's lost opportunity as an Oxford undergraduate. Did he know about this? What had prevented his mother from going to Oxford after the war? *Adam*. She must have married and conceived

36

straightaway. Or…? The 'or' answered itself. Grace was about to say something following the same line of reasoning. Effy flashed her a familiar warning look and Grace understood in an instant. Should she broach this with Mack to confirm her suspicion? Or was it the kind of question best not asked?

Mary MacKinnon's cheery response came as a salve. "Now, Jane, I can remember when the boys were young. You bought a so-called fashionable 'wiggle' dress. It did look good on you."

"What's a 'wiggle' dress?" Grace was amused by the name.

Both Mary and Jane looked surprised by her question.

Effy intervened. "It's a calf length dress or skirt where the hem is much narrower than the hip. It emphasises the 'wiggle' of the hip when you walk or dance."

Grace stood up and clutched the hem of her skirt tightly, taking a few tottering steps. "I see what you mean. Didn't Marilyn Monroe wear these kind of 'wiggle' skirts?"

Mack and his father were enjoying listening to Tony Bennett. It was better than watching The Black and White Minstrel Show. A John Wayne movie, *The Comancheros*, would be on at quarter to nine. "Thank you for buying me this LP. I do appreciate it but it was a lot of money."

It was. Yet Mack was sure it had been the right gift to get his father. It was better than a pair of socks. At least with music his dad would always have it to listen to it. Socks wore out, got darned and in the end got binned. No one else would think to buy his father something he would enjoy with genuine long-term pleasure. It was a man thing.

"The lyrics of that second track sum up the generality of women." Rob addressed his son with a wicked grin. "Listen and learn, son, listen and learn."

Mack checked out the title on the back of the album cover. "Do you mean 'Girl Talk'?"

"That's the one." Rob rose and went over to the radiogram to turn the LP over to the A side. "Listen to the words again and tell me what you think."

"You must think a great deal of your friend to make her such a beautiful dress," Mary began. "Tell me about her."

"What would you like to know?" Effy was cautious, noting Jane's

37

instant interest prompted by the question.

"You know, what's she's like as a person? How did you get to know one another? Those sorts of things, dear."

"We met for the first time when I went to Halifax with James. She was a friend of Tom's and James'. I got to know her that same evening. Afterwards we became friends. We share an interest in fashion, music and dancing. We like window-shopping and chatting about girl things. As a person she's very confident and knows how to put men in their place. She also has a wicked sense of humour that makes me laugh. I suppose in some ways we are opposites but we get on so well, it's as if we've known each other all our lives."

"Does she have a boyfriend of her own?" asked Jane.

"No. Not at the moment. Angie's choosy. She always says she hasn't found what she's looking for." *No.* She wasn't going to fall into one of Jane's trap questions. Mack had warned her against his mother's clever interrogating techniques.

Grace's expression displayed a peculiar relief. Effy would have to find out what Grace knew.

"Is she a student like you?" Mary went on with the questioning.

"No, she left school and went to work as an apothecary assistant at a chemist's. However, and it's a bit hush-hush, she's going to evening classes to take her O Levels in summer. Please don't say anything to James or Tom. Both Ellen and myself have been encouraging her to stick with it. Oh, she passed her driving test and bought her own car, too, with her Uncle Den's help. Angie comes over to see me on Halifax half-day closing. She picks me up at St. Jo's so we can go round clothes shops."

"But aren't you supposed to be in classes?" queried Mary.

"No. I have the afternoon free for study periods so I sneak out. We both work Saturdays, so it's the only opportunity we have to get together."

"And does James go too?"

It was obvious where this was leading. Yes, Effy suspected Angie might have a crush on Mack, although Angie had never once given her cause for concern.

"Heavens, no! Girls only. That's the whole point. James wouldn't appreciate getting dragged round clothes shops by us."

"I see." Mary studied Effy while exchanging a quick glance with Jane. "Jane seemed to think she was wanting to replace you in James's affections."

Effy let out a little laugh. "I don't think so. She's never ever given me cause to think it. Besides, she only spends time with him when we're all together at the weekends."

Grace chipped in. "Anyway James only has eyes for Effy. I doubt very much he's interested in Angie. Nice as she is, I don't think she's his type."

The question took Mack by surprise. It wasn't quite what he was expecting from his father. "Do you think this friend Angie has any designs on your affections? You don't think she's trying to take you away from Effy?"

"Dad... really?"

"Well?"

"Put it this way, if she did then it would be a lost cause, wouldn't it? Effy's my girl. Angie's her best friend, although she was also a friend of mine and Tom's before they even met. I like Angie a lot but she's never going to replace Effy. Never ever."

"It's surprising she hasn't a boyfriend of her own. A pretty-looking lassie like Angie ought to have been snapped up by now."

"Well, it's not for lack of trying by the fellas. She's really careful. I know she's had some awful experiences so that's the most likely reason. Also, from what's she's told Effy, her parents' marriage isn't perfect. She has no intention of falling into the same trap."

"I see."

"I hope you do, Dad." Mack put a stop to any further conversation on that topic.

"Do you have a secret crush on Angie?" Effy asked in her most matter-of-fact voice. "Or do you think she has a crush on you?"

"What?" Mack couldn't believe he was hearing these words. "Do you know my Dad asked me the same thing when you were all upstairs. Is there some reason for you asking?"

"No. Not especially. Now, give me an answer. Do you have a crush on her?"

"Straight answer is a definite no. Can't make it any plainer. If she fancies me then it's not going anywhere, is it? Anyway, she's your best friend. You tell me. Has she ever given you any cause to think so? Because she sure as hell has never given me cause to think so."

"No. You're right. Angie's never given me cause, either, even though I suspect she has some kind of thing for you." Effy's next words shook him. "Mind you, if I wasn't around she would be perfect for you."

He took her in his arms and the words came tumbling out. "Don't say things like that. You're the only one for me. You'll always be number one in my heart. Always." That was true. And yet...

# CHAPTER 9

**He's Just a Playboy – The Drifters (UK Atlantic 4008 B Side 1964)**

*New Year's Day, Sunday 1 January 1967*

"Hang on, so what if Den was a Teddy boy back in his teens? What does it matter?"

"What do you mean, was? Just 'cos I'm married with kids and in my twenties don't mean I've hung up my blue suede shoes. Once a Ted, always a Ted."

Den was Angie's Uncle. Mack, Tom and a couple of Mod lads were in the kitchen enjoying Angie's eighteenth birthday.

"Let me get this straight. You're what? About twenty-five?" Asked Tom Catford.

"No, I'm twenty-six for a few more months, nearer twenty-seven."

"And you did National Service when you were eighteen?" Tom pressed on.

"Yes. Not like you lucky young bar-stewards getting off light without having to do it."

"Yeah! That's our lucky break, and your tough titty." Alan Holmes whooped.

"I don't get it. You did National Service, so why do you still want to be a Teddy boy when you don't qualify as a boy anymore?"

"Okay. Let me put it this way. Why are you guys Mods?"

"Because it's cool," replied Stingray, one of the Mods.

"There's your answer. Us Teds are cool. Maybe not in your eyes but we are in our eyes. Without us, you young 'uns would be nowhere today."

Stingray sniggered. "I don't think so."

Mack cut in. "Den's right. I agree with him. If it wasn't for the Teds things might be different. Without them breaking the rules over clothes back in the Fifties things wouldn't have changed."

"How do you figure that?" Alan Holmes asked, fidgeting with his beer bottle.

"Think about it. Rock and Roll broke the music mould. Would you want to be listening to the likes of Ruby Murray and Dickie Valentine? Given the choice of Rosemary Clooney and Ronnie Hilton or Elvis and

41

Chuck Berry, which would you choose? No contest. Rock and Roll opened the door for the Blues and R&B. It wasn't only the music. All the coffee bars and milk bars got opened up for them to hang out in. With jukeboxes they got to hear the latest records. Then they went out and bought the records. Like it or not, their dress sense, hairstyles and attitudes said *we want to be different*. That's like us saying *we don't want to be like everyone else*. I hate to say it but the Teds broke the door down for the Sixties to go Mod. We may have a different idea about fashion and music but it comes down to the same thing. It's an attitude, a state of mind, saying you want to be different."

"Yeah, I get that," responded Alan. "When you put it like that it makes sense. I never thought of it that way."

"Gawd help us! We've got to be thankful to Teds for letting us become Mods! What a turn-up for the book! Too weird to get yer 'ead round," chortled Stingray.

"Bloody hell, you're a clever bugger. Even I never thought of us Teds doing that but I suppose you're right. We did knock the doors down." Den seemed pleased with Mack's words. "Angie was right when she told me you were a bit of a bright spark."

"Aye, and he failed his Eleven Plus. Went to a modern, not a grammar. They thought he was good enough to get into a grammar school Sixth Form when he left the modern," Tom informed Den.

"What's the story with the small RAF decals on your scooter fly screens?" Den changed the subject.

"You mean the targets?"

"Yeah. You know, the round things the RAF has on its airplane wings."

"Do you want to explain that one, Tom? After all, I heard it from you first." Mack was feeling as thought he'd talked enough already.

"Last summer during the Wakes holiday a bunch of us went down to Torquay. We met up with some London Mods. One had a target on his parka back. Others had target stickers on their scooters. Of course I had to ask, like you do. They were a bit reluctant to tell us. Anyhow, long story short, cutting to the chase, one of them let it slip when he was well pissed. He let on that it referred to the Battle of Britain 'Few'. Real Mods were 'the new Few'. Sounded plausible. When I told Mack he understood straightaway, didn't you?"

"I could relate to it," replied Mack. "We don't want to be like everybody else. Compared to most young people our age Mods are few in number. We look as if we conform to the expectations of the establishment but we don't. We want to do things our way, not what's expected of us. Mods look smart, sharp and stylish to get accepted. The fact is we're doing it to undermine the status quo by appearing acceptable."

"You say that but you don't say why. Come on, give me the low on it," pressed Den.

"Like I said, we don't want to be like everyone else. We don't believe in entitlement but in working to get what we want and to live the way we want. Nobody's going to tell us otherwise. Bottom line is, we hate the establishment because they think they're the only ones entitled to run things the way they always have. Mods are the radicals who are going to change it from the inside."

"Nah. Now you're trying to bullshit me." Den dismissed the idea, putting his beer glass down on the kitchen table. "Most of you don't think like that. Being Mods, it's a passing teenage fad."

"You mean like still being a Ted at your age?" smirked Tom.

Mack smiled, mischief evident. "Maybe it's a fad. Maybe it's not. Only time will tell. The Tickets and the Numbers may be like that but the leaders of the pack, the High Numbers and Faces, will always be Aces. You want to know something, Den? The real enemy is the so-called wealthy ruling elite of this country. The enemy tries to condemn so many of us so *we'll live and die in these towns* never knowing anything different or better. The times are changing but the enemy is always going be there and I won't let them drag me down."

"What's a Ticket?" asked Stingray.

"It's a weekend Mod like you." Alan and Tom pointed at him, causing a burst of laughter.

"Fuck off, you twats! I'm no weekend mini-Mod."

"Now, now boys! Play nice! No swearing. I don't want my birthday do spoilt." Angie entered the kitchen, followed by Grace. "Move out of the way of the oven. Let me see if the sausage rolls are ready."

"Mack's taking the micky. Trying to make out him and his mates are some kind of revolutionary movement changing the system."

Angie pulled the oven tray out. "They're ready but too hot. Yes, Uncle Den, you need to be careful with Mack. He's well-known for taking the micky-mouse. I heard him convince one of the scooter lads that Nuneaton was named after a nun eaten by wolves."

"Never!" exclaimed Den. "You're pulling my leg?"

"No. He did. Honest. Didn't he, Tom? Stingray?" They nodded, grins all round.

"That was bloody funny," cracked Alan. "Like Angie says. I couldn't keep a straight face. It was hilarious."

"Not as funny as the one about zebras," blurted Tom.

Mack looked embarrassed.

"Oh, I heard about that!" Stingray butted in. "Didn't you convince Sy Hayward they painted zebras brown to use in movies because horses didn't look real on the big screen but painted zebras did? Sy swallowed it hook line and sinker. Went round telling everyone they used painted zebras in films."

"Sy. What a dummy! A real live Simple Simon," chuckled Alan.

A chorus of voices broke out into a spontaneous chant.

> "Simple Simon met a Pie man
> Going to the fair.
> Asked Simon of the Pie man
> What you got there?
> PIES you moron!"

"He's never lived it down, the dozy cu… prat," chortled Stingray, moderating his choice of words. "A reyt thicko. He was well narked when people kept chanting that to him."

"If you think that's bad," Angie grinned, "one of their mates walked into the Vic Lounge proud as a peacock wearing his brand-new green mohair suit. This lot started singing *Robin Hood, Robin Hood riding through the glen* just like on the TV. The Vic crowd howled their socks off. Poor Grantsy. I felt for him. It was embarrassing. Blame TC for that, he started it."

Den choked back a laugh.

"It was only a bit of fun, Angie. Grantsy took it well." Tom grinned. "Even though everyone's been calling him Sherwood after that."

"Yes, Mack. I wonder who started calling him Sherwood?" She gave him an accusing look.

"It was in fun, Angie. How was I to know it would stick as his nickname?"

"Most of us have a nickname. 'Cos my name's Steve and my surname's Wray, I got my nickname at school from the telly programme and it's stuck ever since. That's why they all call me Stingray."

44

"It's like Acky's mate Yamaha. He got seen riding a Yamaha motorbike so they all called him that even though he rides around on a TV175," added Tom.

Den stepped out of the way to let his niece put the sausage rolls on a large plate. "How do you lot afford to keep buying all the new gear as dedicated followers of fashion?"

"Trade secret," joked Tom. "If I told you we'd have to kill you."

"Come on, give us a straight answer." Den grinned. "It's what Mods are all about, isn't it?"

"It's not easy," piped up Stingray. "I spend most of my wages."

"Yeah, it does cost me a fair bit too," added Alan. "I'm always skint by Tuesday. Don't know how Mack and TC do it."

"It's not about the quantity," Mack answered. "It's about the quality. You don't need to be spending all the time to look sharp. Few of us can afford it. It's about being creative and knowing where to go looking for bargains. It's also about trying to keep one jump ahead of everyone else and not wearing the same thing. A lot confuse fashion with style. They're not the same thing."

"Go on, I'm listening." Den showed genuine interest.

"Casual's easy," continued Mack. "For a basic set of must have's, you need some Levi jeans, straight-leg Levi Cords and Sta Prest trousers. Top half: a sports jacket, herringbone or check. These should be three buttoned with vents. I got my sports jacket second-hand. Effy helped me with the tailoring. Changed it from two to three button fastening with new buttons, extended the vents from four inch to ten. Apart from that I've got a Harrington and a monkey jacket. Found a pale blue and a white Fred Perry top going cheap in the sales. Don't think the shop knew what they were selling. A couple of check short sleeve shirts with button-down collars. Sewed the buttons onto the collars myself. They pass for Ben Sherman and look as smart but cost less than a third of the price. The best of it is they're better quality shirts, too. That's it. Mix and match the lot and you're well away. Now suits, they're another matter. They have to be top quality, as do the shirts to go with the suits. So do the cufflinks and tiepins you wear. I've picked up second-hand solid silver cuff links and tiepins for next to nothing. Even found a nine-karat gold tiepin going cheap at the parish jumble sale. The shirt cuffs have to show from the jacket sleeves. I borrow my Dad's cuff links sometimes but you can find plenty second-hand. Ties are easy but you do need decent tiepins to match. I've got two suits so far, and a third getting made up."

Den gave a low whistle. "Blimey. That's more clobber than I own now. If your suits cost anything like my drape jackets did, I take it they don't come cheap."

"If you go to Burton's or one of the High Street tailors, then it's not going to be cheap. It's also going to be a bit too High Street. A lot of the lads end up looking samey. Get yourself a local bespoke tailor. That's what Tom and I did. Then we did the rounds of the local mill shops to get a roll of cloth. It's not only less expensive it's about the quality of the material, the mohair wool mix. It's also about the different patterns you can't get from the chain tailors like Fenton's or John Collier."

"And it's brilliant quality cloth, believe you me," chipped in Tom. "You'd never get the same from the High Street. The bloke we use can knock up a made to measure for about fifteen quid and it includes the cost of the roll of cloth. That's cheaper than the High Street even when you add in the cost of the cloth. And when it's finished it looks like it cost fifty or sixty quid."

"I thought you told me your last suit cost thirty quid!" This revelation upset Stingray.

"No," replied Mack. "You said *you* thought it cost thirty. I didn't deny it. I let you think it."

"It may be cheaper but it's still not cheap." Den rubbed his chin. "But then, quality don't come cheap, does it? I paid a lot for my drape jackets. What about these leather coats? They must cost a packet?"

"Don't own one," Mack replied, "nor a Crombie copy. Be original and be different is the name of the game. I try not to follow the herd. Saturday night and how many of them do you see down the Square with imitation Crombie coats? Loads. I found a heavy three-quarter-length grey wool and mohair overcoat with a breast pocket for a silk hanky. That overcoat stands out amongst all those black Crombie-style coats."

"Wish I'd seen it before I bought mine," Alan muttered. "I would have bought one like Mack's. Half the price of mine and much better quality."

"Stingray got his leather coat from Brunskill's in Bradford. Twelve quid it cost, didn't it?"

"Real peacocks, these two, Uncle Den. Mack's got a passion for fashion. It's rubbed off hanging around Effy and Grace," commented Angie. "I got my leather coat from Brunskill's too."

"Have you opened your birthday present from Effy and Grace?" asked Mack.

"Not had a chance yet." Angie placed the fresh sausage rolls on a serving plate, slapping Tom's hand as he tried to help himself. "As soon as I've finished in here I'm going to open it. Grace, would you take these through for me? I want a word or two with this lot."

"They've been behaving themselves, Angie," reported Den. "We've had some interesting chat about Teds and Mods. Very amicable."

"I thought you'd get on. I never doubted it. No. It's Stingray and Alan. I saw you two eying up Grace. Don't get any ideas. She's well under age even if she doesn't look it. So don't bother chatting her up. She's too young for you two."

"How old is she? She's got to be sixteen."

"Looks can be deceiving. She's not fifteen yet. Steer clear. Now, what about joining the rest of us? Strange thing about you blokes, you always spend time in the kitchen when it's a party. Any other time and you're nowhere to be seen."

"That's 'cos there's usually no beer, only washing up," joked Stingray.

"Watch it! Don't let your brain go to your head!" Angie reprimanded with a smile.

"Why's everyone taking the piss out of me tonight?"

"We love you really." Angie smiled as she went out.

"That's told you straight. Never tangle with my niece. She quick with the clever put-downs."

Back in the living room Mack could see Effy and Ellen deep in conversation with Gillian, Angie's older sister. The conversation stopped as they saw him making his way over to them. Strange how that always seemed to happen whenever they were chatting. What was so secret about their conversations?

"You must be Mack. Effy and Ellen have been telling me all about you." Gillian introduced herself. Mack noticed that Effy was blushing. What on earth had she been talking about?

"That's me. A pleasure to finally meet you, Gillian." The resemblance to Angie was striking. Same black hair and very dark brown eyes framing a pale complexion. So this was Gillian who saw Effy at Family Planning. He felt embarrassed, knowing she knew the score.

"Angie's has told me all about you," Gillian continued. That felt awkward, too, though not as awkward as being in this house again. The last time he'd been here Angie had taken his virginity. It was a peculiar feeling seeing Effy, Ellen and Gillian sitting on the same sofa where Angie had seduced him.

"Where's Grace?" He asked, feeling uncomfortable as the three girls kept looking at him.

"She's gone upstairs with Angie to open up her and Effy's present," Ellen informed him.

"Oh, I do hope she likes it." Effy sounded worried.

"I'm sure she'll look great in it," he responded immediately, trying to put her at ease. "It's a fantastic looking dress, beautifully made. She'll love it."

"Excuse me a moment. I can hear someone knocking on the door." Gillian rose. "I hope it's not gate-crashers. I'll get Den to come with me although Angie mentioned there was a possibility of some friend from Manchester coming over."

"Friend?" Mack's curiosity got the better of him. "Has she found herself a bloke there?"

"She's mentioned she'd met someone." He sensed Effy knew more but she said nothing further.

"It might be this guy called Nate," Gillian informed him as she made to go to the door. "Angie met him at The Twisted Wheel. He's part of a local older crowd that goes. Seems like a gen bloke according to her. She told me he's a bit of a smooth operator."

Mack felt a sudden unexpected inexplicable pang of jealousy. He tried hard but he couldn't shake the feeling. Why should he feel this way about Angie? She was only his friend, unlike Effy. There should be no reason for him to feel jealous. What had happened had happened. It was in the past, never to be mentioned.

"What's wrong, Mack?" Trust Effy to notice his reaction. Was it so blatant?

"Nothing, Eff. It's nothing." The look she gave him was worrying.

"Eh, up Nate!" Tom called across the room. "Glad you could make it, mate."

Mack and Effy glanced towards the doorway as the conversation in the crowded room stilled. Mack wasn't quite what they all expected. Ellen was right. Nate was not the kind of bloke they'd imagined Angie choosing as a boyfriend. Standing no more than five foot six he epitomised Mod cool. His hair, styled in a shorter than usual backcombed French cut, framed an olive complexion. The suit was one of the best tailored that Mack had ever seen. In his left hand Nate held what looked like a champagne bottle. The Drifters' *He's Just a Playboy* was playing like some appropriate overture, making Mack smile. Exuding total confidence, Nate made his way across to Tom while taking in everyone in the crowded room. The handshaking ritual followed as Tom and Nate greeted one another with requisite Mod etiquette. Their mutual verbal exchanges drowned as talk in the room returned to its previous noisy level. Ellen rose and made her way across to them.

Mack looked at Effy, the smile turning into a smirk. "I can't see it, Eff. Honest I can't. He's not Angie's type, no more than I am."

"Are you sure you're not?" Her response worried him.

He placed a hand on each shoulder. "I thought we'd sorted this already. Don't go imagining what doesn't exist, Eff. There's only room for one girl in my life, not two. It's you. Don't ever doubt it. But he's not Angie's type, I'm certain."

"The trouble is, you *are* her type." Effy was watching his reaction to her words.

"So? That's not my problem, even if it were true, which I don't believe it is. She's your friend more so than mine these days. Anyway, I thought we'd put this silly idea to bed."

Angie walked into the room, wearing the dress Effy and Grace had made. Mack admitted to himself she looked stunning. Glancing over for the briefest moment, Angie looked straight at him before seeking out Effy.

"Angie!" Tom attracted her attention. "Look who's here?"

Her face lit up in delight as she spotted the arrival. Mack and Effy scrutinised Nate and Angie's every move. Captivated, they watched Nate hand the champagne bottle to Tom. Taking Angie by each hand to admire her dress, Nate made her twirl before giving her a peck on the cheek.

Mack had never seen the dress worn until now. Whatever words Angie and Nate were saying to each other, their reaction was one of mutual delight. Tom passed the champagne bottle back to Nate, who gave it to Angie. Then he produced a small gift box from his jacket pocket and handed it to her. Blushing, she appeared embarrassed by Nate's gifts. It was fascinating yet somehow peculiar.

"Has she mentioned this guy to you?" Mack turned to Effy.

"Kind of... sort of. She mentioned she'd become friendly with some guys at The Twisted Wheel and that they were from North Manchester, but she never said anything about someone called Nate."

"You surprise me. I thought as her best friend she'd tell you everything. Look out, here they come." They rose from the settee as the trio approached.

Mack towered over Nate by a full six inches.

Angie did the introductions. "This is Nate Silvers, a friend of mine from The Twisted Wheel." Mack found himself sized up by the newcomer who had a strong, firm handshake. There was nothing limp-wristed about him. What came next was as surprising. He took Effy by both hands in the same manner as he had with Angie.

"Angie, you were so right. She is stunning. In fact, Effy, you are fabulous. We can and we must use you, Effy. You could be a new Jean Shrimpton. And there was I thinking your sister Ellen was a looker as well as Angie. What an incomparable beauty we have in you."

Effy blushed at the compliment. Mack felt anger welling up as possessiveness took hold.

"Angie, you, Ellen and Effy must have a private talk with me this evening before I head back to Manchester. I've found what we're looking for at Silvers Fashions. You girls are the business."

"That shy redhead by the door is their youngest sister Grace."

Nate gushed to Angie. "Wow, wow, wow. You were so right to bring me over to meet them. We can use the three of them as well as yourself."

Turning to Effy once again, he became business-like in an instant. "You designed and made this dress for Angie?"

Before Effy could say any more he continued. "It's amazing. The combination of colours, the choice of fabric, the way it flows as Angie moves. Angie says you are a real dab hand with design."

Effy was flattered. "I can't take all the credit. Grace is a great seamstress. She did all the cutting."

Maintaining strong eye contact with Effy, Nate asked, "Without using patterns, is that right?"

"She makes her own," Effy answered.

"We'll all have to chat shortly. I don't have much time. I have to get back to Manchester in less than an hour." Focusing on Mack, Nate startled him with his next words. "And you are the legend. The guy who kicked Scooby's hard men into touch."

"How do you know about that?" Mack was taken by complete surprise.

"The one who bolted told me what happened. At the time he didn't know who you were. He knew you were a couple of guys from Yorkshire. It was only after a minor incident near The Wheel involving 'Ratty' or Scooby that the story came out."

"Is that his nickname?" Mack grinned, remembering Scooby the pusher.

"C'mon! He looks ratty. Anyway, the guy who ran away told me you demolished two of the local hard cases in a flash. Made a point of saying it was all over in less than twenty seconds. Said he'd never seen anything like it."

"What's that all about?" Effy looked aghast. "When did that happen? You never told me."

"There's a lot these two don't tell us," Ellen grumbled. "You only learn third-hand later on and then only by chance. You know what Mack can be like. He'll only tell you what he wants. I only found out after we had a near run-in with this character 'Ratty' near The Twisted Wheel. If it hadn't been for Nate and Angie, god knows what would have happened. Tom made me swear to say nothing about it to you."

Effy gave him a glare. Words would come later, he could tell.

"I'm sure you'll tell me all about it, El." Effy followed up the glare with a frost-cold look he didn't like. "Yes, I can already see the shine coming off Mack's halo."

This was not going well. Angie intervened, giving Ellen a sharp look that ordered her to clam up. "Okay, Halloran sisters, as Nate has to get back, can we three go up to my room with Nate so he can explain what's going on."

"Aren't we invited?" asked Tom.

"No. You two have to mingle. Actually, I'd like you and Mack to chat to those two girls over there, real friendly like. The tall gangly one is Alice Liddell and the other is Cathy Manley. I was at school with Alice. Alice died in hospital last year. They thought she was dead and they were taking her to the morgue when she came round. She couldn't remember

51

anything about her life before that. Total amnesia. They've both started coming down the Plebs since the summer. You will have seen them but not taken any notice. You might find Alice a little strange so play nice. She's found it tough having to relearn all about her life and family."

"And don't get any ideas, lover boy." Ellen made it clear they shouldn't overstep the boundaries.

"Message received and understood." Tom gave her his broadest smile. "As if I would, doll."

"Okay, let's do the hostess bit," sighed Mack as he watched Nate and the girls disappear from the room, taking Grace with them. Turning to the two girls he remembered seeing them down The Plebs. He recalled how friendly Angie was with them.

"I kind of know Alice. She used to live not far from us. Never spoke to her. Well, that's not true. I did try to chat her up once when I was about fourteen. She was a right shy thing. Giggled a lot and gave me the brush-off."

"Why doesn't that surprise me, Tom? Far more important is what went on at The Wheel with you and Scooby. I have to know to get my tale straight when Effy gets back to me. I don't think she's well pleased with me tonight for one thing or another."

"Later, sunshine, later. It's not as bad as all that. Hi there." Tom addressed the two girls. Alice was the tall Twiggy thin one with honey-coloured bobbed hair. She had a confident manner, standing almost like a man would when Mack studied her close up. The other was a shy-looking brunette. Tom began with, "You'll probably not remember me…"

"I don't remember you," Alice replied, looking him up and down as she spoke, "but I know you live along the road from me. To be honest I don't remember anyone after my 'accident'. I've seen you down The Plebs with your girlfriend Ellen. Angie's told me about your cousin. I've seen you with your beautiful girlfriend, she's called Effy, isn't she?"

Mack confirmed with a nod. "You've just started on the scene. I've seen you dancing when we've been down the club. I understand you're an old friend of Angie's?"

"So I've been told. We're getting to know each other again. Truth is, my mind was wiped clean. They tell me I died and revived. I didn't know who I was when I revived."

"You mean you didn't even know your name?"

52

"No, not even my name. I was a blank canvas. I've no memories of who I was before."

"So you don't remember seeing the Pearly Gates when you were dead?" quipped Tom. "Or was it the hot spot down below?"

Mack elbowed him. "Take no notice of my cousin. He's a joker and too clever for his own good sometimes. How about you… Cathy, isn't it?"

They made polite conversation until Effy and her sisters returned with Angie and Nate. Mack had found Alice unnerving yet fascinating at the same time. There was something he could not quite come to terms with about her. She had the confidence and conversation of a grown man, someone his father's age, yet she was only Angie's age. There'd been a few moments when he'd wondered if he was conversing with a girl. Alice came across like an adult with years of experience behind her. Not that he could ever describe her as masculine in any way. Quite the contrary: physically she was attractive and feminine. It was her self-assurance and composed manner that suggested mannish qualities, unlike her shy friend Cathy. Alice was definitely peculiar. Mack could not work her out. This would become to be another fated meeting. Alice would come to play a part in his life and those of his friends in the future.

"A pleasure chatting with you." Mack broke off the conversation, seeing Effy and Angie returning. "It was great getting to know you. No doubt we'll see you around and chat some more."

Effy and her sisters were excited. Angie was beaming. Nate looked pleased too. What had gone on? Sneaking a look at his wristwatch, Mack realised time had flown while chatting to Alice. The girls had been gone forty minutes.

Nate extended his hand towards Mack. "It's been a pleasure to meet you, Mack, but I have to dash. You must get over to The Twisted Wheel with Angie and meet everyone. You and Effy have to come. There's nothing like The Wheel. It's the top Mod Soul spot in the country. We get the best acts from the U.S. as well as home-grown bands."

Mack's response was guarded. "We'll look forward to going. A pleasure to have met you."

As Nate made his farewells they followed him out into the cold night air. His Mini Cooper S wasn't any old Cooper S. It had a custom-sprayed Union Jack flag roof with a broad stripe on the bonnet and a matching one on the boot. Each door had the obligatory blank white racing circle on the

53

Mini's racing green paintwork. The guy was not short of a penny piece, that much was clear.

# CHAPTER 10

**Maybe I Know – Lesley Gore (Mercury MF 829 – 1964)**

Once inside Mack turned to Effy. Curiosity had the better of him. "Okay, Eff. Spill the Heinz. What's been going on?"

Effy stopped smiling and glanced at Angie and Grace, who both shrugged their shoulders. "You never tell me the half of anything if you tell me at all. Now it's your turn to wonder what's going on."

"Oh, for God's sake, Eff…"

"I thought you didn't believe in God?"

"Why are we falling out? What's wrong?"

"Nothing."

"Listen, Eff…" Tom began, seeing a spat developing.

Effy turned on him. "Going to make excuses for Mack?"

"Yeah, I am. The Oldham gig was my fault. He didn't want to go along with it, not really. I persuaded him. Blame me, not Mack. We thought it better not to advertise it because we knew you'd get mad. Some things are better left unsaid."

"Don't spout song lyrics at me, Thomas Catford!" she snapped. "Nothing surprises me about the pair of you. Goodness knows what else you two have got up to and kept it secret from Ellen and me."

"Don't go spoiling Angie's party, Eff." It was Mack's turn to be sharp. This was a tone he'd never used with her. The reprimand was instant. Turning to Angie, his tone warm and conciliatory, he said, "I'm going to be blunt. Has Effy anything to worry about you and me?"

"Grief, no. Effy, you can't be serious? For heaven's sake, I thought we were friends? How on earth could you think any such thing?"

Grace joined in, upset by the conversation. "It's Mack's Mum and Gran's fault, putting ideas into Effy's head."

"What do you mean? It's their fault?" Mack's astonishment was obvious. Angie went pale.

"They both kept mentioning it over Christmas even though I kept saying it wasn't so." Grace looked Angie in the eyes as she spoke. "Of course it isn't, is it?"

"You're right, Grace. It isn't."

55

Grace's recounting of the conversation made Effy redden with embarrassment. The distress was clear in her eyes as the words tumbled out of her sister's mouth.

"Oh, great!" Mack threw his hand up in the air. "I'm glad we cleared that up. Satisfied?"

"I'm sorry, Jimmy Mack." Effy eyes welled up and the tears began to fall. "I'm so, so, sorry Angie. I'm being awful and spoiling your party."

Angie sat down beside Effy and hugged her. She wasn't going to spoil their friendship, even if lying was her only choice.

"I'll always be your friend, Effy. Nothing will come between us as far as I'm concerned. Perhaps if I didn't come over it would be better, if that's how his mum thinks?"

"Stuff and nonsense! You come over as often as you want to see Effy. I'm going to put my mum in her place about this." Genuine anger seethed in Mack's words. "Now let's put a stop to this nonsense. If you want to know what I've got up to, ask and I'll tell you the truth."

Except neither Angie nor Mack could ever tell Effy about that night. Like the song's lyrics, some things were better left unsaid.

# CHAPTER 11

**Just A Little Misunderstanding – Contours (Tamla Motown TMG 564 – 1966)**

*Sunday 1 January 1967 – Later still*

"So you see," Tom confessed to Effy and Ellen, "don't blame Mack. He refused to have any more to do with pills. In fact, he's made me think hard about what had happened. I hate to admit it but since I've met Ellen I'm avoiding doing daft stuff. She's told me I've got to grow up if we're going to be together."

At least Effy now seemed convinced. She clung to Mack's arm like a limpet. He hoped Grace coming to his defence had put Effy's suspicious thoughts to rest. If Angie harboured feelings for him they were well masked. Yet it had him wondering if there was some truth to it. There was no fire without smoke and no smoke without fire.

"TC owes Nate big time. Ratty's hard men had it in for him after what Mack did to them." Angie continued the tale. "If Nate hadn't stepped in they would have beaten Tom to a pulp. They have a terrible rep for violence. I heard they stabbed a guy from Bradford during a pill deal."

"There were five of them," Tom continued, "I could have taken one or two but not all five. Then Nate stepped in. He said something like, *you lot need to take care or something nasty is going to come your way.* They backed off immediately. I've never seen guys look so shit scared."

"He's hardly scary-looking," admitted Ellen, "but Tom's right. A few words from him and thank heavens they backed off. I've never been so frightened."

"If Angie hadn't known him from previous visits to The Wheel and if he hadn't been passing... well, I'd have been in hospital instead of seeing The Coasters," Tom confessed.

"Who is this Nate bloke? Is he some kind of local gangster, one of the local mafia or a Black Belt karate expert? Let's face it, he didn't strike me as a fighter – more like a lover," Mack joked.

"He's the man in the know." Angie's quiet voice intruded. "That makes the local scumbags run scared of him and his North Manchester Mods."

57

"So what was he after tonight?" Mack was insistent.

"He wants me, Ellen and Effy, and now Grace to do some modelling for his family business. They're in the rag trade. They make and supply clothes for catalogue companies – usually inexpensive knock-offs of the latest fashions. They also own some boutiques in Manchester."

"So how did this all happen?" he persisted, suspicious of what he'd heard.

Angie had met Nate some months earlier. At first she'd assumed he was trying to get off with her and was making himself sound big. It was only over a few all-nighters that she had learned the truth. He was what he claimed. After stepping in to save TC from Scooby's mob he'd seen Ellen and said she'd make a great model, too. So Angie had thought of Effy, saying she was stunning and real model material. Learning Effy designed and made her own outfits also interested Nate, especially when he'd seen Ellen wearing one of Effy's creations. It had sparked his interest further. All this had been back in November. Then the family problems had set in with the girls' parents. Angie kept getting telephone calls from Nate and had to put him off, explaining the situation as it stood. Her eighteenth birthday do had seemed an ideal way for Nate to meet everyone. So she had invited him, not actually expecting him to show. Seeing Effy and then Grace had only made him more determined they should model for his family firm.

"What kind of 'modelling' are we talking? Underwear?" Tom's smirk and smutty innuendo earned him a reprimanding slap on the arm from Ellen.

"Trust you!" she said reprovingly. "No. He wants us to do a photo shoot of their range for teens and under twenty-ones. They want them for the catalogue companies. Although other things he told them suggested his father's firm wanted to branch out. They would also like us to model their gear at a special session for buyers."

"When?" asked Mack.

"Don't know. Nate didn't say," sighed Angie. "For their summer collection, I imagine. He must be serious. Why else would he have come all the way from Manchester with a bottle of bubbly and an expensive dress ring for me?"

It was no cheap junk jewellery as they saw when they'd inspected it. At least a fiver's worth at any quality jewellers was the consensus. He had to be serious about the modelling.

"He must fancy you something rotten." Grace voiced her opinion.

Ellen and Angie exchanged knowing smiles before Angie revealed, "I don't think so. None of us girls are his type. Tom might be, possibly Mack, but we ladies aren't in the running as playmates."

"You're jesting?" Tom was in genuine shock.

"I don't think they're joking," Mack chuckled on hearing Angie's words, "I'm not bothered as long as he doesn't think I'm his cuppa tea."

"No, I don't think you are Mack." Angie added straight-faced, "I suspect Nate thinks Tom is."

"Holy Batshit!" Tom exclaimed, consternation writ large on his face. "Foooook a duck! You cannot be serious?"

"Oh, but we are. It's that tight bun bottom of yours that's done it." Angie struggled to keep her unsmiling expression.

"My arse? Never!" The beer glass almost slipped from his grasp. Then it dawned.

Ellen couldn't stop herself. Seeing Tom's face she whooped with laughter. Gasping for air she spluttered, "We had you going there."

"How do you know he bats for the other side?" Mack directed his question at Angie.

"It's what they call 'uncommon' knowledge. The kind of thing you don't go around advertising, knowing what the law's like. If it's not clear to everyone I am not, nor have been, nor am likely to be his girlfriend, only a friend who is a girl. He's a bloke I'm friendly with, got it?"

"What are you going to do about this modelling job? I take it you're all interested?" Mack asked.

"If the money he mentioned is as good as he promised, then we'd be fools not to take up his offer," Angie replied.

"How much is he offering to pay?" Mack pressed.

"Five guineas for a photographic session. Plus return train fares."

"What? Each?" Tom queried.

"That's what he said," confirmed Ellen. "Worth doing for a day's work."

Tom let out a long low whistle. "You're not kidding. You don't think he wants any male models, do you? For that kind of money I'd model underwear."

"With your bottom he'd probably want you to." Angie giggled.

"I'd do it for half the money," murmured Grace, cheerful and grinning, "but I've no problem with five guineas."

"Do you know Twiggy earns two hundred quid a week?" Mack left the question hanging.

"How do you know?" Ellen interest was instant.

"I borrowed a library book called *The Young Meteors*. She earns fifteen guineas an hour and over forty pounds in the States."

"I wondered why you'd borrowed it." Effy sounded bemused, remembering him reading it one evening. "I didn't think it was your usual reading. Well, we're not in her league and what he's offering will do me."

"What did you think of Alice and Cathy?" Angie asked Tom and Mack, changing the subject.

"Cathy was okay. Shy and not very talkative, couldn't get much out of her chat-wise. As for Alice, she's one weird chick. Not just weird, downright peculiar." Tom put his beer glass down on the mantelpiece. "Ask Mack the master interrogator what he made of your back from the dead friend."

Mack pulled a face. "Give over, Tom. I was nothing of the kind. Yeah, I did find her strange. It was like having a conversation with my Dad, not like talking to you girls. Was she like that before it happened?"

Angie frowned, clearly deciding what to say next. After a short pause she admitted that the Alice she had known was nothing like the girl she had been a friend to since primary school. Alice looked and sounded like Alice but it wasn't the Alice she'd known. "It's as if she's become another person."

"That makes her sound creepy." Tom gave a pretend shudder.

"Imagine if your mind got wiped clean?" Mack put his glass of lemonade down. "And you had to start over from scratch? I bet you'd be different. Can you imagine what starting over would be like? I can't. Knowing nobody, not even your own mother or brother and sister. Talk about being born again. How do you even begin to do that? We need to give the lass a break."

"Now you put it like that I have to agree with you, Mack," was Ellen's considered response.

Grace and Effy agreed.

"They were down at The Plebs on Boxing Day. Stayed to watch the Victor Brox Band. Alice told me their mums were none too pleased. Alice's mum was having kittens worrying over her. Not surprising given what happened to her. Alice's brother Frank took Cathy home on his motorbike before coming back for her. Anyway, Alice told me she's getting into the scene, so I said she and her friend could hang out with us," Angie told them.

"Can they cut it with the rest of us? You know what I mean? Style is key to being Mods. They don't seem quite there yet. I mean…"

"Don't be awful, Tom." Ellen cut him off.

"No, don't!" Effy sounded hurt by his comment. "That's no way to treat anyone."

"Can you imagine the rep they'll have getting seen on the back of a Rocker's motorbike?" Tom continued, immune to their words. "Can you imagine how we'll look associating with a Rocker?"

Angie glared at him. "He's not a Rocker. He's not anything; he's a lad with a second-hand motorcycle. If that's your problem, don't let it sweat you. If they miss their last bus I'll give them a lift home."

"I'm sure Effy won't mind waiting in the Square if I give one of them a lift back, will you." Mack glanced at Effy for support.

"No, I don't mind as long as you're quick. Do they live far out of town?"

Tom looked sheepish as he admitted, "Alice lives close by. I suppose I could give her a lift if Ellen doesn't mind. Either that or we get her brother a scooter and a Parka."

Mack's parents' arrival brought the talking to an end.

Jane MacKinnon noted polite but cool and awkward pretence from the teenagers as she and Robert entered. Angie's mum and dad were far warmer in greeting them.

It was late and the Christmas holidays were over. Effy and her sisters had travelled over with Mack's parents. Robert and Jane had used Angie's party as an excuse to spend some time with Tom's parents. The three sisters squeezed into the back of the Ford. Mack found himself riding home alone in the freezing cold, narrowly avoiding running over a cat as he raced through Shelf. Even with the near empty roads he couldn't beat the car on his Lambretta but it was close.

# CHAPTER 12

**That's What Love Is Made Of – The Miracles (Stateside SS 353 – 1964)**

*Tuesday 3 January 1967*

At Effy's insistence Mack promised to say nothing to his mother. He gave his word. Effy never mentioned his father, an unwitting error on her part. The lawyer in him knew how to skirt his promise. He expressed his feelings in an emphatic, vehement delivery about his mother's suspicions. Robert MacKinnon found himself dumbfounded by his son's words. Mack made it clear how he felt about the resultant fallout over Angie and the effect on Effy.

"Are you done, James?"

He snorted. "Not quite. But I would appreciate you having a diplomatic word with Mum without mentioning what I've said."

"And how exactly am I supposed to do that, son?"

He knew exactly what to say, having planned it out. "Say I told you in confidence. You can tell Mum we've had a *tete a tete* and that there is nothing going on between Angie and myself. That's on Angie's public admission. Neither I, nor Effy, nor Angie want it mentioned again. Definitely tell her not to say anything to Effy because it'll upset her and it's best forgotten."

When Angie came visiting his mother was a model of warmth and welcoming. Quite what his father had said to his mother he could only guess. Whatever it was it worked.

Now was the time to strike. Using the incident as leverage he persuaded his parents to let them go to The Twisted Wheel. When they pointed out that Ellen and Tom would be there and Angie would go too, they agreed, although with some reluctance. They would all travel over in Uncle Den's Bedford van. Of course they implied that Den would be driving. Mack omitted to mention that it would be Angie driving. As long as schoolwork was not neglected it was fine but they already knew that it never was.

"…And what does Jane Austen have to say to you about love in the nineteen sixties?" Miss Thorpe asked Effy. "Now that we've gleaned so little from the rest of the group."

Effy smiled, not surprised that Miss Thorpe had left her until last to pass comment. "Her best advice is to get a real man, not a man who is no better than a boy. Frank Churchill falls into that category. He's a playboy and that's what Austen would call him today. A real man's actions say more about him than those of a playboy. That's the difference between Knightley and Churchill or creepy Elton. It's the same difference that exists between Darcy and Wickham in *Pride and Prejudice*. Austen's other sound advice to women is to look at how men treat others. Churchill, Willoughby and Wickham are selfish and deceitful; Knightley and Darcy aren't. Knightley's conduct with others is kind, patient and that of a gentleman. Early impressions may be misleading too. Take Willoughby in *Sense and Sensibility*. He fools everyone, especially Marianne. By so doing he almost destroys her reputation. Sensibly, Austen points out that you shouldn't fall in love too quickly. A woman needs to know what she expects to find in a relationship. Marrying for money or prestige alone guarantees nothing but it should not be dismissed. You may not have to look too far to find the man in your life. Knightley is always around for Emma. It's an interesting choice of name, Knightley. Smacks of knightly chivalry and courtly love. Reflects well on him."

"And do such perfect men exist in real life, Fiona?" probed Miss Thorpe.

"Perfection is impossible. The short answer is *No*, they don't. None of Austen's heroes are perfect. Then again, neither are her women. They all have faults. That's human nature. This is why they are Austen's heroes and heroines. As for members of my sex, woman like Austen may appear astute when it comes to men but they seldom are. Too many women today still end up choosing the wrong man. For other women it often proves to be a case of caution over fear. It may explain why Austen remained a spinster."

"Caution over fear?" queried Miss Thorpe. "What do you mean by that?"

"By being over-cautious or indecisive you avoid the fear of making a wrong choice."

"Is that so dreadful?"

"Is life without living life?"

# CHAPTER 13

**Stop Look and Listen – The Chiffons (Stateside SS 550 – 1966)**

*Wednesday 4 January 1967*

"You've got to have the lighting and you have to set the mood to capture the mood. That's what makes these trendy fashion photographers like David Bailey such a success. Take a look at these I saved from magazines."

Mack started looking through Tim Smith's collection of magazine clippings. Tim was right. His first pictures by comparison were pedestrian and tame, stilted and with cast shadows. They did nothing to enhance Effy and Grace nor their dress designs. Studying the clippings, he could see how he could improve. The importance of angle shots and poses was clear. He took it to heart and to mind.

"What a couple of pervs." Dzerzhinsky leaned over their shoulders. "So this is how you guys spend your free study periods. Ogling birds."

The ground floor of the Sixth Form common room was empty. A few students were up on the second floor, studying in the cubicles.

"You got to admit, Jersey, it's better than going brain dead studying those notes on a mixed economy versus a centralised one," Tim replied. "Don't tell me. You've gone through them and written the essay already?"

"You must be kidding! It's going to take me all week to do that. I'm no genius like you two. But I know what I like when it comes to birds. That one of Jean Shrimp looks cool."

"Tell me why you think it's cool, Jersey?" Mack was genuine in seeking an answer.

"I dunno. I know what I like, though." He seemed unsure, but continued after a brief pause. "I guess the way she's standing. Her face. Everything. It's like the photographer snapped her at an important moment in time."

"Hey, Jersey, that's a great answer." Tim seemed taken aback by his observation. "I don't think I could have said it better. There you are, Mack. That's what you should try to aim for. Catching that moment in time, like it's part of a story."

"There's something else. It's how she displays the clothes. No matter what she's wearing in these different photos she looks at home in them. It still doesn't get round my problem of not having studio lighting," Mack mused aloud.

"Lighting?" queried Jersey. "What sort?"

They explained. He answered. Theatre stage lights, would they do? No problem. Need a studio? No problem. He knew where. That's how it began to fall into place. This was when the future began to take shape.

"You want to use our parish hall before they pull it down," Jersey continued with complete confidence. "They used to do a lot of am-dram productions there. Tim's girlfriend Chloe used to be in them. She did all the make-up for the actors too, didn't she, Tim?"

"So she's told me." Tim appeared miffed. "Fancies herself as an actress but she's too short and chubby to ever make it."

His unflattering comment didn't sit well with Mack. Turning to Jersey, he asked, "Are we talking floodlights and theatre-style spotlights?"

"We are," replied Jersey, pleased with himself. "The whole shebang. Mind, most of it looks ancient but it still works. I bet if you made an offer for the lights they'd shake on it to get shot of them. I know the woman with the keys. Want me to ask if you can use the hall?"

"If you would. Sounds excellent to me," Mack smiled.

"His mum's the one with the keys," Tim crowed. "That's the bit he hasn't told you."


Sitting round the dining room table that evening Mack, Effy and Grace drafted a plan of action.

"We can't do Saturday afternoon, I'm working. Sunday we'll be in no fit state after going to The Twisted Wheel." Effy, who was acting as the scribe, paused and then suggested, "What about next Sunday?"

Mack checked his diary. "That's the fourteenth. The Soul Sisters are on at The Plebs on the Saturday night. We can't miss seeing them. It's bound to be another late night. We could do it one evening straight after college? That might be an alternative, what do you think?"

"How are we going to get there? It's all the dresses we'd have to carry." Effy paused, sweeping her long hair behind her ears and starting to fasten it up. "You don't even know if the lights work. It's the make-up as well – that'll take time."

"Ah," smiled Mack, "turns out your mate and Tim's girlfriend is a dab hand make-up girl. She used to act in the local amateur dramatics and do the make-up for the parish's distinguished thespians. We could always ask her to help out. As for the lights, I'll do a recce with Jersey first and start checking the place out. See if there are any props or backdrops we can use for the shoot. I need to catch you girls in the moment."

Grace, having paid close attention, began sniggering. "Get you, MacKinnon! The next David Bailey and Terrence Donovan in one."

He had to smile as Effy joined her sister laughing along with Grace's description. He must have come across as a bit pretentious.

"Then there are your parents. I can't say they'll being pleased with us doing something midweek when we should be studying." Effy looked serious but after the laughter the hint of a smile was still there. When she looked at him like this, he was overcome with blissful joy.

"They won't mind," he said, trying to reassure them. "Well, not much, and given the situation as long as it's not a regular occurrence I can't see it's going to be a problem."

"What about Ellen? Don't you think we could ask her to come along and take part? She might not be too pleased if we left her out," Grace offered. "Now she's stopping at White's Terrace she's nearby. Have you thought about doing it on a Friday evening instead of going out?"

"That's an idea. Actually, it's a damn good idea. TC may like to come over and help out. I'm sure he won't mind giving up a Friday night to help us out. Especially if we wanted Ellen in the shoot." The idea had occurred to him earlier. Tom's presence and scooter could prove useful in helping make it all happen.

"I can't understand why you haven't mentioned asking Angie to be involved." Effy directed her gaze at him. He felt her reading his reaction. After what had transpired Mack wanted to keep Angie out of suspicion's way.

"You know why. Besides, she only has the two dresses you made for her."

"We're exact body doubles. She could wear some of my other dresses. That could speed up the shoot. And think of it…" Effy almost purred. "A dark-haired beauty surrounded by the strawberry blonde Hallorans."

"Hey! I'm a redhead," flared Grace.

"Besides," Effy brushed aside her sister's words, "Angie's car would be perfect too. And let's not forget who got us the modelling work with Nate. Silvers?"

"We could always ask Adam to help out with his car," Grace suggested. "Effy's friend Chloe lives in West Bowling. It's a fair way to get over to this side of the city."

"If you're sure, I'll leave it with you. You can ask Angie." Mack felt like saying, *as long as you don't start getting silly ideas about us.*

They thrashed out a logistical plan for using the parish hall.

"Could I ask you to do something?"

The sisters listened as he explained what he was wanting from them to get the best result from the shoot.

"Grace, are we looking at the next David Bailey?" A faint hint of mockery in her voice blended together with an impressed air. "Mack's taking this seriously, aren't you, my love? I think we ought to give his idea a go, don't you, Grace?"

"We should, Eff, for our Manchester modelling debut. Yes, we should study how models pose and see why they make the clothes look so good."

*****

"What on earth are you doing, Grace?" Ellen had come up to their attic bedroom and had caught sight of her sister flouncing and pulling faces in front of the wardrobe mirror.

"Practising for Mack's fashion shoot. Hasn't he mentioned it to you?"

"Actually, no. He hasn't. I said 'Hi' and he mumbled something back. He was too engrossed doing his Statistics homework, muttering 'bloody' this and 'bloody' that and looking annoyed. I imagine he was having a bit of a problem getting the answer. Okay, so now explain your bizarre behaviour, sis."

"Well, it's like this. He suggested we should prepare for our modelling by trying out different poses and expressions. You know, like the real models do. He said their poses are a moment in time, like in a story. The trouble is Effy can't keep a straight face. She keeps falling about laughing at my efforts."

"I can't help it, Grace. I'm sorry, love. You over-exaggerate the poses and the faces and it looks ever so comical." Effy was barely able to keep her laughter under control. "You need to try and be as natural as possible."

"Well, I don't see you doing any better or looking all that natural."

"Gawd, you two," Ellen grinned, "you need to go to a modelling school if you're serious. Still, he has a point. We ought to make an effort if we're going to get paid. Mack's little effort could be a good place to start our careers as fashion clothes-horses. I think we should act as natural as possible. Remember our deportment classes? Just keep our postures straight and pretend we're chic elegant young women."

"What brings you up here? Bridget driving you mad as a substitute mum?" asked Effy.

"No. She's not. She's lovely and treats me like a grown up. Actually, she's not home tonight so I'm kind of on my own."

"Oh, aye?" queried Grace.

"Before you say anything more, TC's not round or coming round. Deidre's arrived back home from her adventures at her beatnik boyfriend's home. I've come to ask a favour. She's kicked me out of our old bedroom. Says I should sleep somewhere else, would you believe?"

"She wants you out of your room?" Effy looked astonished. "Use our old room. You can sleep in my bed or Grace's. We won't mind."

"She meant I shouldn't sleep in the house."

"What?" Exclaimed Effy, angered by Ellen's words. "The cheeky she devil! How dare she kick you out of our house and your bedroom?"

Ellen nodded, aggrieved. "I can't go to Bridget's. You can guess why. There's no room at Caitlin's now they've moved little Jane into the spare room. That only leaves here."

"Have you asked Mack's mum if you can?" Effy checked.

"She's told me it's okay. But I didn't tell her why. Told her Bridget was over at her flat in Shipley and wouldn't be back tonight. Pretended I didn't want to spend the night on my own in the house. So is it okay to bunk up with one of you tonight?"

"Our Deidre's up to no good. What a cheeky cow behaving like a slut."

Effy and Ellen exchanged looks but said nothing. This was no time to contradict Grace. It was better not to let their youngest sister know about their own behaviour. The youngster already knew about Bridget and her married man. That was unfortunate enough.

# CHAPTER 14

### Chain Reaction – The Spellbinders (CBS 202622 -1966)

*Saturday 7 & 8 January 1967*

Angie had impressed Tom. "Well, you're amazing, Angie. I'm truly amazed at how you've managed to drive a Bedford van. I'll have to let your Uncle Den know what a great job you've done getting us to Manchester in one piece."

Angie tried to look shocked and disbelieving. "I'm almost lost for words."

"That'll make a change," Tom shot back before she could say another word.

"It was alright for you and El up front with Angie," Linda complained.

"We were rolling over one another in the back," Mack added. "Effy was almost seasick as we went round all those twisty turns and bends. Alan banged his bonce on the wheel arch."

"Was that the wailing 'ouch' we heard?" came Tom's cheery response. "Sounded if he was in genuine pain."

"I was, you twat, and it hurt. Bet I've got a lump or cut on my conk." Tom's jibe irritated Alan. "You can travel in the back in the morning and I'll sit up front."

"How's Stingray?" asked Angie.

"Well smashed. He's higher than a kite already. Take a look at his eyes. Well dilated. If he chews gum any harder his bleeding jaw will drop off. It's a wonder it hasn't," replied Linda, Angie's other long-time friend.

"I'm brill, guys, I'm brill. Blues are outta sight, man. I'm ready for the action, man." They couldn't stop him blathering on and on, one of the symptoms of a dozen or more amphetamines.

"Will the van be safe here?" Mack asked Angie. "We don't want it being nicked 'cos your Uncle Den's not going to be happy if it happens."

"Genius mechanic here took a leaf out of your scooter's book," she replied, glancing over at a beaming TC. "He fitted a secondary ignition disabling switch. Uncle Den was well chuffed with him."

"What if they pull the wires out of the ignition and try to fire it up that way?" asked Mack.

"Won't work. It's a by-pass job. And the switch is well concealed. The only one who knows how to start it up again with no ignition and the disabling switch is me and gorgeous there."

"No, I don't!" Ellen piped up.

"He meant me," Angie grinned as the two girls shared the joke. "Okay, boys and girls. Ticket money now if you don't mind."

They made their way down into Piccadilly before heading to Whitworth Street. The queue for the all-nighter had already begun to form.

"Blow me down. It's true. The police station really is opposite the club." Alan couldn't believe his own eyes. "Easy peasy to raid the place and find pills."

"It happens now and again," was Angie's cool response. "The club's owners shop anyone selling pills straight to the Feds. They won't put up with it. They don't want their business ruined. Besides, anyone with an ounce of common will already have taken them before they get in. You'll see more than a few zombies like Stingray in there."

They joined the queue, the four girls huddling together amongst the young men. Hunched in their coats, they sheltered from the bitter cold air blowing down the street.

Located a short walk from Piccadilly Station, The Twisted Wheel was on Whitworth Street. The club was on the ground floor and basement of a large three-storey Victorian building. Surrounded by other red-brick commercial buildings, it was typical of the city's architecture from the same era. The queue continued growing. Friendly banter punctuated by laughter filled the night air. Mack and Effy were busy chatting with one another when Angie let out an unexpected and, for her, unladylike expletive.

"Shit! Ratty and his mates are coming down the street. I hoped he wouldn't turn up." She looked concerned. "Do you still want to go ahead with this?"

"Nothing surer. No worries, Angie, no worries." Mack's tone instantly turned steely and ice-cold. "Stingray, you and Alan stick with the girls. Don't get mixed up in this, okay? It's nothing to do with you. It's mine and Tom's problem."

They nodded in response.

"Mack, it's not Ratty you need to worry about. It's those Moss Side thugs that he's palled up with as well as his Oldham mates. Don't look at them," she tried to warn him. Effy froze.

Mack stopped Scooby and his accompanying bodyguards in their tracks.

"Hello, Scooby. Or should I call you 'Ratty', you fucking double-crossing bastard?"

Scooby stopped, startled by Mack's sudden appearance. Mack had struck a nerve. An instant venomous glint played in the dealer's eyes.

"And how are the teeth, *Smiler*?" Mack recognised one of the two he had beaten up that night. "See the dentist hasn't fitted you with dentures yet. You need to get them broken teeth fixed."

The Smiler was about to launch himself at Mack but Scooby held him back with one hand.

"Glad you stopped him. Otherwise he'd be sucking through a straw in hospital for weeks."

"Don't make threats you can't carry out." Smiler bared his broken front teeth.

"I never make threats." Mack's iciness was an object lesson in intimidation. "Only promises."

"You must be fucking stupid. Who the fuck do you think you are? Do you think you're going to get away with strolling into our patch after what you did?" Smiler snarled back.

"Keep your pet mutt on his leash, Ratty-arse." Mack's scary confidence was intimidating as he eyed up the opposition. "You tried to roll my guy in a deal. Not on. Not then. Not now. Not ever. So don't act like the snake you are and think you can bite back. You were in the wrong and you're damned lucky I don't beat seven shades of crap out of you right here, right now. So listen up, you crooked shyster twat. Anything happens to any of my friends when they come over to have a good time and you'll wish you were in Australia. Even then I'd find you no matter what stone you hid under. Try anything tonight and you'll end up resting at the bottom of the Manchester Ship Canal keeping company with a lump of concrete."

"And who do you think you are, one of the Kray mob?" Scooby sneered.

Mack continued unruffled, the menace in his voice so genuine it even convinced Tom. "The Krays would approve of how I deal with pricks like you."

It was his sheer intimidating presence more than the words that unnerved Scooby.

71

"Besides, Nate Silvers wouldn't like his friends having problems with you bunch of weenies."

Scooby's expression changed as Mack mentioned Nate's name. The sight of TC backing Mack up served as a reminder of what had passed before.

"You know him?" stuttered Scooby.

"You could say that. We're his associates from across the Pennines, know what I mean?"

"And we're good mates." Tom glared at Scooby over his shoulder. "You haven't forgotten what Silvers warned you about the last time. So tell the guy with the flick knife to put it away before he ends up in hospital."

Angie intervened. "You know who I am. You've seen me with Silvers here at The Wheel. Don't even think about stirring it, not that these two couldn't handle you and your lot. One word from me to Nate and you've had it."

Scooby gave a sickly smile. "Why? What would he do? He's not so scary."

"Okay, I'll tell him what you said when he's down tonight."

Scooby paled. It was noticeable even under street lighting.

"Oh, and if Mack says he'll come looking for you you'd better believe it," she added, "assuming Nate doesn't get to you first. Comprende?"

"Okay, okay. I get the picture." Scooby tried to walk round them but Mack stepped in front of him, his icy eyes boring into the weedy malnourished drug dealer.

"I know your type," Mack hissed in his ear. "You'll be looking for a chance to have a go because your sort never lets it go. You'll think I'll think it's over. Wrong. You'll bide your time and let me think it's all forgotten. I won't. That'll be your biggest mistake and also your last. Don't forget I didn't warn you. If you think you'll catch us as we come out in the morning, you won't."

Mack let him pass with a deliberate crashing of shoulders against the one he'd nicknamed Smiler. "You need to get them teeth capped, handsome." Smiler didn't take it well, clearly itching to have a go at Mack.

"Don't think this is over," he grunted.

"The next time it will be. You'll wish you'd never come across me."

Stepping back into the queue, they watched Scooby and his bodyguards walk past the waiting crowd of Mods. Mack spotted his old school mate from Bradford, Dave Bean, stepping out in front of Scooby.

Some kind of brief conversation went on between Dave and the Ratty. Scooby turned, looked back at Mack, shrugged his shoulders and carried on walking.

"Dear God, I didn't think you'd be so stupid," Angie couldn't believe his audacity. "Let's hope we scared the brown stuff out of him."

"Thanks for the added bit about Nate. You and TC definitely put the frighteners on mentioning his name. I hope Nate doesn't mind."

"Fucking 'Smiler'," Tom chortled. "That was funny."

"Stop swearing," Ellen scolded. "You know how I hate that. And you, MacKinnon, don't you have any common sense? You were asking for trouble confronting him and his mates like that."

"What on earth were you thinking?" Effy joined in, visibly trembling, having seen and heard everything. "Couldn't you just let him walk past?"

"No, he couldn't." Tom answered for Mack. "He's a rattlesnake. It's not over until it's over."

"Tom's right. I was getting the licks in first to intimidate him."

"You certainly did that," added Angie. "He'll think twice about it but the real problem is reptiles like him don't think. Mind you, he'll be wary knowing Nate's a mate of ours."

"His gang are packing flick knives." Tom sounded grim. "We'll have to watch out for those if they come looking for us if your chat hasn't work."

"Thanks for spotting that while I was gabbing. If it goes to plan there'll be no more problems after tonight." Mack exchanged glances with Angie and Linda.

"Smiler, what a nickname," Tom carried on. "You must have smashed all his top teeth…"

Effy suggested. "Maybe we should go home."

"No way, we're going to have a good time and put that behind us." Mack smiled, making light of it. "Nothing's going to happen tonight. Or when we leave in the morning. Snakes like him bide their time. Besides, there's only one way to remove a problem like Ratty. I could have kicked his head in, and those of his mates, but they'd still come back for more. No, there's better ways of dealing with the likes of them. The sooner it's done the better."

Tom chortled. "You wouldn't actually send him down to the bottom of the Ship Canal weighted down with concrete, would you?"

73

"Don't be daft, cuz. Where would I get concrete blocks this time of night?" Turning to Linda, Mack said, "You and Angie still up for dealing with him? You're sure he's the one who got your ex banged up?"

Linda nodded.

"After this, we've got to sort him," Angie stated. "He's never going to let it go, is he?"

"No, he's not. He's the type who'd slit his own throat to get his own way."

Effy heard Angie saying to Linda, "Do you still want to go ahead? It's risky… but solves the problem if it works." Linda nodded; nothing more passed their lips. Mack took Effy by the hand, smiling. The questions were writ large on her face. The answer was writ large on his. She understood it was better not to ask. There was a dangerous dark side to Mack that was revealing itself as past events surfaced. She'd thought she knew him but now she realised she didn't – or not as well as she'd believed. His dark side frightened and thrilled her in equal measures. The queue began to move, gathering pace. They took out their brand-new membership cards and tickets.

Marvin Gaye's *Ain't That Peculiar* was playing as they entered the club. Hearing this song was a promising sign of a great time ahead of them. The top floor contained a coffee-bar area. The main part of the club was downstairs. The DJs, as they discovered, were in their own caged area at the back, away from the raised stage area at the other end. The bent and twisted bicycle wheels explained how the club got its name. There were a series of what looked like dividing alcoves. Speakers mounted high up on the walls, almost on the ceilings, poured out the music. The club soon filled. They had formed their own dance circle near the stage area. The atmosphere was definitely something special. Still feeling anxious, Effy stayed close to Mack. Gradually her anxiety began to fade as they danced. Nate and his crowd arrived in style and came over to join them. After a while Angie and Nate broke away from the group and went back upstairs. Angie returned, beckoning to Linda and Mack to go with her as Jackie Wilson's *Whispers (Getting' Louder)* gave way to Edwin Starr's *Stop Her on Sight*.

They were up to something and Effy intended to join them. Tom took her by the arm. "Stay with me and Ellen and the other lads. He won't be gone long." They weren't. Effy couldn't help spotting Ratty and his mates hanging round the alcoves on the other side from the stage.

"They're not going to start anything, are they?" She felt alarmed. "I don't trust them."

"Nobody does," Tom replied, adding almost as a casual afterthought, "They shouldn't have started something they aren't going to be able to finish."

"What do you mean?"

"Nothing to worry about. It's getting sorted real soon."

Turning to Tom with fear in her eyes, Effy asked, "Mack's not getting involved in another fight, is he?"

"Nah." Tom's smile broadened, "Mack's too Machiavellian for that. He'll be back soon with Angie and Linda. This won't come to blows but Ratty won't be too happy, you can bet on it."

The three returned and joined the circle again, giving nothing away.

Some of the best sounds they'd heard were finding their way onto the turntables. Sue Record classics like Ernestine Anderson's *Keep an Eye on Love,* Bobby Parker's *Watch Your Step* and Billy Preston's *Billy's Bag.* There were familiar Motown and Stax records, too, and others like *The Cheater* by Bob Kuban and In Men and *Soul Sauce* by Cal Tjader. The music was outstanding and the dance area became packed. Their circle became compressed into a small area. As the band came on stage to warm up Mack nudged Effy indicating where she should look. It was a shock. Was that who she thought it was?

Raising her heels and putting her lips to Mack's ear, she said, "Am I imagining him?"

"You're not imagining him. It's Jimi Hendrix. I can't understand what he's doing here. Not exactly his scene, I wouldn't have thought."

Pretty much everyone noticed the guitarist gracing the club. Effy noted Hendrix wasn't quite as tall as Mack who stood at least a couple of inches above him. Seeing him was an unexpected bonus. The night or rather early hours turned into musical heaven as the group performed their latest double-sided release *Help Me* with *Chain Reaction.* Mack had bought the 45 on its release. The recordings had blown him away. He told Effy the group hailed from New Jersey and the female singer was called Elouise something or other. The group's live performance was excellent. Effy was delighted, and the ugly incident from earlier on had disappeared from her thoughts. Mack stood with his arms wrapped round her while they watched. She never noticed Angie and Linda slipping away from their little group and melting into the crowd. Before the end of the performance the two had returned, squeezing through the mass of watching bodies. Effy noticed the glances they exchanged with Mack and Tom. Even Ellen looked puzzled. Something was going on but no one revealed anything further.

After the final call back of the band they went upstairs to cool off and get some soft drinks. Effy saw Nate Silvers speaking to some men. Not Mods. Later it transpired they were the management. Then, conversation over, he came over, his face lit with a broad grin. "That's tonight's nastiness taken care of."

Grins all round.

Not much later the truth leaked out as two plainclothes policemen arrived. Accompanied by two uniformed men they disappeared downstairs. They returned dragging a strenuously protesting Ratty behind them in unceremonious fashion. Over the music and chatter they couldn't hear exactly what he was saying but he seemed to be a mixture of angry, disgruntled and panic-stricken.

"It'll be interesting to see what they'll find in his rat-infested lair." Nate's smug smile almost told the tale all by itself. Linda and Angie exchanged knowing looks. Mack and Tom were also smiling but nothing was said. Something devious had this way come. Effy instinctively knew this had Mack's pawprints all over it. His recent obsession with reading Machiavelli's *The Prince* and that Chinese book about warfare had something to do with it.

Recalling Tom's uncharacteristic use of the word Machiavellian was the clincher. Mack kept the two well-thumbed paperbacks close to hand in the house. He was always dipping into them and jotting down quotes in a notebook. Effy recollected a quote she had read in secret that went something like: *if you hurt someone it should be so bad you wouldn't ever fear them seeking revenge*. Recollecting this made her feel concerned.

During the early hours Angie, Ellen and Effy found themselves involved in a further conversation about modelling for Nate's family firm. He needed them to get the shoot done sooner than expected. The trouble was, it would have to take place midweek. That was awkward and clashed with school for the sisters and work for Angie. Nate would complete the arrangements and confirm these with the girls. Mack, meanwhile, was having a catch-up chat with Dave Bean.

"I saw you talking with Ratty?"

"Yeah, I saw you looking as if you were going to kick the crap out of him. I know what a crazy fuck he is. Too much double-crossing on deals, that's his problem. He's a Grade A nutter."

"So what were you talking about?"

"I warned him and his hard men to steer well clear of you. Told him about the fight with Osborn. You, know, when you kicked him and his four mates down the hill towards Thornton Road."

"Five? There were only two of them."

"Talk on the grapevine says it was five. Tale goes it was hell of a beating you handed out. You're like a bogyman legend down there. One of them told me he'd crap himself to death if he thought you were coming to get him. Anyway, how do you like The Wheel?"

It was freezing cold when they emerged. The van engine needed warming up on the choke. This gave them time to scrape the windscreen clear and get the asthmatic heater blowing some warm air. As they drove back in the Bedford Alan and Stingray spoke about Scooby's arrest.

"Feds collared that bloke you were squaring up to. Alan and me watched them dragging him out. Kept protesting he was innocent and it was a set-up."

"Claimed someone had slipped pills into his pocket. Wasn't half effing and blinding."

"Did he now? What a shame. It's all I can do to stop the crocodile tears causing a flood," Mack responded with a wry glance at Linda. "A light-fingered Lil may have set him up."

"Light-fingered 'Lil," chortled Tom. He was about to say more until Linda gave him a cutting look, placing a finger on her lips. He smiled back with a nod. "The less said the better."

Effy tried to put two and two together but couldn't quite make it add up to four.

Linda concluded with her own mysterious words. "We've got even for Steve. He will be pleased when he finds out. Getting even is the least I could do for my ex."

# CHAPTER 15

**Sweet Thing – Detroit Spinners (Tamla Motown TMG 514 – 1965)**

*Sunday 8 January 1967*

"Jimi Hendrix was at the club!" squeaked Grace in pure delight, and then, almost as if to confirm her disbelief, "*The* Jimi Hendrix of *Hey Joe*? You're making it up, aren't you, sis!"

Effy showed her the back of The Twisted Wheel membership card where she'd managed to persuade him to sign. "There! That's his autograph!"

"Can I borrow it tomorrow?" Grace snatched it from her sister's hand.

"Why?"

"So I can show Jean and the girls in my form? They'll be green and you'll be even more cool than you are already."

"No. I don't want you showing off. I don't need the publicity. I'm cool enough."

"Oh, go on, Eff! Don't be a spoilsport."

"No."

"Mack, please ask her to let me. She will if you ask her nicely?"

Mack looked at Effy and smiled, shaking his head.

"Okay, Grace." One glance at Mack and Effy conceded with reluctance. "Don't you dare lose it or damage it! It's my membership card and I want to get in again next time we go! In one piece looking as it does now! Do I make myself clear?"

They'd made it back to Bradford after nine o'clock picking up Mack's scooter outside Den's house in Halifax first. There had been a snow flurry on the way home but it had stopped as they dropped down from Queensbury. Both of them were chilled through. After some toast both went to their beds to catch up on sleep, begging Grace to make sure they were up by two in the afternoon. They slept through until three. Grace roused them when Robert MacKinnon became fed up with waiting. Sunday dinner had been moved to three rather than the more usual two o'clock. Even so they both still felt tired.

"I hope you two night owls aren't planning on doing this every weekend." It was more like a question than a statement coming from Mack's dad. "Going over to Manchester every weekend is going to interfere with your A levels."

"No, Dad. Only if there's an American Soul act that's too good to miss."

Effy nodded in agreement.

They tried doing some work but were too tired to do more than some required reading and making desultory notes. Effy dozed off at one point. She had a book in her left hand and a pen in her right with the nib moving on her pad and making strange patterns. Grace's laughter woke her with a start.

"Look at the state of you, Eff! What a sight!" Grace crowed.

"I'd better have a bath." Effy rose, looking annoyed with her sister. "Then I'll get ready for an early night."

"That might be a sensible idea, Effy," Mack's mum commented as she began to wind some wool ready for the next phase of knitting. "James can do the same. Your clothes could do with a wash. And your suit will have to go to the dry cleaners. You both smell of cigarette smoke."

"Point made, Mum. Call me when you're done, Eff, and don't use up all the hot water," Mack called after her as she went up the stairs.

"Check on your sister in a little while, will you, Grace. I don't want her falling asleep in the bath tub and drowning."

"Mum..." Mack protested.

"Don't mum me. It's known to happen. Poor dear's exhausted staying up all night and gallivanting across the country with you." Of course it was his fault. Effy could do no wrong in his mother's eyes.

"Manchester's hardly the other side of the country..." he began. Seeing his mother's expression he realised it was wiser to say nothing more. Grace cupped her hand to her mouth, amused for some reason. Mack gave her his best dirty look. That only made her giggle and stick her tongue out at him. His mum had a point. At least he could agree with her about that much. They couldn't be going over every weekend as much as it seemed like a great idea. It would cause a lot of unnecessary friction if they did. It was the last thing they needed. They would have to pick their times for going over to The Wheel. That might prove hard given the future acts that were getting booked.

Mack and Effy had made a secret pact in the days leading up to the New Year. Their shared futures were too important. Whatever each chose to do in the next couple of years they wouldn't jeopardise their joint future.

79

Living for today was well and good but not for them. There was too much at stake. Studying for A levels, working weekends in part-time jobs, and going out Fridays and Saturdays was tough and demanding. Work hard and play hard was the plan, because they wouldn't be teenagers forever. They were going to make the best of their youth without endangering their future prospects.

"Let's be honest," Effy had said, "neither of us would settle for anything second-best. I know you wouldn't. I'm pretty sure I won't. Our futures are together."

"True," he had echoed with absolute certainty. "Our futures are together."

Effy was waiting for him as he came upstairs. "God, I'm so zonked I could sleep for a week."

"Me too." He whispered in her ear, "Wish I could cuddle up with you tonight."

Effy kissed him. "Think of me as you drop off and in your dreams you will." She made her way up to the attic bedroom. Mack found it strange how she insisted on wearing his dressing gown instead of her own. She looked wonderful in it and left him feeling loved. Effy was such a sweet thing.

Pausing upstairs at the bedroom door Effy turned round with a cryptic comment. "I keep adding two and two together but somehow I still can't make it add up to four." Then she was gone. What the heck did she mean by that?

# CHAPTER 16

**Keep Looking – Solomon Burke (Atlantic 584026 – 1966)**

*Wednesday 11 January 1967*

"What do you think? Any good as a place to shoot photos?" Jersey asked as they looked round the dilapidated parish hall. It was a glorified wooden hut erected on a brick base. The place was past its best. It was easy to see why it needed demolishing. A small kitchen area was on the right at entry with a cubicle room and toilets on the left. There was a decent-sized stage at the far end with some small storage rooms behind. The hall was dank, unaired but clean.

Examining the footlights and stage lights stacked in a corner, Mack asked, "Do they still work?"

"Yeah, course they do. I know they're not much to look at, a bit ancient, but they should be more than bright enough. They're going to start clearing out in a month. If you make an offer for the lights they can be yours for a cheapo price."

"How cheapo would cheapo be?"

"Real cheapo. Giveaway cheapo."

Mack had to admit the place was ideal for the shoot. An outdoor session at this time of the year was out. You couldn't rely on the weather in January let alone the temperature.

There were bits of old scenery from past productions. These might be usable as backdrops together with an old sizable white projection screen. The hall was a fraction warmer than outside. They could see one another's breath as they walked round; in the kind of outfits the girls would be modelling, they could suffer exposure standing around. Jersey said the radiators and boiler still worked. They'd have to get their own coal in to fire it up. A hundred weight sack of coal would get it toasty if they lit it an hour or so before starting the session.

Mack didn't have a tripod but he noticed some old sets of stepladders that would come in useful as substitutes. Some creative thinking would help him make the best of it.

Jersey offered to help him set up the lighting, having lots of previous experience from helping in the am-dram productions since he was thirteen. Mack gave him his home telephone number.

"You're dead lucky having a telephone at home. My mum tried to get one but there's a long waiting list. And then it's only going to be a party line when the GPO gets round to letting us have one."

"My dad's a bank manager and needs it for his work. He got it installed as a business priority when we first moved here. The only other person I know who has one at home is Angie, a friend of Effy's and mine. Her dad's job requires one for emergency callouts. My uncle and aunt don't have one. When Tom needs to call he has to use a phone box like most folks. Eff's house has one because of her father's printing business, but since he's been in Ireland you can only make incoming calls. Sean Halloran wanted to make sure none of his daughters racked up his phone bill while he was away."

"Smart move. I reckon women have a problem stopping on the phone for ages. My mum says if we get one she's getting a lock on it so my sister can't use it without getting timed. Me? Who am I going to call? No girlfriend, not likely to find one the way I am. M-Mack…" Jersey stuttered with nervous embarrassment. "Y-you always look dead smart. I can see why the birds go for you. Me, I always look a mess. My mum keeps going on at me. What do I have to do to get a girlfriend?"

Jersey dressed like a slob. His creased and shiny trousers, his scuffed shoes looking like they'd never seen polish, Mack wondered what he could do or even say. Jersey's hair was lank and there was enough dandruff on his jacket shoulders to give the appearance of a light snowfall. Still wearing the Sixth Form tie so late in the evening did little to enhance his appearance. Tied in a half Windsor knot the size of a peanut, it made Mack smile. Blackheads on his face looked like a spray of shotgun pellets. He shaved but with no accuracy, leaving random bristle patches round the lower jawline. The guy was clueless yet brave and honest enough to ask for help. Mack felt sorry for him. Did he want to do a Henry Higgins on Jersey? Jersey presented a challenge; that was certain. He was asking for help and it must have taken a lot of courage to ask.

"Never say never Jersey, things change." Mack made a start. "There are things you can do. I can give you some tips. Anyhow you're still going to help with the lighting on the night, aren't you?"

"Course I will."

"Great. We'll chat as I set up and I'll give you some tips on to how to smarten up so you can get yourself a girlfriend. Okay? We'll organise for me to come round to your spot to get you sorted."

"Okay, Mack." The relief on Jersey's face was clear.

"I'll make a Mod of you yet."

"A Mod? Me?"

"Yes, you. Why not? When I've done with smartening you up Professor Higgins style you'll be my fair gentleman." Mack grinned. "Do you know what Clearasil is?"


Later in the evening Mack talked with Effy and Grace. They drafted a plan of action on paper with a timetable for the shoot. Effy agreed to ask Chloe to help with make-up and to call Angie. The date was set and the parish hall booked for a week on Friday. Angie agreed to come over and take part in the shoot and act as an extra taxi helping to bring Chloe over from West Bowling. They dragooned Adam into helping to get the girls and their clothes from home.

Mack had raided the Carlisle Road library as soon as it reopened after New Year. He'd stripped the Junior section bookshelf on photography. What better way to come to grips with snapping photos than using kid-simple explanations? You could teach yourself pretty much anything if you wanted it enough. How hard could it be? If he had learned how to take apart and put together Lambretta engines and fix them, as well as a hundred and one other mechanical jobs besides, why should he find this any more difficult? He'd also picked a lot of tips from his dad. Robert MacKinnon had once been a keen amateur photographer until they'd moved away from Halifax. Then he no longer seemed to have the time, with his new job.

If Mack was going to master this photography lark he would have to get smart and sharp fast. There was no time in his life to join a photography club.

# CHAPTER 17

### Sock It to 'Em JB – Rex Garvin & The Mighty Cravers
### (Atlantic 584-028 – 1966)

*Saturday 14 January 1967*

If the weather hadn't been so awful he and Effy might have gone over to Halifax on Friday night. Neither fancied the ride over on the scooter. The weather was lousy: sleet, then rain, then more sleet. They'd settled for an evening at the pictures so they could spend some time alone together. Luckily they had taken the trolley bus into the city. In any case he didn't like leaving his scooter unattended in the city after dark. Some of Osborn's pals might spot it and trash it in an act of revenge.

Two hours into the morning at the Jenkins's scooter dealership Mack watched Dave Bean arrive. Sloping in through the glass front door after shaking his brolly dry Mark Mates followed him. One swift look told him Dave was still flying in the wild blue yonder from last night's amphetamines. The showroom was empty, which was as well if they wanted a chat.

"No plumbing emergencies today, Dave?"

"Gaffer and me don't do weekends. Well, gaffer might turn out if someone's desperate. Won't take me, though, he's not keen on paying us more for working weekends. Brought 'Check' with me." He indicated Mates one of the known local 'Faces'. Mack knew 'Check' from his schoolboy days.

"So what brings you both here this fine morning? It's peeing cats and mutts outside. Not the best of to be out and about." Mack liked Dave but he didn't want to pass the time of day listening to any rambling amphetamine inanities this morning.

"You are definitely going to want to hear what we're going to tell you in a mo."

"Is that right, Dave?"

Mates nodded, shaking hands with Mack.

"Definitely."

"Shoot."

"Last night, while we were down with some of the Faces at the Pack Horse, we had some visitors from Manchester."

What Mack heard made him cold. It wasn't going to be over until he settled it. There were unpredictable consequences for past actions. This was one such a consequence and the final solution would have to be his. Tonight he would go down The Plebs with Effy, together with Tom, Ellen and Angie and their friends. Nothing was going to prevent them seeing The Soul Sisters. But first he would need to deal with a problem.

Dave informed him that 'Smiler' had turned up looking for him in Bradford. He hadn't been alone but with a bunch of Scooby's thugs. Given some of the local Faces had recent form dealing drugs with Scooby's mob this was not a bright idea. A few were itching to have a go at the Moss Siders over soured deals that had ended in violence. Mark 'Check' Mates was one among a number who had a score to settle, according to Dave.

Mack had known 'Check' as one of the hard men at the rival secondary modern over the road. Whilst they were never friends, the two knew one another by reputation. They had never tangled. Both had been feared locally for their fighting skills and looked on as the best in their schools. They had shared a few bus trips into the city after school. The Rhodesway lad had always treated him with cagey respect, exchanging friendly banter. Neither had ever experienced any personal animosity towards the other. Mack and Tom were not the only ones with a problem.

'Smiler', as Mack had dubbed him, was Ronnie Sykes: a Moss Side thug who led Scooby's strong-arm pack. Last summer Sykes and his pals had tried to roll Tom and himself. The mugging had failed. Mack had broken his accomplice's nose with a Glasgow kiss before delivering a blow to Sykes's jaw that broke his front teeth. That should have been the end of it. Now it had resurfaced and what surprised Mack was Sykes's desire to get even. Pride, they said, came before a fall. He would not fall nor fail. If Sykes wanted a return match he'd get one. On Mack's terms and turf.

Check spoke. "I have a score to settle with that bastard's pals. It's personal. Some of the guys would have had a go at him last night but there's a time and place for a rumble. Not when you've had a pint or three and you're with your bird. Besides I was wearing my new suit, you know what I mean? No way was I going to get it ruined."

"Anyway," continued Dave, "someone shot their gob off saying you were a Halifax lad. Sykes and his mob thought you came from Bradford so that's why they came looking. The bad news is they're coming over to

85

Halifax tonight because I heard them say so. Worse still, someone accidentally tipped them off."

"How many of them?"

"There were five or six of them including Sykes. They boasted they were going to do you over so you'd end up spending a year in hospital if you survived. That's exactly what they did with a friend of ours." Dave enlarged further. "They kicked the crap out of him, then stabbed and robbed him."

"Thanks for the heads up, guys." Mack took in the grim news, his mind racing for solutions. "Looks like I'm going to have my work cut out."

"They all carry flick knives and knuckle dusters. They're evil bastards. A bunch of pill heads from Moss Side who like to think they're running the local drugs scene. They knifed my pal Geoff after rolling him. No witnesses and they never got done for it."

"I'll sort it somehow."

"Not on your own, you won't. I'll help you out 'cos I... we have our reasons. There's a score a few of us need to settle. This is the best opportunity we're going to get. We know what you did to Osborn, real rough justice. He had it coming so the story goes. Do you know Kev Finch and Chris Smith? Well, they're up for it. They'll help even up the odds. Kev will bring something useful to the party. We'll come over – just say when and where we meet you tonight?"

"I hope you're not talking about a firearm."

"Nah." Check was dismissive.

Mack was reluctant to get anyone else drawn into it. Check seemed determined not to be left out. After Dave and Check left the shop Mack rang the Halloran house. Maybe Tom had stayed over with Ellen and was still there. He wasn't, having left early to work in the garage. Mack's luck was in as Ellen had the number of the garage, otherwise he might not have reached him until the evening. He wasn't going to get Tom involved this time. Four on six were reasonable odds but the thought of confronting knives and knuckle-dusters was chilling. He would have to work out how this was going to play out. The last thing was to end up with a blood bath. He remembered something *Thirty Seconds* had told him. He'd jotted it down at the time. *The best fighter never gets angry. He keeps calm. He keeps a clear head to make sure he comes out the winner*. Mack needed some inspiration. It came to him recalling the words of Sun Tzu that he'd also jotted down on reading *The Art of War*. *The supreme art of war is to subdue the enemy without fighting.*

How on earth could he do that with a head case like Sykes?

Not fighting wasn't an option. Then it came to him. He would dictate the terms of the fight.

Tom listened to what Mack told him. What came next shook him. Mack told him in blunt uncertain terms he was not to get involved under any circumstances. In spite of strenuous protests, Mack made it clear what he wanted Tom to do. Tonight Tom's job would be keeping Ellen and Effy out of it and safe. Mack stressed that Tom would be his alibi with Effy and Ellen. Nor was Angie to know, nor Stingray and Alan or any of the others lads. It was his problem and his fight alone. Angie could help him out by keeping the girls occupied while he was dealing with it. How Tom managed it Mack left up to him.

Check was already down the Pack Horse when he walked in at the back door. Kev Finch and Chris "Smithy" Smith were there too. They were couple of brawny likely lads, both working in the building trade. Kev Finch had gone to school with Mack. They knew one another although they had been in different form groups. Finch had played in the rugby team and was no walkover who had specialised in unseen deliberate fouls on opposing players. These fouling incidents had frequently spilled over after the game. The lad loved to rumble. Smithy, he didn't know. He was a year or maybe two older and had access to a mini van. They agreed to drive over early and meet him in The Beefeater. On the way home he stopped off at a local hardware shop to buy two rubber-coated toilet flush handles and a WC flushing chain. Within fifteen minutes using his dad's tools he had fashioned what he was going to need.

Mack spun Effy a yarn about needing to go over to Halifax earlier to fix someone's scooter. He hated himself for the deception and for lying yet again. Ellen was already at Tom's, having gone on the bus in the afternoon. Tom arranged for Angie to pick up the girls and himself from his house in the evening. Suspicion aroused Angie forced Tom to tell her the real reason.

Mack and Effy set off for Halifax earlier than usual. Effy couldn't understand why he wasn't going smartly dressed, wearing Levi's and a Harrington instead. He shrugged it off, saying if he was looking over someone's scooter he didn't want to risk getting his best threads dirty from grease and oil. Effy found it unusual but didn't question his words. Mack often sorted out scooter problems for some of the Halifax lads, though never before on a Saturday night.

As arranged they met at The Beefeater coffee bar. The only advantage the four of them would have would be the place of their choosing.

Mack took them down the Upper George pub to explain what he had planned.

"Okay, let me get this straight. You want me and Kev to hold back two or three of them outside of here?" Smithy rubbed his chin, glancing at red-headed Kev who returned a wicked grin. "No problem. What we've got in this bag will scare the shit out of them. I'll take one and you can take the other."

Mack examined the bag's contents. "Guns!"

"They're powder actuated nail guns. Not real guns. These'll fire nails into concrete. We use them all the time at work. Just point and pull the trigger if you have to."

"For fuck's sake…" Mack swore in disbelief.

"Don't worry, mate. We don't plan to shoot 'em. Not unless we have to. Nor should you. The idea is to scare the fuck out of 'em. So get your best Oscar winning performance on when you tackle him. If you can scare him and his pals shitless, job done. So don't pull the trigger unless you've no choice. He may be fucking hard but he won't be fucking stupid enough to risk it. If you do shoot him, shoot him though the foot or the hand. Don't forget. One of these can send a nail clean through someone." Finch looked Mack straight in the eye. "What do you think we're going to do? Nail 'em to a cross like Jesus? They'll think twice about getting shot with one of these. But here's the thing. We need you to keep Sykes occupied. I'm going to cover Smithy so he can kick the shit out of the guy who stabbed our mate."

"So that's it?"

"That's it," was Kev Finch's nonchalant response. "We want one of the other twats. But we'd have to deal with Sykes to get at his mate. We'll leave him to you 'cos he's your grudge. It's his mate we want. And anyhow, we reckon you could bury him one on one."

There was something in Finch and Smithy's eyes that Mack didn't like. They were up to something. This could go so wrong, so badly wrong. Lenny had warned him never to use a weapon. So had Tom's dad when they were young. Mack was torn. Using a weapon was a no go. They were jail tickets if you got caught. Using them could only result in GBH, or worse. Even carrying something like that would get you arrested.

He was reluctant to even use what he had made earlier. It wasn't as if he could run away from the confrontation. Sykes was a psycho like his pal Scooby, a head case looking for revenge. Even if he beat the crap out of him there were no guarantees Sykes wouldn't come looking for him again. There was no way out. He couldn't run away. He had to stay, dictating the battleground to his advantage as best he could. How else could he cope with a flick-knife wielding thug with a knuckle-duster unless he was armed too?

Lenny hadn't shown him how to deal with armed thugs. Mack's sole hope was that Check and his accomplices didn't end up using the lethal nail guns. *Fear was going to be the key to ending all this.* Kev Finch was right. He'd have to put on an act that would scare the guy shitless. As Lenny had instilled in him, in a fight it was not about courage or bravery. Courage was mastering your fear and bravery was the decisive action to end the fear. The time had come to end it. All this trouble was the consequence of the ill-fated drug deal Tom had drawn him into last summer. How he wished he could turn back the hands of time but that was impossible. Instead he steeled himself hoping, whatever the outcome, Effy would never know about it.

The choice of the Upper George pub was deliberate. The pub had a front and a back door. The back door led into a narrow alleyway that fed from the front side of the pub snaking to its rear and past Shirley Crabtree's Big Daddy's club. It was ideal as a battleground. If it came to a fight Mack reasoned the best way to overcome these loonies was in the alleyway's narrowness. They wouldn't have room to come at him from different sides. One at a time was the idea. He planned on hitting them like ninepins in a bowling alley. Tom later nicknamed it the *Spartan Gambit* after the Battle of Thermopylae. It wasn't quite how it worked out.

He left word in the square with a few of the regulars to direct anyone looking for him to the pub. This excluded everyone and Tom and the girls in particular since it was hush-hush. Everyone assumed it was a dealer transaction going off. Kev Finch and Smithy were posted outside the front door. They were to prevent the last three going through the door of the pub. Meanwhile he and Check would be seated close by the back door. The way it went down wasn't quite like Check and the Bradford lads envisaged.

Mack reasoned Sykes wouldn't dare to start a fight in the pub so he planned to give the Smiler one last chance to back off. The pub wasn't busy when Sykes and one of his gang entered the smoke-choked room. It didn't take him long to spot him. As he strode over Mack noted the hate-filled expression on his face.

"Outside, you fuckin' cunt."

"Sit yourself down, *Mister* Sykes." Mack gave him an irresistible smile as if he were with an old friend. "A few words before we go outside. That is if we have to."

For a split second Sykes couldn't believe his hearing. "We 'ave to. Outside."

It was a quiet corner tucked out of sight. A few older blokes were propping up the bar blocking the bar staff's view. No one would hear what was going on in the corner.

"So you warned him, did you, Mates? I'll fuck you over when I've done with him."

Check grinned. "Us Yorkshire lads stick together. And you've got an effing short memory. We've not forgotten the stabbing. As for that threat of yours it's not happening."

"I ain't scared of you lot."

"Sit down." This time Mack changed his expression, hoping it was as chilling and as hard as steel. The commanding tone made Sykes take serious note. That and the sudden slick appearance of the nail gun pointing straight at him. He sat down across the table. His tough-looking pal shuffled uncomfortably at the unmistakable threat. Everything now depended on doing an Academy Award winning performance. Could he bluff enough fear into this Moss Side hard man to avert scrapping? He continued trying to sound soft-spoken yet gritty in a way he hoped Clint Eastwood would approve of. "This here is a powder actuated nail gun. It shoots four-inch nails into concrete. Imagine what it'll do to you if I pull the trigger? Do you want to find out if I'm bluffing?"

"You haven't the bottle. You wouldn't dare."

Mack surprised himself. He fired. Even Check found himself shaken by Mack's casualness.

Sykes paled as he looked where the nail had embedded in a doorjamb. It was not what he'd expected Mack to do. Fear crept into his thoughts for the first time in a long while.

Mack had to play it just like in the novel by Alistair MacLean because fear was the key. Somehow he had to scare the hell out of Sykes and his sidekick.

"Maybe. Maybe not. I've enough nails left to fucking crucify you if I decide to do it. Do you want to find out?" It sounded nonchalant, almost unreal in his ears. Both Sykes's and Check's faces were tense and white. The unexpected thump of the nail gun had been lost in the bar-room hubbub. No one else had heard the discharge over the noise of clinking glasses and chatter.

"I said, do you want to find out?" Mack was insistent, demanding through clenched teeth.

Sykes stared in silence at the unwavering nail gun pointed at him; his accomplice was shaken. It was an act and Mack was making it the best acting he'd ever done. What did scare him was the thought he'd go beyond acting and pull the trigger for real. There was no turning away now. Recalling how he'd thrashed Osborn Mack found himself in inner emotional turmoil. Driven by a cold calculated fury, he realised that his actions from that night still preyed on him. The beating had been brutal. Like it or not it was the kind of pain he'd have to inflict again. There'd be no choice. Sykes was a loony with a reputation for violence. It was going to be a case of him or me in the brawl and Mack had no intention of losing.

"Your problem, Smiler," Mack goaded him, breaking the unnatural silence, "is (a) you don't get your broken teeth fixed at the dentist and (b) you're stupid enough to think you can keep coming looking to get even. Well, you can't. If you leave tonight it'll be on my say that it's over. Peacefully it ain't going to happen. I've got you taped. So let's settle it one on one. Check here's going to make sure your pal doesn't interfere. In a few seconds we're going out this back door, you and your pal first. We'll settle this outside like men do. No weapons. Got that? Try anything and Check here will nail your foot in the ground."

Mack knew that wasn't going to happen. He no more trusted Sykes than a sane person would a venomous scorpion. As soon as he left the pub by the back exit Sykes would go for his flick knife or knuckle-duster or both. He doubted Check would have the bottle to use the nail gun. On the other hand, he had a feeling Kev Finch wouldn't hesitate. Sykes would expect his mates to be waiting outside. Mack hoped Finch and Smithy had sorted out Sykes's mates. Otherwise there would be a scrap and a half on his hands. As they rose to leave Mack passed the nail gun to Check, eyeing Sykes as he did so. Check took the gun from him, covering it with his maroon leather coat. "Okay. Let's go."

Check wanted to go in front of him but Mack restrained him with a shake of his head. He needed Sykes out first, and then his chum. Going through the door he watched Sykes sink his hands into his pockets. As he did so Mack's hand was already in his Harrington pulling out the weapon he'd fashioned. Like a shadow he kept right behind Sykes's chum. As they stepped through Mack didn't wait. In a simultaneous action he delivered a tremendous kick in the back of the knee to the tough in front, sending him sprawling into Sykes as he was about to turn. The lad was lucky enough not to get skewered on the flick-knife blade.

Mack's handmade flail smashed into Smiler's face, sending him crashing backwards to the ground. A vicious push ensured Sykes ended flat on his back. The blow not only dazed him, his face had erupted into a volcanic explosion of blinding splattering blood. Before the Moss Sider could react, Mack stamped on the hand holding the lethal blade using the full force of his foot. An excruciating yell of agony burst from Sykes's lips. Mack's foot remained on his enemy's hand. "Watch his chum," Mack hissed as Check covered the stunned sidekick.

"Tut, tut. Smiler, that wasn't very nice, was it?" He hissed in Sykes's face. "I didn't think for a second you played by Queensbury rules. And I was right. You had to fight dirty, didn't you? Trouble is, I'm a way filthier bastard in a scrap." The words were tough but left him sickened as he took in the damage he'd inflicted. It was an act of abhorrent violence he'd known he'd have to commit. He hoped the blow to the face hadn't fractured Sykes's skull or concussed him causing bleeding in the brain. This was the kind of barbaric act he'd wanted to avoid but there had been no avoiding it. It wasn't over yet. The next bit had to be convincing. Wrenching the flick knife from his opponent's hand he prodded the point of the blade under Smiler's chin. As much as he detested doing it he couldn't afford to show any weakness. The threat needed to sound, look and be vicious. "Should I cut his face as a reminder not to play with knives? What do you think, Check?"

"Step too far, man. But I'd understand if you did it," came the reply, although Check's voice was shaky.

"So tell me Smiler Sykes? How d'ya fancy a full-length scar across your mush? Or should I cut one of your ears off for a souvenir?"

Smiler was still in pained shock from the flail blow; his blooded face was unable to conceal cowering fear. Mack caressed the side of his face back and forth with the point of the blade.

"So here's the deal," Mack continued. "You pack and leave the North. I'm going to let my mate Nate Silvers know what you intended to do to me. I wouldn't give a brass farthing for your chances after he finds out. Oh, and if you happen to bump into your pal Scooby, tell him he'll be next if he pisses me off. Got it?"

Sykes nodded.

"Don't forget. If you go down the Smoke I've got friends there who make Check and me look like angels. One telephone call tomorrow from me... you get the picture? So if I were you I'd be real careful." It was all a shameless bluff... lies, but Mack reckoned at this precise moment they were believable.

Taking his foot off the hand he could see the shattered fingers. Sykes had worn a knuckle-duster. When he'd stamped on his hand to make him lose the knife, it had done the damage.

"Naughty boy, Smiler, you're such a very naughty boy," Mack mocked him, roughly pulling the metal object off the broken fingers. Sykes screamed in agony.

"What the hell's going on out here?" It was a bouncer from the Big Daddy club. It looked like Shirley Crabtree's brother.

"Nothing, mate." Check replied. "Lad's drunk too much and crashed into the wall as he came out of the pub. We'll sort him out. My pal's helping him up, aren't yer?"

"Sure am," smiled Mack. Turning to the young Moss Side tough who looked scared out his wits, he said, "You're his mate, aren't you? You'll see he's okay getting back home, won't you? Well, don't just stand there. Help him up."

They watched the two of them disappear down the alleyway.

"Fuck me. You had me going. I didn't think you were acting, Mack. I was shitting myself thinking you really were going to carve his face up or cut his ear off. What on earth did you hit him with?"

Mack dangled the toilet flush handles linked on a short flush chain. "Did I look as if I was kidding?" A little ambiguity would do no harm.

"What the hell is it?"

"It's my version of a rice flail. Chinese farmers have something like this to beat harvested rice plants. They also used them as weapons."

"Jeez. I couldn't believe the speed you went for him. It was a blur. You must have known he was going for the flick knife."

"Call it educated guesswork. I had a fair idea what he'd do. And there's only one thing you can do when it's like that."

"What's that?"

"Do unto others as they would do unto you. But do it first and do it bloody quick. Let's see how Kev and Smithy are getting on." Mack closed

93

the flick knife and handed it over together with the knuckle-duster, "Here. Have a couple of souvenirs. Do what you like with them."

As they rounded the pub back into the Upper George Yard there was no sign of the other Bradford lads or any of Smiler's gang. Angie was standing near The Plebs Club entrance, shivering in the cold night air. Seeing him emerging from the passageway she ran over to him. The relief on her face touched Mack's heart. Throwing her arms round him she hugged him tightly, a torrent of words berating him. "You're so bloody stupid I could kick you over and over. I've been sick with worry. If anything had happened to you I don't know what I would have done. Or how Effy would have coped. Are you okay? I made Tom tell me what you were up to. I know you. I sensed you were up to something. And no. Before you ask, Effy and Ellen don't know I know. I'm not going to tell them either."

"I'm okay. Whatever you know you don't. Nothing happened. Nothing took place."

Angie let go of him with a reluctant slowness. "That's your story, is it? And you're sticking to it, are you? That's so typical of you, James MacKinnon."

"Angie, you sound like my mum. You and I know what we have to do. Say nothing. Some things are best kept on the QT. Got another favour to ask you. Can you ring Nate Silvers and tell him what's happened?"

"Okay. What did happen?"

So he told her and watched as she paled, horrified at his account of what had gone down. Mack spared her the details, glossing over the fight itself. Subdued by what she heard her instinctive reaction was to say, "Effy can never know. Nor Ellen. We have to keep this secret. I'll tell him to make sure he keeps his trap shut and says nothing to either of them. The less everyone knows the better. Let's hope Sykes doesn't go bleating to the cops."

"What? And lose his hard man reputation? Not a chance. After I told him I was making a 'phone call to Nate I think he'll be clearing out of Manchester to pastures new."

"Don't want to interrupt this touching get-together but… have you seen a couple of lads from Bradford round here?" Check asked.

"No. I heard there'd been a bit of a scuffle outside the George as I came out of the club about five minutes ago. Someone had nails punched through their feet by some lads with what looked like a gun. At least that's the tale I got told. Tell me that wasn't you two, was it?"

Mack looked at Check who still had the nail gun under his coat. "No. Not us two. We wouldn't do anything like that, would we, Check?"

"Nah, never."

The club was so packed Mack only got in because Angie pressed her red pass-out stamp onto his hand. As he was a well-known club regular he wasn't challenged going in. Otherwise there would have been no chance of seeing The Soul Sisters. The Plebs was rammed to capacity. After the cold outside the club felt hot, sticky and sweaty. The atmosphere was permeated with a distinct almost sweet-smelling female odour. Wilson Pickett's *Land of a Thousand Dances* was coming to an end. Effy was dancing in the middle of a larger outer group with Ellen and Tom while in the outer he could see Linda, Stingray, and Alan as well as a few others. Effy didn't notice him until Angie broke through into the dancing and said something in her ear. Another Wilson Pickett song came on, *Ninety-nine and a Half (Won't Do)*. Moments later she had him wrapped tightly in her arms.

"What took you so long? I thought you were never coming. I was missing you."

"It was a tough problem. It took some sorting. Sorry it took me so long."

She kissed him with passionate intensity as if it was their first ever kiss. He felt himself merging into her. His life with her was precious and nothing without her. He promised himself nothing would ever come between them if he could help it. Then, seeing Angie, he began to wonder as they exchanged looks. For a split second he glimpsed a heart breaking.

# CHAPTER 18

**Shoot Your Shot – Jr. Walker  (Tamla Motown TMG 559 –1966)**

*Friday 20 January 1967*

"What did you think of the Soul Sisters last week? I always think the records sound better than the act but I thought they were brill. Big women though!" Tom was helping Mack stoke the boiler in the Parish Hall.

"Yeah, they were terrific. I thought they were even better live." Mack watched the flames take hold. "It's a bit slow firing up."

"Give it a minute. You need patience to get it going. When it gets to full heat it won't half warm up the place," Jersey muttered over his shoulder. "It'll get that warm you'll be able to do a bikini fashion shoot."

"Huh! No chance of that, young man," complained Ellen, shuddering from the cold even though she was swathed in layers of clothes, a coat and even Tom's parka over the top.

"I hope there's some hot water to wash my hands before we start," muttered Mack.

"What time are Grace and Eff coming down?" Ellen asked, stamping each knee high booted foot to keep warm.

"Whenever Adam gets to pick them up with all the clothes." Mack was getting stalled listening to Ellen moan about the cold. "Anyhow, stop complaining about feeling cold. You women have ten per cent more body fat than we do according to my Human Biology teacher. If anyone should complain it's us."

Ellen stopped stamping her feet. "Is that true?"

"He's right. We're both doing APH and I heard the Bio teacher say it. He ought to know," confirmed Jersey.

"Well, you're not one of the fair sex." Ellen wouldn't let it rest. "You men are meant to be hardy and tough unlike us females."

"Don't waste your breath, guys," Tom chuckled. "El's got an answer for everything. I've given up arguing with her."

That was Mack's cue to start singing a recent Rolling Stones number in a quiet voice, changing the words from *my* to *her*. This annoyed both Tom and Ellen as he sang *under her thumb*. At least Ellen stopped complaining about being cold much to his relief. Jersey kept chuckling under his breath.

Adam had been delayed by having to finish a customer's repair job at the garage. It was a frequent Friday evening occurrence but it panicked Effy and Grace into thinking he'd forgotten. They arrived, flustered, with two suitcases and two large bags filled to the brim. Angie arrived scant minutes later with a self-conscious Chloe Johnson overwhelmed by all the activity. Mack noted she began to lose the diffidence on seeing Effy and Ellen who greeted her with undisguised enthusiasm. A beaming smile lit up her face on seeing Jersey.

"Anton! What are you doing here?" Before Jersey had time to splutter a reply Chloe bubbled over. "It's so lovely to see you again and what a lovely surprise. I haven't seen you since last year when we did the panto here."

"Call me Tony, Chloe. Lovely to see you again."

"The girl has the hots for him." Tom smirked with his back to them. "Can't you tell?"

"She already has a boyfriend, dearest," Ellen answered in a low voice. "So much for your powers of observation."

"Put your money where your mouth is. I'll bet a quid within a month these two are an item."

"Done," Ellen replied archly. "Show me your money."

"Bad idea, Ellen." Mack shook his head. "Kiss that quid goodbye."

"You want to put a quid on it too?" Ellen became annoyed with him.

"No. I don't want to take your pound. Least of all after Tom takes the one you bet him."

"Scared?"

"No. You don't know what I know and what psychic Tom here has sussed."

"And what's that?"

"Tim Smith's days as her boyfriend are as good as over."

"How do you know?"

"Effy told me."

"See, El," crowed Tom with his usual cocky self-assurance. "And I didn't even know about them splitting up. But I'm great at sussing out when a girl fancies a guy."

The rest of the evening was organised chaos. Preparing the girls took the better part of forty minutes. Chloe Johnson was a whizz with the make-up. Each of the girls took it in turn to act as her assistant. The guys were amazed at how much she managed to enhance their looks. Tom was almost open-mouthed listening to Chloe's tutorial on how to look like Twiggy or Pattie Boyd. It was intriguing listening to the complexity of the information about prepping and using foundation, shadows, creases, liners and final mascara. Even Mack marvelled at the transformation in all four of his models. The end result was that four stunning-looking girls were even more stunning. Jersey seemed immune to it all as they worked on the set to eliminate shadows while Mack, anxious to get the light right, kept taking meter readings and finding the best angles. He had brought enough 35mm film to shoot an extravagant hundred plus photos. Every camera click was going to have to count to try and capture the twenty-four outfits Effy and Grace had designed and made as well as the two that Angie possessed. After hair and make-up came the dressing where the girls busied deciding which colour tights they would wear with which outfit. At least they'd all agreed on who was going to wear what dress or skirt. And so the shoot began. Having abandoned a story theme Mack concentrated on matching their outfits against a quick choice of pre-selected scenery. They'd even dragged a mirror onto the stage, cleaning it up so he could try a handful of trick reflecting front shots. Ellen had proved helpful with useful suggestions during their planning session. He'd taken her advice and the shots looked like they would pan out.

From the start he called the shots. Working from a short list he'd penned he dictated the ways the girls should stand, alone or in various groupings. This included guiding them on what expressions to try. Jokes were told to create spontaneous laughter and smiles as well as comments provoking shock and surprise. When instructed to stand with legs apart or interlocking their legs as a group with unsmiling faces they did so without a murmur. The best of it was the almost professional manner in which they responded as models. No matter what he asked them to do they acted as he imagined real models would. The best of it was they seemed instinctively to know how to flaunt the outfits to their best in front of the camera. Later he would understand how important this was. The best models knew how to relate to the outfits they displayed. What pleased him most was realising how the four seemed to have this natural ability. Grace surprised him the most, displaying flair that he and her sisters had never suspected. By the time he had finished the three rolls of film he was wishing he could have afforded another three. It was exhaustive and exhausting work that took far longer than he'd anticipated. Where possible he'd used a stepladder as a makeshift tripod. Most of the shots were handheld.

The Leica was no lightweight. He needed all his concentration and strength to keep the camera rock-steady to avoid blurring. Jersey had followed him with dogged determination, giving him sound advice on where to look for the best angles to avoid shadows. They tried some black-and-white shadow shots, too, using up one of the rolls. Jersey had been a star, moving the heavy lighting around with surprising speed and with an expert feel for what Mack was attempting. All those am-dram and pantomime productions had turned him into a dab hand at the art of illumination.

Effy had wanted him to try to capture the flow of the dresses as they moved but Mack said no. He had no experience of capturing movement on film. He was unsure if the Leica's aperture would open far enough to cope with rapid movement. Nor was he prepared to waste the limited stock of film he had. Instead he'd taken up some of her ideas. She had suggested emulating a modern-day version of Reuben's painting *The Three Graces*. Effy had shown him the painting in one of her art books. He had rolled about laughing on the sofa in the lounge. She hadn't seen the amusing side of it and he didn't explain why he was laughing. Reuben's three fat naked ladies were the complete opposite of the three sisters. What had kept him smirking and bursting out into uncontrolled bouts of laughing was the thought of seeing Effy, Ellen and Grace in the classic nude pose.

This evening, the sisters did the take on the Three Graces, wearing convergent outfits and colours. He'd snapped what he hoped would turn out to be an amazing series of shots. Well, the dark room would begin to reveal all tomorrow afternoon when he finished working at Benny's Scooters. Then he'd soon know if it had been worth the effort.

"That's it, girls. It's all in the can. Thanks for being such fantastic models. I hope I can live up to your expectations and come up with the results."

"So do we!" Angie gushed. "Who knows? We may well have worked with the next David Bailey. This could be the start of a glittering new career and champagne lifestyle."

Angie was known for mickey taking but her comment was serious.

"I mean it, Mack. You could have fooled me you weren't a pro fashion photographer. Either that or you were doing a clever David Hemming's take-off in that *Blow Up* movie we all went to see."

99

"Oh, cheers for that. I was so good, was I? So should I take up acting as a career too?"

"Honestly," Grace gave him the once-over, rolling her eyes, "nah. You're far too ugly. Well, actually, yes you could on second thoughts. Hammer Horror movies could always find a part for you. Only joking."

"Effy, you need to do something about your kid sister before I stick my fangs in her throat," Mack joked as he chased her round her sisters.

"Oh, grow up Grace!" Ellen groaned. "Act your age not your shoe size. As for Mr 'Handsome Looking' he's a class act so I think she has a point. You had me going tonight. There were moments when I thought, who is this guy?"

"I have to admit..." began Effy, only to get interrupted by Chloe.

"I was trying to work out if you were the real you or an actual fashion photographer? I've done plenty of plays here with the amateur dramatics. You just went from you to this other person. I couldn't believe it was you. You had me going. How do you do it?"

"Do what, Chloe?"

"Change from you to someone else. It was amazing."

"Okay, enough mickey mousing me."

"No, the lass has a point." He heard Adam speaking from the back of the hall. "You even had me going. You weren't you. You were like somebody else. A fecking good actor, I have to agree with them."

"Looks like RADA or Goldsmiths for you, my love." Effy smiled, trying to conceal her feelings.

"When are we having this fish and chip supper then?" pressed Angie. "I'm starving. I haven't had anything to eat since lunchtime."

"I'm going to fetch them now," they heard Adam shout as he disappeared through the parish hall door.

# CHAPTER 19

**I Got What It Takes – Brooks & Jerry (Direction 58-3267 – 1967)**

*Saturday 21 January 1967*

Some of the photographs were astounding. Far better than he'd dared to expect. Out of the hundred or so thirty odd looked almost professional. He'd run them off as contacts. Then, choosing the best, he did eighteen six by fours of the standouts. Another twenty or so were okay. As for the rest, well, he'd work out later why they'd not worked. Effy was still down at Dorothy Perkins and wouldn't be home until the store closed.

Grace, not having a Saturday job yet, had insisted on helping him in the makeshift dark room. He was still nervous doing the developing and having Grace as an extra pair of hands turned out useful. He was learning as he went along and she was learning what to do from him. Effy's sister was definitely a quick learner of the dark room arts. There was enough photographic paper to make forty more six by four prints. The accidental purchase of bromide paper with its silver emulsion produced a distinct clear cold black finish that gave the photos a greater sense of depth for the black-and-white shots. The rest he would have to take in to develop during the week. That wouldn't come cheap but it would be worth getting the best twenty made up as eight by tens.

The Three Graces shots looked so startling he heard Grace gasp. "You're brilliant, Mack. You actually pulled it off. That's an amazing photograph. But so is this one of Angie surrounded by Effy and Ellen. Wow. James MacKinnon, I think you could actually be the next David Bailey. You haven't just made us look fantastic. You've made Effy's designs look fab. You could put these in *Petticoat* or any girl's mag and they'd look brill. I don't know which bit is better. Us looking so gorgeous or the clothes looking so good."

"Can I come in?" Mack's dad took them by surprise.

"In a minute, Dad. We're waiting to develop the last one."

"Has that homemade developing tank been alright? I was worried it might not do the job."

"It's worked fine, Dad."

"How's the red light worked? Not over-exposed any of the prints?"

"No. It seems to have done okay. We kept the photographic paper safe using the safelight as Tim advised."

Seconds later, he pulled back the two layers of black curtaining. "Okay. Take a look at these and tell me what you think?"

"He's done a brill job, Mr MacKinnon. I can't get over how superb they are. Effy is going to be thrilled when she sees her clothes modelled like this."

"But aren't they your clothes too? After all, you've helped to make most of them and made some of them all by yourself. You should take some credit."

"Don't get me wrong, Mr MacKinnon, but it's my sister's designs that make them look so good. She has the ideas. All I do is to turn her design into clothes."

"Yes, but you're the better seamstress and cutter, so don't be so modest. Effy always praises you and tells me how much better you are than her at cutting and sewing."

"I'm not that much better than Effy. Well, a bit but I don't have her flair for design. She knows exactly how it'll look and what colour and fabric will be best before it's even made. Take this baby doll dress she's modelling," Robert MacKinnon's eyes nearly popped out of his sockets as he studied the photo Grace showed him, "Empire line with under bust ties and in emerald green satin effect chiffon. We've made two versions; this one is sleeveless and the other has short puffed Regency type sleeves."

There was silence. "What's the matter, Mr MacKinnon? Don't you like it?"

"How far above her knees is the hemline?" His father's expression was of a man who'd touched an exposed live mains wire. "Don't you think it's a little on the short side, a bit too revealing and risqué?"

Mack chuckled. "Looks okay to my eyes, Dad."

"I bet it does," his father replied with a wink, "but do you want other young men gawping and leering at Effy in what looks like nightwear?"

"It's going to be the trend this year, Mr MacKinnon. All the girls will wear them so short, even me."

"It'll just make 'em even more envious, Dad." Mack grinned. "Not only will she look beautiful but they'll all be wishing they had a girlfriend like Effy."

"Or me," Grace added with more than a faint hint of annoyance.

Robert MacKinnon was going to say something further but thought it wiser not to. Then, after a thoughtful pause, he added. "I hope her mother and father aren't upset if they see her dressed like this."

"Not a case of 'if'. They will, and lots of other girls and young women too by summer time. In Bob Dylan's words, *the times they are a changing'.*

"What do you think of Angie in this sapphire blue A line shift? I love the way Effy worked the fine silky silver piping into the Peter Pan collar and sleeve ends. Doesn't she look fab, Mr MacKinnon? I think those white tights and shoes just set off the whole outfit."

Mack was in silent stitches watching his dad's face. "Er, um, yes Grace. She looks very pretty, very lovely indeed. To be honest I haven't got a clue about anything you've said. You lost me with piping and Peter Pan."

Mack's laughter echoed around the cellar leaving Grace and his dad staring at him.

"What's so funny?" they asked at the same time, thunderstruck by his outburst of laughter.

"It's my Dad, Grace. He's no idea about women's fashions. I've never forgotten when Mum dragged him and me off to Leeds to buy some new outfits. My mum wanted our opinions on her choices. Everything she tried on got the same answer: *that'll do fine, Jane.* He was sweating with fear every time we set foot in a women's dress shop, he didn't know where to look. When we passed ladies' lingerie in Marks, he went bright red like a crab. When it comes to what women wear he's all at sea."

"Nonsense, James. Ignore him, Grace. And I suppose you know more?"

"I've been learning loads ever since I got to know Effy and Grace. And of late a heck of a lot," he added. Pausing he gave his father a reminder. "Even why women shave their legs and underarms."

"Actually, Mr MacKinnon," said Grace, sounding almost apologetic, "he's surprising! Mack knows a fair bit when it comes to trendy fashions for girls. I think that's Effy's doing because he's always looking over her shoulders at the fashion pages. I've even spied him checking out The Sunday Times colour supplements fashion pages."

"Is that so? Next thing he'll be reading his mother's *Woman's Own.*"

"Been there and done that," Mack smirked. "Lots of fashion shots in them. The clothes may not be for teenage girls but the models still have to know how to pose. Anyway, you should take more notice yourself and compliment Mum on her appearance a bit more. I'm sure she'd appreciate a compliment now and again."

"Hark at you," mocked his father, "trying to teach this old sea dog well-worn tricks. I'll have you know...'

"...You already do. I'm a fast learner, Dad. Got my best tips from you, especially when it comes to the fair sex. Mind, Grace has yet to join the fair sex..."

"Oi, you cheeky monkey! What are you implying?" Grace gasped.

"I'm only jesting, lass," Mack teased, "you're quite fair already. You look amazing in these photos. No one would think *you* were only fourteen. Astonishing what some war paint can do to age you."

"I'm almost fifteen," she protested. "Well, I will be in ten days."

"Don't forget to switch off this electric bar fire when you've cleared up. I don't want it racking up my electricity bill more than necessary. I'll leave you to it ."

"It's a bit nippy down here. I'll leave you to tidy up, Mack. Can I take these prints up to show your mum?" Grace grabbed some of the photos, leaving him annoyed at being left.

Jane MacKinnon was surprised by her son's impressive photography. Effy couldn't wait to get Ellen and Angie's reactions; she described the photos as breath taking. Then came her disappointment. Mack was reluctant to take the prints over to Halifax on the scooter but his mum's suggestion went down well. She told them to invite Angie over for Sunday tea as well as Ellen and Tom. It made sense. It was cold and drizzling. The ride over wasn't going to be pleasant. The few prints could so easily be ruined. There was a bright side to it all.

Mack's dad was so struck with the photos he agreed to buy Mack all the photographic paper and chemicals he needed in future. This he did out of earshot of his wife, father to son. The girls weren't to know either. He also agreed to stump up the cash to buy the lights from the parish hall providing they were cheap enough. Mack gave one mental sigh of relief after another. This photography game was too expensive for his limited means. Thank goodness his father was stepping in to help out.

*****

The smell of stale beer and a choking acrid haze of blue cigarette smoke made Effy cough. It was a stench ingrained in the pub's tobacco-stained walls and ceiling. The Vic Lounge was always packed Saturday nights. Tony

Clarke's *The Entertainer* was fading out on the jukebox as they found their friends in a tight group near the rear door. It was an all-nighter down The Plebs with Root & Jenny Jackson performing.

Ellen was berating Tom who was laughing and teasing her. It had to be hilarious. Angie was laughing too, as were Linda and Stingray.

"What've we missed?" grinned Mack.

"Glad you finally made it." Tom had to raise his voice to be heard over the hubbub.

"He's embarrassed me again." Ellen's peevishness was clear. "I didn't know where to put myself."

"You've missed tonight's funny." Stingray grinned, while Angie and Linda were still giggling. "He even made Angie laugh."

"Go on, what did he do?" Effy gave her sister a pitying look.

"It wasn't so bad," smirked Tom. "Sherwood was getting a pint in for Dick Wilson and shouted across to him *have you got a glass Dick?*"

Angie cut in delivering the punchline before he could finish. "TC shouted back, *I hope not for his girlfriend's sake.* The whole pub wet itself. Dick Wilson didn't find it funny."

Effy glanced at Mack convulsing. She tried to prevent herself laughing. Not even Ellen's annoyed look could stop her shaking her head and bursting into a giggling fit.

"It gets worse, Effy," Ellen continued. "Noddy here humiliates me in front of everyone with a limerick. The whole pub must have heard it."

"But it's true, doll! You should find it flattering. And don't go exaggerating. Only half the pub heard it and they all cheered."

"Go on. What did you say?" Mack knew he was expected to ask.

"Don't you dare say it again !" Ellen warned Tom.

Linda grinned. "I'll tell you!"

Tom stuck his size tens in his mouth some more. "I said it to all the girls at school."

Linda ignored him, *"Roses are red, emeralds are green and your bum's the best I've ever seen."*

"Actually, Ellen, you should be flattered." Mack failed to keep a straight face.

"I might have known you'd stick up for him. You're opposite sides of the same damned coin, you two. Go on. Why should I be flattered?"

Effy jumped in, steering the conversation in another direction. "Wait until you see Mack's photos from last night. You look incredible in them. Tom may well be right about your bum."

Her description of the photos improved Ellen's humour no end. She brightened on hearing her sister's glowing report, the peevishness fading into undisguised delight.

Later on Angie turned down the invitation to come over to Mack's. Problems at home meant she felt she and her sister Gillian needed to be there. It was cryptic but Mack and Effy worked out whatever was happening wasn't good. Angie had other news she had to relay. Nate had been in touch with possible dates for their modelling work. All the suggested dates were midweek. The news brought them down with a bump.

"How are we going to get round it? Angie's at work and we're in school?" The girls looked at Mack for suggestions.

"I've got a problem with one of the dates," Ellen sighed, sounding unhappy. "I've got to go for an interview for a teacher training college place."

Mack and Effy both noticed Tom's sudden sheepishness.

"You never told me you'd got an interview? Where? St. Mary's in Strawberry Hill?" Effy asked, excited at her sister's news.

"Huddersfield." Ellen answered, taking Tom's hand while he gave her a supportive glance.

"Huddersfield! Why?" Effy exclaimed in astonishment. "Are you joking, sis? I didn't even know they had a teacher training college there."

"Why? Because it's near home and it's near Halifax," Ellen replied with a half smile.

"Has Tom something to do with this? I thought you couldn't wait to get as far away from home as you could?" Mack challenged, expecting Tom to say something.

"It's my choice. Tom has had nothing to do with it."

Tom remained silent.

Angie looked at Ellen, a wry smile forming. "No. I imagine he wouldn't. Tell me something, Tom. You'd be happy if she did though, wouldn't you?"

"I'm saying nothing on the grounds it may tend to incriminate me."

Effy looked daggers at Tom. "No. You might have implied it, knowing you."

"Stop right there, Eff. It was my choice not his. Tom never ever said anything to me about where I should apply. Nor did he imply anything, so don't go imagining things and blaming him. He didn't even know where I'd applied until after I'd got the interview."

"Okay," Effy sighed. "I take it back, Tom. I still think you're daft, sis. You always wanted to go down south to Twickenham and St. Mary's. I only hope you're not making the decision for the wrong reasons."

Ellen looked at Tom, a blissful smile forming. Tom broke into an uncharacteristic bashful smile of his own. Mack noticed them squeezing each other's hands. It was a near instant revelation. Closely observing others reveals everything to the wise watcher. Never was this more so than at this moment. It was all in perfect focus and not so surprising.

# CHAPTER 20

**Aim and Ambition – Jimmy Cliff (Island Records WIP 6004-B – 1967)**

*Tuesday 24 January 1967*

"I'm worried, Mack. Really worried about the future." It had not gone unnoticed. Effy hadn't been the same since Ellen had told them of her choice of a backwater teacher training college.

"Is this because of Ellen choosing to go to Huddersfield?" He reached across the table and put his hand on hers. They had taken to doing their homework on an evening in the dining room. Effy's confident cheerful manner had become subdued since the evening in the Vic.

"Yes and no. It's about us. I'm scared, Jimmy Mack. What am I going to do? What are we going to do? I keep wondering about what's going to happen to us next year?" She sounded so plaintive, it was upsetting. They had avoided talking about the uncertain future. Both knew they had to confront some serious and hard choices. Now Effy was raising the matter. "I don't think I can bear imagining us separated."

Mack swallowed hard. "We're going to have to talk about it. It's been preying on me too. I don't want us to separate either."

"I love you so much, Mack. I couldn't stand it if we were apart and maybe far away from one another for any length of time."

"Have you given any thought to what you want to do?" His voice deepened to a husky concerned whisper.

"My teachers keep saying I should try for an Oxbridge place."

"What do you think you should do?"

"I don't know what to think or do. Your mum wanted to go to Oxford, didn't she?"

"Yes. The war and marriage put a stop to it. I take it she let that slip."

Effy nodded. "She let it slip when your gran was here. Then there was the parents' evening. Now she keeps encouraging me to try for a place."

"Is it what you want to do?"

She shrugged her shoulders.

"Listen, if it's what you want to do…"

"…That's the problem. I don't know. Everyone thinks I'm good enough. Everyone says I should go for it but it's not what I've imagined myself doing. I love art. I love designing clothes. I've always imagined that's what I'd end up doing. What about you?"

"I have no idea, Effy. No idea at all." He sounded despondent even to himself. "I know I've no chance of getting an Oxbridge place. I might get into a Uni or a Poly to do something but I've no idea what. I do know I don't want to stop you from whatever you set your heart on. If it means an Oxford scholarship then fine."

She sighed. "Everyone expects us to aim high. I overheard what your father said to you the other night. About Business Studies and Marketing? You didn't sound terribly keen."

"I wasn't." And this was the problem. No matter what came to mind he couldn't find any enthusiasm for it. "I sometimes wish I'd been like Tom and got an apprenticeship to learn a trade. If I'd taken up Benny's offer I would almost be a qualified motorcycle and scooter mechanic by now."

"You'd never be happy doing that." She spoke in a hushed soft tone, putting her other hand on top of his. "You know and so do I. There'd be no challenge in it for you."

She was right. Effy did know him. "So what do you think I'd be good at?"

"That's your problem…" She stopped abruptly.

"My problem? Go on. Say what you were going to say. I promise I won't get annoyed. If I can't trust your honesty whose can I?"

It was her glowing half-smile that made his heart beat faster. Sighing, looking him in the eyes, she said. "Your problem is you'd be good at whatever you put your mind to do. You might not know what you want to do now. When you work it out you'll be the best at it. That's you all over. You could become a famous photographer. I could see you doing that after our little fashion shoot. You have an eye for it. And yes, I can see why everyone round you thinks you could be an actor. It's not because you've got the looks but it's how you've got this knack of becoming somebody else. It's marvellous how you do it. To tell the truth, that's what I find scary about you. I do wonder at times who is the real you when you start playing games."

"You tell me this but I've no idea I'm doing it," he lied, conscious that was what he did all too often. Effy knew him better than he did himself.

"…And you've always been so grown-up and mature ever since I've known you. Your mum's even told me you've been nothing like a surly ill-tempered teenager. In fact the complete opposite of Adam, grown up long before your time. Her exact words were *James is seventeen going on thirty.*"

"She's right. It's not only me is it? You're no longer the same sweet innocent young girl I met at the library two years ago. We've gone through so much and we're still going through more. I suppose that's what it means to grow up. Coping with everything. It's not only us. Everyone we know is changing too."

"Life's going to change everyone we know. We won't be able to do anything about it. Everything we do will make us what we become. There's no escaping it." There was a gentle sadness in her murmured words. "It's what growing up is all about, isn't it? Change. There are days when I wish everything would stay the same. Forever. No growing up, just staying as we are."

Mack steered the conversation back to the reality confronting them. "All the top photographers are in London. They've all got connections. Even models like Twiggy and the Shrimp are from down there. If you want to be an actor or pop star or anything at all you have to be down there. There's nothing here. Even Dad says so. The textile industry's dying. Mills are closing, the dye works are shutting down. In a few years it'll all be gone. Folk haven't woken up to it yet. There's no future here for young people like us who want to be to be someone and do something. The action is all down South. We need to ask ourselves hard questions. What do we want from life besides one another? That book I was reading, *The Young Meteors*? It had a simple message. If you want to be somebody you need to go where the action is."

"Mack, wherever you go I will follow you."

"No. No, you won't. If you decide on Oxford or Cambridge I'll follow you. I never want you to end up like my mum wondering what may have been. Not because of me. You're bright and talented and it would be a waste like my mum thinks."

"But I can't wreck your future, Mack. I couldn't expect you to give up your own dreams and ambitions. I couldn't live knowing I'd done it. No. If we're going to be together, we're going to stay together, someway somehow. We can work it out."

"Listen, Effy, I don't have any dreams or serious ambitions at the moment. You don't have to worry about me. Whatever I choose to do I'll come out smiling and on top." It was pure bravado and she could tell he was acting.

# CHAPTER 21

**It Ain't Watcha Do (It's the Way How You Do It) – Little Richard**

**(Sue Records 4015 – 1966)**

*26 January 1967*

Nothing annoyed him more than a pontificating prick. Parfitt was a pontificating prick and a pain. It was the worst thirty minutes of the week and clearly this week's session wasn't going to get any better.

The day had begun well. The Grade 1 GCE English result had given Mack a glow of satisfaction. His CSE Grade 1 English Language and Lit results hadn't been seen as good enough so they'd entered him for the November re-sit. Where others were desperate re-sitting just to get a pass, this was his first and only attempt at the exam. The results were pinned on the Sixth Form notice board. Top grade.

His English teacher "Merton" Mullarkey, an Oxford graduate, inspired him with no confidence. Merton had a habit of sneering and making snide comments. He'd even pulled Mack up in a rather vociferous manner over a minor grammatical error. "I see they didn't teach you English grammar at the secondary modern, MacKinnon. No doubt they considered it beyond the scope of secondary modern pupils."

This snooty arrogant condescension had incensed Mack. As if he was not fit to be in this grammar school because he'd once failed the Eleven plus? Or maybe because he was Adam's brother and they thought he'd behave in the same way Adam had? Mack noticed Merton hovering over his shoulder, studying the results. He should have said nothing but it was irresistible. "I got a '1' in GCE English."

In a breathtakingly supercilious manner Mullarkey dismissed his achievement. "A fluke result. Has to be. They always mark the re-sits easier." Walking away he left Mack mentally balling his fists ready to have a verbal swing at the arrogant fart. Who the hell did Mullarkey think he was? If he was such a hotshot Oxford graduate what the hell was this poxy arrogant git doing working in a grammar school in Bradford? Blood still rushing to his face, he somehow contained the seething anger from exploding. It was inevitable how things panned out later in the afternoon.

Mack had grown to despise religious instruction long before coming to St. Bede's. Now it aggravated him no end. Parfitt was a Holy Joe, a pain in the theological arse. Even Gaylor, the group's tutor, found listening to him uncomfortable. As a rule Mack kept his peace during these half-hour sessions, though usually with gritted teeth. It was an endured waste of time. He'd never uttered a word in previous sessions. Most of the time he idled in switched-on deafness while working out economics essay answers or maths questions. It took some doing, Parfitt's voice was difficult to tune out.

Considered scholarship Sixth material he was one of a select bunch kid-glove groomed for Oxbridge. His domination of discussions earned him no favours with the rest. Like Mack, they suffered in silence. Today Jersey, head thrown back, was staring at the ceiling mouthing something. He could just make it out. 'Please God, make the twat shut his gob.' Tim Smith, eyes glazed over, sat with his head sunk in his hands. Mack reached his limits of tolerated annoyance.

When he cracked the others in the group woke out of their stupefied slumbers. His reputation for controversial comments was well established. No one present would forget today's words.

"So let's clarify what the Church expects me to believe, *Father* Parfitt."

Mack's heavy sarcasm was unmistakable; chuckles spread round the room as the group sensed major sport looming. Speaking with ponderous deliberation, articulating every word with judicious resonance, he continued in the manner of a B-movie courtroom barrister.

"My so-called saviour was born of a virgin. A virgin impregnated by God's alter ego 'the Holy Ghost'. This was so God could give birth to himself as his other alter ego, the Son. Talk about a God with split personalities. Then there's Mary. Committing adultery by cheating on Joseph with the Holy Ghost. Doesn't that qualify your Saviour as (a) illegitimate (b) a fornicator and (c) incestuous? It doesn't stop there, does it? It gets a lot worse. He gets nailed to a cross to save us from our sins. Dead and buried, he brings himself back to life after three days to magically ascend to heaven. His followers then tell everyone they can live forever. All they have to do is breakfast on his body and blood every Sunday while praising him with hosannas. Why? So he can cleanse them of their sin. Sin he put there in the first place when he created all things.

"And don't you think, *Father* Parfitt, it's a tad outrageous? Blaming all women for introducing sin into the world? Why, because one woman got

112

conned by a snake? Not just any ordinary snake. Oh no, no ordinary snake. We're dealing with a talking snake no less, aren't we? A snake so clever and so cunning it tricked this poor woman into eating magical forbidden fruit from a magical tree? And, since God knew all things past, present and to come, the end result of her action was never in doubt, was it? It was a foregone conclusion. Original sin becomes the birth right of generations ever after. Guess what, Parfitt? I'd sooner believe in fairies at the bottom of the garden. Not this load of tripe which passeth all understanding, especially yours."

Parfitt sat open-mouthed, disbelieving his ears. Mr Gaylor's reaction veered from stricken to horrified. Tears flowed from Jersey's eyes, he was laughing so hard. Others joined in with some wit in the corner clapping. Tim grinned idiotically, shaking his head. "The Spanish Inquisition's going to get you for this."

His chat with the Spanish Inquisition in the shape of the School Chaplain left Mack damned in the eyes of the Church and the school. Jersey later claimed the priest came out from the lengthy chat sheet-white. Word got around fast. The upside was, Parfitt stopped pontificating, some Sixth Formers cruelly joking he'd suffered a crisis of faith.

It proved a bad week in other ways, too. Seeking his father's opinion on the current state of the British economy for an essay made him realise his father was down. And it was unusual for him to be down. By nature his dad breezed confidence. At first Mack thought perhaps he was tired or maybe going down with a winter cold. It was a deeper malaise. As a bank manager he was in tune with the economic changes happening in the country. Many of the measures being introduced by Harold Wilson's Labour government were proving ineffective. The balance of payment had a large deficit and appeared out of control. Unemployment had reached a new high, rising before Christmas to over six hundred thousand. The trade unions were playing up and labour relations were at a new low. Rob MacKinnon reckoned Jim Callaghan, the Chancellor, would end up devaluing the pound later in the year. If that happened it would be disastrous. It was all the fault of Reggie Maudling for allowing spending to get out of control on imports when the Conservatives were in power. Added to this, the taxes people were paying were way too high. Some of this came as a shock. Especially when his dad mentioned that for every pound he earned he had to pay 8s 3d income tax – a rate of 41.25 per cent. No wonder people were unhappy and no wonder the trade unions were making increasing demands. The seaman's strike last summer hadn't helped matters even with England winning the World Cup.

Robert MacKinnon was the youngest son of three, with his younger sister Ellen the only girl. William, his older brother, had been destined to take the reins of the family businesses from his father. Instead war intervened and William was killed at El Alamein. Thomas, his other brother, died during an air raid on Malta. Serving as a Hurricane pilot defending the island, he'd been with fellow pilots when the bombs fell. The loss of their two eldest sons had almost broken his parents. Then there was the unexplained mystery of what had happened between Robert and Mack's grandfather. Whatever the reason, his father shied away from explaining. In his late grandfather's will Robert MacKinnon was excluded from running the family businesses. Mack sensed the decision had delighted him.

Granny MacKinnon kept her promise to her husband. With considerable unwillingness she had not involved his father in the running of the businesses. Irrespective of her late husband's wishes she had every intention of seeing her son takeover the family enterprise in due time. During her stay over Christmas, long closeted discussions had taken place between mother and son. It didn't seem unusual at the time. Since those secretive chats his dad had lacked his distinctive bouncy optimism. Mack suspected the future was nearer than his father had expected. Whatever had transpired between them, it had affected Robert MacKinnon.

He tried to tackle his father on the subject without success. Tonight he tried again.

"Okay, Dad. What gives? It's not like you to be like this. I'm old enough to work out all's not right with you." It was cheeky. He half expected getting slapped down.

Robert MacKinnon gave his son a long hard stare and sighed. Mack knew straightaway what that meant. His father was weighing up what to say. "Let's talk upstairs in your room, son."

Once there his father opened up in a rather rambling and uncharacteristic manner.

"It's hard for me to know how to say this. I suppose I've got to share with someone. Adam ought to be in on this but then again maybe not. Your Aunt Ellen, bless her, was never one with a serious head on her shoulders. When we came out of the Navy Ellen ran away from home and came to stay with us. Your mum and myself were already in her father's bad books for getting married. That was the same with my father. I was the youngest son but I was also the least favoured. Not going into details, he and I were at constant loggerheads. When I joined up it proved the last straw. He'd already lost his favourite son William in North Africa. Thomas's death made things worse. I was the last surviving male."

Mack's dad paused. There was the taste of bitterness in his next words. "Even before I enlisted in the Navy he'd disowned me because I wouldn't do what he wanted. From when we were small, we were told William would inherit everything. Thomas and myself would have to make our own ways in life. I never had a problem with this. What I had problems with was how he'd attempted to control and manipulate our lives to suit his own ends. He treated us like puppets, pulling all kinds of mental strings. I have no kind words for him. Frankly, the best thing I did was to cut the strings he was trying to pull. A friend I served alongside during my time in the Navy helped me get a job with the bank in Halifax, of all places. It was an offer I couldn't refuse after we left the service. I needed work. I thought I was getting a career. Instead I got a salary. But I had to do what I had to do. That's how your Aunt Ellen met your Uncle Phil. The rest is history. That's how we ended up in West Yorkshire."

"I can guess where this is going."

"Can you? Yes, I suppose you can. You've inherited your grandfather's sense of astuteness. I hope all his better qualities, not the others. He could be utterly ruthless, manipulative, revelling in toying with the emotions and feelings of those around him. A singularly unpleasant man I'm saddened to tell you. In his younger days he had a reputation for getting his way using violent means. I'm rambling. Your gran wants me to return to Edinburgh to run the business. She's getting too old, she says, to deal with running things."

"And you don't want to go?" Mack left the question hanging.

"No, I don't," came the blunt reply. "I like the life I have here. I've made my own way in the world and am beholden to no one. My family is here and so is my sister's family. We've stood by one another over the years. Besides, we have our granddaughter here. Why would we want to leave Adam, Caitlin and Jane? There are also things you may not be aware of at the moment. I'm not at liberty to tell you what they are but they involve both Adam and Tom. No doubt they'll let you in on their plans in due course. Then there's our wider 'adopted' family, Effy and Grace."

"What's this about Adam and Tom? Or is it Tom and Ellen?"

"Tom and Ellen?" His father looked puzzled.

Mack told him about Ellen's decision to apply for a teacher-training place at Huddersfield, surprising him. His faint smile spoke more than words.

"I think they're serious, Dad. They've not even been together two minutes."

"Looks like our family can't escape the Hallorans." He ran his hand through his son's hair. "He could do worse. No. We're faced with another problem. I believe your mum's talking to the girls at the moment. They'll have to tell you themselves when they've had time to think and decide what they should do."

Mack panicked. "You're not going to ask them to leave, are you?"

"Good heavens, no. Your mum and I would never do that. Having Effy and Grace around has been a revelation. We often wondered what it would have been like to have daughters. Now we know. If they were our daughters I'd be Larry happy. Like we've said before, the girls can stop as long as they want. Especially Effy, if it keeps you two from doing something foolish."

"Can you afford to keep us all?"

"Yes, son. I can. That's the least of my worries."

"As I see it, Dad, you don't have to go back to Edinburgh if you don't want. Gran can always sell up and retire. She's your mum but she should have stood up to your father."

"Don't blame your gran. She wasn't responsible for his actions or behaviour. Nothing's ever as simple as it seems, James. Life's not a novel. There's no plotted story line. Life writes itself as our choices mount up and the consequences become clear."

"So are you even considering going back to Edinburgh?" Mack persisted.

It was obvious his father was in a quandary. There was more going on than Mack was privy to knowing and he intended to wheedle it out of his father.

"The answer to your question is no. I will not go back even if the bank gave me a promotion there and that's not likely. No. The real problems are right here. Banking is undergoing rapid changes. I'm expected to take up new responsibilities as my bank innovates. We're talking about installing card machines so customers can make withdrawals out of hours. There's also a strong likelihood of banks merging and with it an air of uncertainty at work. I'm praying they don't want to promote me to an even bigger branch in London or Manchester. Those are the things concerning me, son. The last thing I need you to do is mention any of these worries to your mother. Let's not share this with her; she has enough to worry about with the new baby coming. We may have left it a bit late in life to have another child. Let's keep my words to ourselves, father to son. These are matters I can share with you and only you. They're not ones I could share with Adam. Even now he's not as mature as you. Until I know what's what let's keep my worries to ourselves."

"You can rely on me, Dad. Thanks for confiding."

His father's next words were surprising. "No. Thank you for letting me share my worries with you. As a father, it's my job to prepare you as best I can for the life ahead of you. I can only do this by sharing the problems I face so you can learn from them. We none of us ever know better, no matter how old we get. Sometimes all we can do is wait and see."

Mack was pleased his father had confided in him. Nothing in life seemed straightforward these days. His father's last words worried him. Could they be true? No matter how old you got you never knew any better?

He kept retracing what his father had said. Life was not a novel. Why was his mum talking to Effy and Grace? What was going on there? And what the hell were Tom and Adam up to? Mack suspected quite a lot had slipped unintentionally from his father's lips. It was not like his father to let things slip.

# CHAPTER 22

### Heart Trouble – The Eyes of Blue (Deram DM 106 – 1966)

*Monday 30 January 1967*

Aileen sat sobbing in front of the dying embers of the living room fireplace. She was no longer dressed as a novice nun. Bridget, seated by her side, looked up and rose. Even though the house had been her home since birth, Effy no longer liked returning here. For her this place had ceased to be home. It harboured too many unhappy memories. Home was where her heart was and that home was Mack.

"I'm glad you're here," Bridget sighed. "Aileen's not right. She's asked for you. You're the only one she says she'll talk to. I've tried but she won't tell me why she won't talk to me. She's insistent it should be you. I'll leave you two together and brew some tea for you two and Jane."

"What's wrong, Aileen?" Effy sat down by her sister and put her hand on her shoulder. "Tell me what's the matter, big sis."

Aileen did not answer straightaway. She was twenty-two, the eldest of the seven sisters. When Effy had first met Mack she and her sister had been as tall as one another. Two years later Effy was a head taller. Aileen had always been diminutive in stature. Effy could see how thin her sister had become. Shrunken, pale, with dark shadows under her eyes, it was clear from her physical state she was not right. Everything that could be wrong with someone was wrong with her sister.

She had never been close to Aileen and put it down to their difference in ages. The fact was, Aileen had never been close to any of her sisters. When they had all lived at home it was as though they'd lived with a shadow. It wasn't that Aileen wasn't affectionate. She loved them in her own way but she had always seemed distant, so aloof from them. Bridget had been the one who took up the mantle of the big sister, caring for the youngest when their mother couldn't. It had been Bridget who had stuck up for them against their father. Aileen had cowered in silence. Effy had thought her strange, never disagreeing when her father was at his worst. She had left a well-paying satisfying job as a bank teller to enter the novitiate, never making clear why she'd taken the decision to do so. Was it a way of escaping? Now she was back from the convent for good, according to Jane MacKinnon. Back and in a desperate emotional state according to Bridget.

"When did you stop believing?"

The question took Effy by surprise.

*****

"I've run out of change, Mack." Tom was in a phone box. "I was going to nip over but what with Aileen back home it's a bit pointless. Ellen knocked it on the head. Told me we'd not get any privacy what with Bridget there and Eff, Caitlin and Grace coming down with your mum at all hours every day. Anyway, it's nothing that can't wait. You can always ask your brother."

Mack put the phone down, exasperated at hearing the pips go. He'd wanted to ring him back in the phone box like he usually did but Tom told him there was a queue waiting. It was frustrating.

Effy was in no mood to talk, either, when she returned from Whites Terrace with his mum. Whatever was going on down there it had taken its toll. They'd been gone a few hours and it was late. She could tell he wanted to know what was happening. When his mother disappeared to make some tea, she said, "Later. Not now. I have to think it through. I feel as if I've gone through a mental mangle this evening."

"Okay." He concealed his impatient curiosity with an amiable smile.

She paused and then asked an unexpected question. "When did you stop believing?"

It was a strange question but he understood it straightaway. "I was in an RE lesson in the Third Form. Father Finnegan tried to stop us sinning again. Silly old Father Finnegan."

"I'm being serious, Mack."

"No, I'm not kidding, He *was* called Finnegan. The good Father tried to awake us to the dangers of the flesh and its temptations. *He thought we were young and easily frightene*d. I wasn't. What made you ask?"

"I'll tell you tomorrow."

Tomorrow came and went and he was no wiser. Grace was uncommunicative and not herself either. When he asked Ellen, she claimed she knew nothing. Mack wasn't sure she was telling the truth. If his mother knew anything it was unlikely she would tell him. Confidences were her forte. Tackling Effy again got him nowhere. Having thought things through, she decided it would be best if she kept it to herself for a while. Adam was more forthcoming.

119

"You're a right nosey git, aren't yer?" Adam's initial response was typical. "You mean Tom's not told you? Fancy. I always thought you two were like twins and shared everything. Anyway, it's no biggy."

What Adam told Mack proved unsurprising and obvious when he thought it through. Adam had been a qualified mechanic for a year. Tom, it appeared, had set records for speeding through his apprenticeship and was set to qualify ahead of time. A conversation one Sunday at Adam's had led to the two of them talking about going into business together. A further conversation between Adam and Mick Jenkins had seen matters go further. Nothing was settled as yet but Mick was keen to persuade his father Benny to expand the business. Benny's Scooters should become Benny's Motors. They could expand by taking on new premises to sell motorcars as well as two-wheelers. And by two-wheelers, he was talking about stocking and selling Japanese motorcycles while keeping the Lambrettas going.

"That'll need a pile of money. Last time I heard, you and Caitlin were struggling to make ends meet. As for Tom, he's got more in his piggy bank than in his post office savings account. So Adam, how's this going to happen? Got a secret backer or something?"

"You could say that." Adam gave him a twisted grin. "Bank of Granny MacKinnon."

"What?" That was a bombshell. "Gran's never helped out any of the family. She's had a downer on Aunt Ellen for years. I'm not even sure she's forgiven her even now for running away and marrying down the social ladder. As for you, you weren't exactly the golden wonder boy in her eyes a few years back."

Adam's twisted grin became a beaming smile. "Things change, young Mack, things change. Don't forget she came to our wedding, that, and us making her a great-gran. Believe it or not she's going to give us the loan."

"Really?"

"Sent me and Tom letters saying she would after talking it over with Dad and Uncle Phil."

"Don't get me wrong. It's a great idea you two getting together. But…"

"But what?"

"…I'd want to see the colour of her money first."

"Don't you trust your Gran?"

Mack said nothing in reply.

"What's going on with you and Aileen? You've not been right since you went down with Mum to see her."

Effy looked up from her copy of Milton's *Paradise Lost*; her tired expression left him feeling rotten for asking. "At first I was going to talk to you about it. Then Aileen has asked me not to say anything. I gave her my word I wouldn't."

"It can't be that terrible? I can't imagine she's committed a murder. Now that would be bad."

There was a long silence. Finally she said, "Would you talk to her if I asked? She wouldn't tell any of my sisters what she told me."

"But she'd tell me?"

"Maybe."

"Why?"

"We're alike. We're no longer believers."

"Is that all it is?"

"No. There's more. Ma wrote and said Da wants to sell Whites Terrace."

"Bummer stunner."

# CHAPTER 23

**Born Under a Bad Sign – Albert King (UK STAX 601015)**

*Saturday 4 February 1967*

"Do you remember when we were little kids?" Tom voice was tinged with unusual poignancy. They were sitting in The Beefeater coffee bar overlooking George's Square towards the parked scooters.

Mack sipped the hot unsweetened espresso before speaking. "What's the matter, Tom? It's not like you being down. Problems with Ellen?"

Tom's face brightened. "No, cuz. Ellen and me are okay. No. It's this whole growing up lark. I've decided I don't much fancy being a grown up."

"You and me too. Let's just stay as we are."

"Wish we could. I was remembering all the things you and me used to do as kids before you moved to Bradford. Like all those games of 'tig' we used to play? Do you remember when my Dad found me that massive 'bolly' and I won about forty marbles? What a killer day that was."

"Half of them belonged to Stingray. I don't think I've ever seen a ball bearing that size since. He's never forgiven you for taking those marbles off him. And I've never forgotten how he teased you about having a girlfriend. You kept denying it till you went red in the face. Little did he realise you were a Casanova in training! What was she called?"

"Dot, or as he and the gang teased me with 'e's going out with Doh – ro – fee."

"Those school dinners were terrible."

"Ugh." Tom pulled a face. "That rice pudding? We used to put loads of jam into it and stir it until it went that disgusting pink. Do you remember me getting caned for putting a drawing pin in Bazza Wilson's shoe after PE?"

"When *The Skull* gave you a couple of whacks with that lead-tipped cane?"

"That smarted. He cut my hand with it, the bastard."

"Fair do, you had it coming. It went right in Bazza's foot. Don't suppose Old Scully had much choice but to whack you. Mind, Bazza was a right twat and had it coming. I wonder what happened to him?"

"I beat seven shades of shit out of him at the secondary modern. It was the talk of Tommy Moore's for a long time. Afterwards he steered well clear of me. He left before we got to the Fourth Form. No idea where he went." They reflected on the memories, each lost in silent remembrances before Tom started again. "Do you remember how your mum made us play in silence when she wanted to listen to *Woman's Hour* on the radio?"

"Not to forget Semprini Serenade. What was it he announced at the beginning? Something like *old ones, new ones, loved ones*. Dad bought a couple of his LPs. It was enough to drive me crazy. I got to hate hearing Semprini."

"I remember when Aunt Jane took us one Saturday to see Elvis in *Blue Hawaii* at The Royal on Manningham Lane."

"And she claimed we wanted to see it when it was really her. We'd just moved to Bradford. Your mum wasn't well so she packed you off to stop with us for the weekend."

"Yeah, then your mum sent you and Adam over on the Number Seventeen bus another weekend. My mum took us all to see *The Young Ones* with Cliff Richards."

"I suspect they took it in turns so our parents could to have those 'special times' without us in the house."

"So Tom, you miss those times? If I'm honest I do too sometimes. Effy and I have to face some big choices. It's not only you worrying about growing up."

"You two are going to be okay."

"I wish I could be sure."

"What does she want to do?"

Mack opened up to Tom, sharing his worries about his and Effy's future. Tom was the only one he felt he could share his problems with, other than Effy. If anyone might say something positive it would be Tom. His cousin listened intently and then it occurred to Mack that it should have been him listening to Tom's worries and problems.

Tom waited until Mack stopped talking, "We none of us know what the future holds. You, Effy, Ellen, me, we'll have to take it as it comes. There are no certs in life. I can't see you two splitting up even if you have to be apart any length of time. Ellen and me, who knows? We're both crazy about each other but we've only known one another for like two seconds compared to you two. Ellen doesn't worry me. If we're meant to be together it'll work out in the end. Nah, for me it's what I end up doing. This thing with Adam and the Jenkins is a big deal. I mean it's a *huge* step to take. I can't help wondering if I'm up to it at my age? All the money it's going to cost. I can't even legally sign for the loan either. My dad and your dad are going to have to sign surety for us. The thought of paying back Gran such a massive loan makes me feel sick. We're not talking peanuts."

The sum he mentioned was *jaw dropping, heart-stopping*. Mack emitted a long low whistle followed by, "Gordon Bennett!"

"Exactly," responded Tom.

No wonder his father hadn't been himself. All this hadn't figured in their recent heart-to-heart chat. Mack also worked out why it hadn't. His father must have known he'd learn about it sooner than later. No wonder Tom was concerned. How was his dad going to square the circle with Gran over Edinburgh and the loan? How was Tom's dad ever going to afford his share? What if it went wrong?

"Look on the positive side. They wouldn't consider guaranteeing the loan if they didn't think it'd work. Where money's concerned, my Dad would never give a loan to anyone unless he was certain the bank would get it back. If he and your dad are guaranteeing repayment you can be sure they think it'll work. Besides Benny Jenkins is no mug. I work for him and he runs a tight business making legal loot, Mick's sound as a pound too. If you're going to work in a partnership there are no better guys than them."

"Your dad says it's a private limited company we'd be setting up, whatever that is. Do you know?"

It was a company with less than fifty shareholders that couldn't trade its shares on the stock exchange, he explained to Tom. This meant that if things went wrong they wouldn't be liable for any debts they incurred but would only lose the money they'd invested. Mack had learned about this when he'd done his O Level Economics. Tom wasn't reassured because the original loan would still need repaying and it was a ton of money.

All Mack could say to him was, "Well, you and my brother and the Jenkins had better make it work. Somehow I suspect you four will do well out of it. Adam's a grafter and so are the Jenkins. You'll be the lazy arse they'll be worried about."

"You cheeky twat, MacKinnon! I'm not a lazy sod, I'm a grafter." Tom pretended to sock him on the jaw, grinning as he did so.

Angie's Triumph Herald appeared in the square.

"Time to go, Tom. Let's put it behind us for tonight."

They'd been waiting for a lift. Edwin Starr was on at The Twisted Wheel. Effy was unwell, laid up in bed with a heavy cold and in no fit state to go out. She'd even missed going to her Saturday job at Dorothy Perkins. After a hot bath she planned to sleep it off with an early night.

Ellen was busy revising but was stopping over keeping Effy and Grace company. Her excuse yet again was that she didn't want to be on her own. Bridget was taking Aileen away for a weekend in York. The truth was much simpler. The MacKinnons's home was centrally heated and toasty warm whereas Whites Terrace was freezing cold. Tom had persuaded Mack to go to Manchester with him and Angie. He didn't want Ellen getting jealous and suspecting him of getting up to no good with Angie or anyone else. Mack had wanted to stop with Effy but she'd insisted he go.

As they walked over to the waiting car Tom passed an unexpected comment. "I reckon if you and Effy weren't such an item you and Angie would be. I suspect deep down our Angela has a secret thing going on for you."

Mack turned to him. "Effy's said the same thing to me not so long ago. Well, I suppose if I hadn't met Effy, we might have been together. We'll never know. I'm not so sure she has a secret thing going on like you seem to imagine."

"It's not a case of imagining. You know me and you know how I can read women. I'm never wrong when it comes to sussing them out."

"There's always a first time, cuz."

"Nope. I don't think so because I'm never wrong." Tom's smugness could be annoying.

'Check' Mates stood at the top of the stairs with guys Mack recognised as Bradford Faces. A steady stream pushed past them as Mack stopped to chat. The Twisted Wheel was busy. Junior Walker's *Cleo's Mood* drifted up from the cellar, its hypnotic melody making toes tap. In their brief exchange he learned Finch and Smithy had got nicked for stealing building materials while working in Baildon. Scooby would be out of circulation for at least a year. As far as The Twisted Wheel was concerned Scooby was on a lifetime ban. There was serious news too. Sykes was still around. He'd been seen hanging out in Piccadilly Plaza with some of his pals. As he listened to

Check's grim news he could see Tom and Angie exchanging looks. Ronnie Sykes had decided to ignore his threat.

What Check told him next made him think. "A word to the wise. Don't get too thick with Silvers. Steer clear. This fella's not only got fingers in pies; he's got his toes, thumbs, nose and dick in them. Dodgy doesn't come close to describing him."

Nate Silvers strolled in about an hour later accompanied by two tough-looking lads. His face lit up on seeing them by the refreshment bar in the upstairs of the club. Giving Angie a kiss on the cheek and paying her a compliment that made her blush, he shook hands with Tom and Mack. Placing a hand on Mack's shoulder, he spoke into his ear. "We have unfinished business outside. I need you to come with me and the guys."

Mack felt himself go cold, the hairs on the back of his neck standing up. Despite Nate's smile and bonhomie there was an edge to his voice. An edge Mack recognised only too well as the kind he used when intimidation was needed.

"Just me, or the three of us?"

"Just you. It's best they don't see what you and I see. We don't need witnesses."

"Sounds ominous."

Nate shrugged. "Let's get this done. We don't want to miss Edwin Starr."

Mack wasn't happy. Nor did he like the look of the two bruisers with Nate. Surely Nate didn't plan on having him beaten up?

As if reading his mind, Nate laughed. "You're not the one with a problem. It's only a short walk round the corner."

Nate seemed to have the entry and exit rights of the owners. As they went out he informed the door staff, "We'll be back in ten."

They walked to a nearby car park and headed for a scruffy battleship-grey mini van. Nobody spoke. One of the two silent bodyguards unlocked the split doors while the other produced a torch to illuminate the interior. Mack stopped himself from gasping out aloud but went cold at the sight.

A trussed, bundled and gagged figure lay inert in the van. His heart sank as he recognised who it was. In the dark it was difficult to tell if he was still alive until one of Nate's guys kicked his ankle. Wriggling round, blinded by the torch, he looked a mess.

126

"See this poor turd here? He was born under a bad sign," Nate joked half-seriously to Mack. "You really need to apologise to Syksie for rearranging his face."

"Are you kidding me? He had it coming."

Without warning Mr Polite Guy Silvers snarled, "Apologise to him, Mack."

Mack readied himself for a scrap. They were professional bruisers but if they tried to do to him what they'd done to Sykes they'd have another thing coming. Even if he ended up wrecking his charcoal grey mohair suit they wouldn't walk away in one piece. Mack complied with reluctance.

"Sorry for making your face a mess, Smiler. Not like you gave me much of a choice." Mack could see the fingers were heavily strapped from when he'd stamped on them.

"Did you hear that, Syksie? He apologised for beating the crap outta you. You heard that, right?" snarled Nate. "You were warned to stay out of my business. You didn't listen. Look where it's got you now. To cap it all you had to have a go at one of my associates, and on his home turf too. You got the kicking you deserved. And you still ignored his suggestion to get out of my city? You'll think twice about it when you sink to the bottom of the Ship Canal."

In the torch light Mack watched a huge wet patch spread from Sykes's crotch down both legs of his trousers. The guy was quaking and in tears. This was way out of hand. It had to be a joke. Nate couldn't be serious about drowning him? Yet somehow he couldn't discount the possibility. This ruthlessness went beyond horrifying and had to be a joke.

Nate turned to Mack and winked. "What do you think? It's up to you. We can drown the fucker and sort it permanent like. Or he can piss off for real somewhere else and never come back? Your choice, Mack."

Mack decided to play along, still unsure if this was only some elaborate charade. "I don't know, Nate. Smiler never seems to learn his lessons. I don't think he's too bright. Dropping him in the canal's a bit much."

Sykes stopped wriggling, making a strangled noise through the gag in his mouth. Eyes wide and tears streaming, he was a sorry mess in his pissed trousers. Mack felt so sickened and sorry for the guy. In his situation he wondered if he'd be braver. Sykes had to be in abject terror. And the facial damage was not Mack's doing. Those were fresh bruises and cuts that must have been inflicted by Nate's heavies.

127

"Let him go, Nate. He knows he's crossed the line once too often. He's got the idea what'll happen if he sticks around. Forgive and forget, I say. I'll forgive if he forgets our differences. What do you say?"

Nate rubbed his chin, hesitating as if thinking it over. "You sure about it? I'd hate to go to all this trouble again if he messed me about in the future."

"You ready to call it a day, pal?" Mack asked Sykes. "Nod for yes."

Smiler nodded so hard it looked like he might suffer concussion.

"Scouts honour, Smiler? You really will behave this time?"

More vigorous nodding followed.

"Thank MacKinnon for getting you a reprieve. After tonight you owe *The Mack* big time. You're only off the hook 'cos I respect him that. Got it?"

Another vigorous nod followed. The menacing intent in Silvers's tone was clear as he added, "Cross me again and they'll be fishing you out of the canal for certain next time."

Mack almost released a sigh of relief.

"Okay, fellas." Nate gestured with a swing of his arm, sounding disappointed. "Take him to Piccadilly Station. Buy him a ticket for the first train outta here, stick a fiver in his pocket and see him on it. I don't care where it goes. I don't want to see him on our patch again."

They heard the van doors slam shut as they walked away without a backward glance.

"He's got the message," Nate stated laconically. They walked back to the club in silence. The future is uncertain. No one knows what the future holds. Causation is strange, divergent and unaccountable; it is what it is and everyone lives with its child, consequence. Mack would encounter Ronnie 'Smiler' Sykes again and be glad of it.

Once inside Nate spoke again. "Let's keep this between you and me. As far as we're concerned we know nothing. In fact, we know less than nothing, *capiche*?"

"I have no idea what you're talking about, Nate. Thanks for showing me the local sights."

Nate winked, giving him a friendly pat on the back. "My pleasure. Now you understand the way I do things here in Manchester."

"Pretty much."

# CHAPTER 24

**What a Sad Feeling – Betty Harris (Stateside SS 475 – 1965)**

*Wednesday 8 February 1967*

Aileen turned out nothing like he'd expected. Effy's sister was perkier than he'd been led to believe. She'd lost weight: quite a lot, he guessed. "Anorexic" was Ellen's description even though it wasn't anorexia. Aileen was pale, tired and care-worn in appearance. But she seemed cheerful enough, greeting him with a peck on the cheek. Effy received a long lingering hug from her sister. Mack had met Aileen on a couple of occasions when she'd returned from the convent during Sean Halloran's illness. Unsmiling and reticent, she had struck him as troubled. As it turned out he hadn't got it wrong.

Aileen was twenty-two or so. He wasn't quite sure but she was at least five years older than Effy. Thanks to what he'd learned from her sisters he felt as though he had a reasonable idea what this eldest sister could be like. This impression didn't match the reality.

Aileen spoke in a hushed, soft voice verging on the languorous. Everything she said was thoughtful and measured, her words chosen with care and precision. At first the mundane conversation went nowhere, leaving him wondering why he was even here. It was all so genteel; why was Aileen reluctant to brass-tack the chat? Then, in a quiet unexpected manner, she asked. "When did you stop believing in God and why?"

"I'm agnostic where God's existence is concerned. Religions are another matter. They're nothing more than a means of enslaving people's minds. I refuse to belong to any religion and be enslaved, indoctrinated and programmed like some organic robot."

"God may exist but you're unsure? Are religious beliefs the issues?"

Mack leaned towards Aileen. "No. Gods and religions both. They try to enslave us."

"Explain to me why you believe this?"

Mack shook his head. What he disclosed next might prove offensive but then if you were true to yourself you had to stand by what you believed.

"Why would such a God, the creator of this and any other universes, expect us to adore him? You'd think such a being would be well above personal vanity. Why would he want or need sycophantic bowing and scraping adoration from mere microbes like us? It's absurd. So absurd I refuse to even entertain the idea. Religions are nothing more than vested interests holding sway using the God idea to promote their own agendas. And can you honestly imagine such a powerful being getting swayed by our prayers? That's real folly."

Aileen gave him a wan smile. "It's the same conclusion I've reached. I lost my faith. That's why I left the convent and religion behind. There is another reason too."

Effy interrupted her sounding concerned. "Are you sure you want to share this with Mack? Don't you think it's a bit too personal?"

Aileen sighed. "I need to share it with someone other than you, Effy my love. I need to hear what someone who doesn't know me well has to say. From what you've told me he strikes me as a young man with an open mind who can keep a secret."

Effy gave him a telling glance. "Only too well, sis, only too well."

"Whatever you say stays with me and Eff and goes no further." Mack confirmed.

What Aileen told him next left him at a loss.

"I'm sexually attracted to men."

Mack spluttered suppressing laughter. "Nothing wrong with that."

"I am also attracted to women in the same way. I am what they call bisexual and I can't help the way I feel."

Tormented, filled with guilt, Aileen had tried to suppress her sexual nature. She had failed. No longer able to reconcile her feelings with the teachings of the church, she had finally broken down, revealing all in the confessional. The priest had harangued her, showing no sympathy, no love and no patience. That was the turning point. During the confession she'd reconciled herself to the truth. Aileen's whole life was a denial and a lie. The lie lay in the self-deception she'd practised while trying to remain true to an unforgiving faith. In the end she had to be who she was, not who she was expected to be in the eyes of others.

"Does knowing what I am shock you?"

Mack shook his head. "Why should it? It's your life. Your sex life's your own affair and no one else's, except the other person with whom you share it. As long you care for each other why should it matter to anyone else?"

A brief silence ensued. Half-joking and half-serious, unsure how to respond further, he asked, "The priest? Don't suppose by any chance he was called Father Finnegan?"

Aileen looked at him, open-mouthed. Glancing at her sister, she said, "How did you know his name? I never mentioned him to Effy let alone anyone else. Are you a mind reader?"

Life moved in mysterious ways, its strangeness impossible to comprehend.

# CHAPTER 25

### Confusion – Lee Dorsey (Stateside SS 552 – 1966)

*Thursday 16 February 1967*

"Thanks for telling me. Now who keeps secrets from who?" It was a degree of annoyance Mack had never displayed before.

Effy had mixed emotions. She felt awful about the deception. At the same time, she was experiencing annoyance verging on anger at his words. There had been genuine reasons for saying nothing and keeping him in the dark. Angie had warned her it would be better to let Mack know what they were doing. Swayed by Ellen and Grace she'd chosen to say nothing to him. At least he couldn't get the blame for them truanting. If they'd been caught taking the day off then it would be their own fault. It seemed like the right way to go about it but thinking it over she wished she'd told him. Calming herself, she understood he was only being over-protective. The annoyance began to dissipate.

"Supposing something had gone wrong?" posed Mack.

"But nothing did. We didn't want you to get into trouble with your mum and dad. And you don't need to be causing any more problems for yourself in the Sixth Form. It was unpleasant enough, the school chaplain coming round to have a word with your parents."

"I should have gone with you."

"Well, you didn't. That's an end to it."

There hadn't been a serious alternative. Nate Silver had made arrangements for the modelling session on a Thursday. Angie had had to pretend she was unwell to get off work, something she hated doing. The four of them had no choice but to sneak off to Manchester. At least they'd managed to catch the early train, changing out of their school uniforms in the Exchange railway station. Nate had been waiting for them at Piccadilly Station with Angie who'd arrived earlier. They had found themselves whisked away in his father's Jag. The photo shoot had taken five hours. Getting back late, they'd made an excuse, saying Ellen had needed help with unfinished housework at Whites Terrace after school.

He knew he shouldn't get annoyed. It made sense keeping him out of it. The priest's recounting of the conversation about his "virulent anti-Catholic notions" had upset her.

"I'm sorry, Eff. You're right. It makes sense. You were only thinking of me."

"I know you. You'd have wanted to come along as a chaperone."

He grumbled, muttering about possible dangers they could have encountered. Effy and the girls had no idea who they'd gotten involved with. Nate Silvers wasn't what he seemed.

After seeing Edwin Starr at The Twisted Wheel that night they'd had a long chat. What Mack had gleaned he liked and he didn't like. Witnessing how Nate had dealt with Sykes, Mack had second thoughts about any further involvement with him. Only the reputable family fashion business tempted him to continue.

The Silvers family were legitimate business people. That was indisputable fact. Reading between the lines, he saw that Nate kept his shady dealings separate. What he couldn't fathom was why Nate was so friendly? What was it about the three of them he found so likable? He and Tom were two seventeen-year-olds from Yorkshire. They weren't rich kids. They were nobodies from nowhere. As for Angie, what possible interest did he have in her if he was homosexual? Mack had his suspicions and those involved amphetamines. So what was his angle? Get the girls to work as models in exchange for favours from Tom, himself and Angie? Nothing was for nothing. There's always a catch and a price to pay.

It was puzzling how Nate Silvers knew all about his and Tom's ultra-brief foray into drugs at Oldham. And what was Nate's connection with Scooby, if any? Did it involve a turf war they'd blundered into? Something wasn't kosher and it all pointed to Nate Silvers.

"So how did the shoot go?"

"Could have been miles better and nowhere as well done as yours. You handled it so much better even if you didn't have a professional set-up. Nate dropped us of at this studio and disappeared for three hours. The photographer was an unprofessional old lecher. He made a pass at each of us at some point in the day including Grace. Angie gave him a mouthful, calling him a dirty old man and child molester. He didn't like that one bit. Then he made the mistake of fondling Ellen's behind. Grace and Angie had to restrain her from throttling him. Ellen threatened to kick him in his man parts. I've never heard Ellen string so many swear words together, ever. I couldn't

133

believe it of her. His assistant had to come to our rescue. She had a quiet word with him. I didn't hear what she said but he calmed down as soon as Nate's name was mentioned. It wasn't funny at the time though but we've had a laugh about it since."

"And you told me you didn't need a chaperone?" Mack exclaimed. "I hope you told Nate."

"We did. We told Nate straight we'd never work with the man again no matter how much he paid us. When Nate saw the photos you'd taken he was blown away."

"You showed him my stuff without asking?"

Effy became upset at Mack's tone. "I didn't think you'd mind. I wanted him to see my designs together with my drawings. He was blown away and so impressed with your photos."

"Oh, was he now?"

"I wasn't supposed to tell you. It was going to be a surprise. Nate wants you to do Silvers Fashions teen and young women's photo shoots in future. When I said he was impressed, I wasn't kidding."

"And does he expect me to go over to Manchester to do his photo sessions? There's no chance of that happening, is there. Not with A levels and working for Benny's."

"You could do them over here, I suppose."

"Where am I going to magic up a studio, Effy, let alone the time? We've nowhere to do that kind of work. We were lucky to get the use of the parish hall but that's not going to be there for much longer. Doesn't sound like a plan, does it, if you stop and think about it?"

"I thought you'd be excited." Effy felt frustrated by his response. "You're the one who's always telling me there are no problems, only solutions you haven't yet found."

Should he tell her of his suspicions about Nate Silvers? He had no definite proof only a gut feeling and a few chary comments that added up to nothing more than conjecture.

"I supposed we could always look into hiring somewhere," Mack mused. "I'll ask dad. He may know somebody who knows somebody through his contacts at the bank. So, when was Nate going to have a chat about this with me?"

# CHAPTER 26

### Get On Up – The Esquires (Stateside SS 2048 – 1967)

*Tuesday 21 February 1967*

They rode into Huddersfield along Bradford Road. Joining the dual carriageway ring road, they reached Southgate. The town was a place Mack didn't know. The previous summer he'd gone over one night with some of the Halifax crowd to the Tahiti club on Venn St. It had been a quiet night with hardly anyone there. Still the DJ had played some excellent Stax 45s. The Tahiti was next to a DIY place called Sydbros. Mack parked his Lambretta outside the store.

"You okay, Ellen?"

Ellen removed her helmet, shivering. "I'm a bit cold."

The grey clouds threatened no rain or snow: a typical dry winter's day. At least it was warmer than usual but not after a scooter ride from Bradford.

"I seem to remember there's a coffee bar not far from here. Better get you some hot tea to warm up before you go in for your interview. The Town Hall is up the street from what I can remember. Isn't the Co-op somewhere up that way?"

"It's somewhere on New Street, wherever that is."

They found two coffee bars close to the Co-op. They went into the one called The Four Cousins. Mack had bumped off lessons for the day. Since he never took time out he could pass it off as a sickie. Ellen had agreed to counterfeit an absence note from his mum. She was nervous about the interview so Mack did his best to calm her down. He even agreed to go into the college and wait while she had her interview. Ellen was usually full of confidence. Not today. She was the proverbial bundle, shuffling about, unable to keep still. At Effy's insistence he'd agreed to take her and keep her company as well as calm.

They still had an hour before the interview. Mack went through a series of questions she might face, starting with the obvious one. Why did she want to become a teacher? He kept her focused, running through a list she had compiled with Effy. He even threw in some he thought might crop up. How would she deal with travelling in every day from Bradford? This elicited a strange smile.

Oastler College of Education was located on the top two floors of the Co-op Department store which he found weird. Most teacher training establishments were self-contained with their own grounds and halls of residence. This was a day college. They walked up the stairs passing shoppers on the way up and students wearing the distinctive blue, white, yellow and black striped scarves on the way down. The first floor of the college was divided into two halves. To the right was the students' common room, to the left a long refectory. At the small corner students' union office they were directed to the reception and offices at the far end of the refectory. At this point Ellen seemed to take courage, hugging him and telling him to wait for her in the students' common room.

Student life looked positively bizarre. The students gave him suspicious looks. Most were lounging about chatting. A Cream LP was playing in the background. A couple of girls sauntered over to ask what he was doing here. Before he realised what was what, these confident young women were chatting him up. Would he like to come to a party Saturday night? The girl with the Geordie accent seemed especially keen. Nothing he said dissuaded her so he played along. Why not? What was there to lose? Ellen came to his rescue, emerging from the interview forty minutes later on a high.

"I'm in! I start next September! It's unconditional too."

"Was it George Wilson who did the interviewing?" asked the Geordie student, assessing Ellen as possible future competition.

"The principal? Yes, it was."

Another girl student showed them round. On the floor above was a lecture hall that also doubled as a gym and theatre. There were various tutor rooms, the most interesting being the AV room with its own TV studio.

"Well, it's not too bad, I don't suppose, for a college on top of a department store. I guess with the main students' union facilities down at the Polytechnic it might be quite good." Ellen seemed pleased.

"Are you sure you'll like it here?" They were having a drink and sandwich in the Olympus Coffee Bar across the road from the Co-op. "The journey from Bradford and back won't be a breeze. It'll be a killer. You'll be spending two hours a day travelling."

"That's not the plan," Ellen confessed.

Mack gave her a quizzical look. "You're not moving to Huddersfield are you?"

"No. I've got other plans." She almost seemed to say *we* before saying *I've*.

"C'mon, Ellen. Spill the Heinz. You know I can keep secrets."

Ellen sipped her coffee and then took a bite from her egg mayonnaise sandwich, chewing thoughtfully. He could see Effy's similar shared family mannerisms with her sister. Alike in some ways, they were so different in others.

"You promise to keep it secret? I mean no one must know for now."

"Not even Effy?"

"You can tell Effy. But Grace mustn't know, or anyone else. I wasn't going to say anything until it was definite. Now I've got a place it's definite." Ellen took another sip of her coffee. "I'm moving into a house with Angie and her sister Gillian as soon as I've left St. Jo's."

"That's a bit of a jaw-dropper, you, Angie and Gillian sharing a place? What's the deal?"

"It's complicated."

"Won't Bridget get upset?"

"She'll be relieved to see me go. Bridget and Greg are pretty serious about each other even though he's still married. She feels obliged to look after me until I'm sorted. Now that Da is planning to sell Whites Terrace and buy somewhere smaller they won't have the room for the three of us: actually, four if Deidre ever moves back, though I don't think that's likely. Deidre's made it clear she'll never be returning no matter what."

"So what about Aileen, now she's back?"

"Oh, Aileen, yes, I'd forgotten her so it does complicate matters. Anyway, having lived with Bridget I've tasted parent-free living. I've loved every minute of it. I suspect Effy won't go back either. She's got her feet well under the table with your mum and dad."

"I hope she doesn't go either. Does Tom know?"

"I mentioned it to him over the weekend. He thinks it'll be great me moving to Halifax. Gillian and Angie have already moved in."

"Why have they left home?"

"There are a lot of family problems. The girls don't get on well with their mum and dad for some reason. Angie didn't really want to say."

"Where's the house?"

137

"In Jubilee Road, sort of between Siddal and Salterhebble, close to Huddersfield Road. It's a three-bedroom terrace. I've seen it already. There's more. Angie's changing jobs too. No doubt she'll tell you herself when you see her. Even I don't know what it is. If anyone knows anything it'll be Eff. Those two have become like you and Tom, two sides of the same coin."

# CHAPTER 27

### Tell It Like It Is – Geno Washington & The Ram Jam Band
### (Piccadilly N.35403 – 1967)

*Friday 24 February 1967*

*4:30 pm. – Leeds Rd. Bradford.*

Robert MacKinnon couldn't understand why his son thought the shop sign was hilarious. It read "Thomas Bowler Photographer". Mack kept sniggering. "I wonder if they call him Tom for short. That'd be just the ticket, eh, dad. It'd be even funnier if his middle name was 'Raffles'!"

"Raffles? Tickets? What are you on about?" His father couldn't see the connection.

"As in Tom Bowler, get it …Tombola, the game?" Mack clarified, trying to control his simmering snigger.

"Yes, very amusing. Pull yourself together, son. Treat this seriously when we meet him. He'll be doing you and the girls a favour hiring out the studio above his shop. And don't forget, as his bank manager I need to keep this introduction on a professional basis. After all, he is a client at my bank. So don't go messing it up with any silly upsetting comments like the one I just heard."

Mack switched on the business-like expression he reserved for customers at Benny's scooters. "I won't," he confirmed as they entered.

Leeds Road was a part of the city he only visited on rare occasions. He'd passed this shop a few times but had never taken much notice of it. On the few occasions when they'd had the family portraits and birthday photographs taken these had been done at another photographer's in the city.

Entering brought them into a small lobby area with a counter. The interior was dated but spotless. The oak surfaces and lustrous panelling exuded an aroma of wax polish. Portraits displayed in tasteful arrangements advertised the considerable quality of the work. Ted Bowler was the son of Thomas Bowler who had retired some years earlier and passed the family business to his son.

139

Bowler was a few years older than Mack's father. The tortoiseshell spectacle frames with their old-fashioned circular eyepieces gave him an odd but distinctive appearance. The combination of tweed jacket, bowtie and a pipe stuck at a jaunty angle from under a moustache only enhanced it. The overall look was that of a perfect stereotypical professor seen in second feature films. The illusion broke when he spoke. The broad distinct Bradford twang emanated from a rather unfortunate high-pitched voice.

The shop premises were larger than they looked from the outside. The three-storey terrace shop contained a secondary studio above the ground floor. This was accessed through the front entrance by a concealed staircase. It was large and well equipped with lights and a variety of backdrops. It was perfect but not cheap. That would be an expense Mack would have to take into account with Nate's father, Alex Silvers. Ted Bowler rented out the studio to amateur and professional photographers alike. He made it clear that the studio was not to be used for any inappropriate photo shoots. The mind boggled at the thought. The photographer was surprised as well as impressed on learning Mack would be doing work for Silvers Fashions. His attitude to Mack warmed, changing from initial coolness.

Mack forced himself not to ask if the photographer's father been called Tom.

Over the coming year they would develop a professional working relationship. Mack would learn and benefit from his acquaintance, starting that same evening. Instead of buying film in rolls Mack discovered the professional photographer's secret. Bowler let him know he could buy film by the hundred-foot length the way the professionals did. Better still, with his father's help, he could buy film and other photographic supplies at wholesale prices making massive savings. Mack also acquired the theatre spotlights from the parish hall, storing these in the cellar next to his DIY dark room. With some improvisation he could make limited use of the rooms in the house.

*8:10 pm. – Vic Lounge. Halifax.*

"Sounds like an amazing deal." Angie replied. Inez Foxx's *Hurt by Love* was playing in the background. It was still early for a Friday night but the pub was already full.

"I'm still not sure about taking on this fashion photography lark."

"You're a natural, Mack," Angie asserted. "Nate was blown away with your photos of us, wasn't he, Effy? I had a chat with him over the phone before I moved out, seeing as we won't have a working phone line in the new place. Gillian's asked the GPO to reconnect the one that was in already but you know what they're like. Anyway, you can phone in to us even if we can't ring out. I've given Effy the number. Nate was keen to emphasise he's prepared to send clothes over to Bradford so you can do the sessions there instead of Manchester. He's got your home telephone number, hasn't he? Have you mentioned to your parents about becoming a photographer for the Silvers?"

"Yes. Why have you moved out?" Mack studied her expression, avoiding the topic of Nate.

"It was time to leave the nest. Gillian was moving out so I thought I would too: new place, new job and new life. Besides, living at home hasn't been too pleasant recently."

Mack thought it better not to ask about her family problems.

"New job? When you've just qualified as an apothecary assistant?"

It was fascinating watching the interplay between Effy and Angie as they exchanged glances. He hadn't asked Effy about Angie and she hadn't volunteered to tell him.

"I couldn't stand the idea of working in a chemist's for the rest of my life." Angie hesitated, glancing once again at Effy before continuing. "You're looking at the new receptionist and filing clerk for Hardacre, Hardcastle and Hewitt."

"The solicitors? That sounds worse than working in the chemist's."

"It pays better. I get Saturdays off too. It's only until I pass my O Levels at Tech in summer. Then I'll look into doing something else."

"O Levels... I didn't know you were doing those. When did you start them?"

"Last September. It was Effy's idea. She convinced me I should. Then when I got to know Ellen... she encouraged me to stick with it..." Angie trailed off.

"That's brilliant. How many are you doing?"

"Five."

"Wow. So that's what you've been getting up to on a night. That's great."

Angie took a sip of her Cherry B. "What did you think I did every night? Come down here to the Vic? Mixing with you and Effy made me realise I was stupid leaving grammar school with no qualifications. When I've passed them I'll see if I can do something more worthwhile."

"I'm impressed. Ellen told me she's moving in with you two as soon as she's done her A Levels. Is that right?"

Angie smiled. "Yes, she is. Should be fun. We get on well and Gillian likes El."

Effy smiled, saying nothing. Later, out of Angie's hearing, she said, "I wonder if Angie and Gillian know what they're letting themselves in for with El as a housemate?"

*10:20 pm. – Vic Lounge. Halifax.*

Effy had gone to the loo with Linda. Mack spoke to Angie out of Tom and Ellen's hearing. "I need to make this quick. We need to talk, no sharing with Eff. No mention to Ellen or Tom or anyone else."

"What's it about?"

"Nate Silvers."

"And?"

"I don't have time to go over it now. It's too involved."

"I'm coming over to Bradford tomorrow to do some window-shopping. I'm seeing Effy during her lunch break. Do you want to meet me somewhere afterwards?"

"The Pack Horse pub. Two o'clock. I'll have finished at Benny's and we can meet there. It's near the Market and Morrison's supermarket."

"I know where it is." She looked unhappy. "I don't want Effy getting the wrong idea."

"Don't worry. We won't be alone. We'll have a chaperone."

# CHAPTER 28

**I'm a Fool to Want You – Ketty Lester**
**(LP Love Letters – London HA – N2455 – 1962)**

*Saturday 25 February.*

*2:30 pm. – The Pack Horse, Westgate, Bradford*

What she'd heard appalled her. Check sat across from them, silent. The pub was quiet for a Saturday afternoon. By this time any City fans going to the match had supped up and headed for Valley Parade.

"If it was anyone but you telling me this, Mack, I wouldn't believe it." Nothing much fazed Angie but this had. Her naturally pale complexion paled even more listening to him.

"There's more." Check joined in. He'd sat in silence listening to Mack recounting the events of the Smiler Sykes episode. "I knew Silver was a prize bastard. When Mack told me what took place I had to add my few jigsaw pieces to complete the picture."

"There are two sides to Nate. He's a bit Jekyll and Hyde. Yeah, he does work for the family business. That's legit. His father is a well-respected businessman. Then there's his 'private enterprises' with Nate using the legit business as a cover. Check and me have had a few quiet chats with various people and this is what we've learned. I'll let Check tell you."

Check took a big swig of his pint, taking care not to spill a drop on his dark-grey three-piece mohair suit. "Seems Scooby's pill supplier used to be Nate Silvers, but nobody can be definite about it, so it goes. You'd struggle to prove it because the guy and his mates make themselves 'invisible', always working through others. Anyhow, things were fine while Scooby towed the company line. Then Scooby and his mates hooked up with some Scouser for getting their supplies, so it goes. Except, rumour only, they were part of the same mob Silvers and his lot were in cahoots with in the first place. He and his lot weren't going to stand by and let Scooby and his pals get away with it. Scooby and his lot could never prove Silvers was their original source, but Silvers knew everything about them. As long as Scooby was small time it didn't matter too much. Trouble was, Scooby's a double-dealing psycho who rolled as many punters as he dealt fairly with others. He's a head case. It was getting out of hand. Your friend Linda's ex-boyfriend Steve was a real case of spite. Sell him the stuff and then set him up so the cops could get him? For fuck's sake why? For kicks, just because he could, is the answer. When he got one of his mates to stab Geoff Greenhall he went too far. Again, there was no reason."

"So how did Tom and I get roped into all this?"

"That must have been my fault." Angie spoke in a subdued voice, her upset evident.

"How?"

Tom had leaked the whole Oldham story to Angie mentioning Scooby. At one all-nighter she had told Nate Silvers the story. Recalling the conversation she now realised how Nate had expressed a considerable interest in what she told him. It was then when things began to change. He started taking a real interest in her as well Tom and Mack even though he didn't know them. When she was offered the modelling job matters developed further. It was all starting to make sense to her. The connections between her and Effy and Mack and Tom became clear. As Mack and Check listened it all made complete sense. The modelling offer, their meeting at the party, and Nate's knowledge of the fight outside Scooby's house with Smiler, setting up Scooby for the police: it was all an elaborate set-up. Why? For a few seconds he did wonder; then out of nowhere it came into sharp relief. Of course, it was obvious. Let someone else do his dirty work, namely himself. How much and to what extent had he and the others been manipulated and lured into playing a part in all this?

"He's not asked you to flog pills for him, has he?" Mack asked Angie.

"No. I wouldn't if he did."

"What about you, Check?"

Check took another long swig of his pint before answering. "He didn't personally but it was suggested in so many words by one of his lot. I reckon he was sussing out some Bradford lads. I know for a fact he tackled Dave Bean but Dave's too much of a pill head. It'd be like letting him loose in a sweet shop. Silver's mob's looking for 'light' users who want to make money. Pill heads can't be trusted 'cos they attract attention."

"I don't think he's going to ask you, Mack," Angie commented. "I told him you didn't use and that after the one time with TC you refused to have any more to do with it. Trouble is, I worry about the likes of Stingray and Alan. They can be a bit gullible."

"Anyway, you two, I got to blow," announced Check. "Closing time's in five minutes. I'm off to buy a pair of brogues I've seen. If you're going to The Wheel I'll see you there. If not catch you both later."

"I could fancy him," Angie revealed, watching him disappear through the back entrance.

"He doesn't strike me as your type, Angie." His quick-fire response was thoughtless.

"So who is my type, Mack?" She reacted with uncharacteristic sharpness.

It was a pointed question not lost on him.

"Okay, don't get shirty."

"Why do you always act so jealous when I mention I like the look of a guy?"

"I don't! Where've you got that idea from?"

"From you? Her dark eyes scrutinised him. "It's like you don't want me seeing anyone else. Perhaps Effy's right, maybe you do fancy me a bit more than you'd like to admit."

"Angie, for heaven's sake…"

"You just don't like the idea of me going with anyone else, do you?"

"I thought we'd sorted this out…"

"…But we haven't so don't tell me we have."

"What do you expect me to say, Angie? That I fancy you and love Effy?"

"Yes. Be honest. I know you love her and as her best friend I know how much she loves you. I have no intention of coming between you two." She hesitated as if deciding what she ought or ought not to say next. Tears began to well in her eyes. "If you have any respect for me, at least be honest with me. I know you like me and it's more than just as a friend. I'm going to be honest with you. I've fallen in love with you and I shouldn't have done. I love you but… here's the 'but'… I will never come between you and her. Never. She's the best friend I've ever had. I love her as a friend. I would never do anything to hurt her. After Gillian's she's the closest person in my life. I want it to stay that way."

"Yet you want me to tell you I love you? Is that it, Angie?"

She fell silent, staring at the half-empty glass of tonic water, tears trickling.

"Well?" he asked. "Is that what you want?"

"In your own way you have strong feelings for me but you just won't admit them. At least be man enough to admit I mean more to you than just as a friend."

Mack was exasperated. He couldn't deny what she was saying and was hurt by her tears. He wanted to pull her close to him and comfort her. Yet he was reluctant to do so and admit anything. Since her eighteenth birthday party he'd begun to tell himself there was a strong physical attraction. There was a kind of inevitability about it, too. She was the first girl with whom he'd had sex. It wasn't just history. It wasn't just the physical attraction. They also got on so well together. Effy was right. If she hadn't been around Angie would now be his girl. Mack still recalled how she'd thrown her arms round him after the fight with Sykes. She was always there. Outside The Wheel she'd stepped forward and said her piece to Scooby. He should have realised it sooner. Then he recollected with complete clarity that heart-breaking moment in the club after his fight with Sykes. She'd glanced at him and Effy and he'd felt her pain. If he admitted how he felt it would have consequences. Every choice had a consequence.

Angie had never revealed what had taken place between them. If anyone could be trusted to keep it secret she could. If, however, she felt as strongly about him as Effy did, what would that mean for all three of them? Dare he admit that she meant more to him than a friend? He loved Effy passionately. She meant everything to him and yet... and yet he had these feelings for Angie, too, and they were not going away. The truth was they had never gone away. Buried deep in a subconscious grave those feelings had refused to stay dead. If he admitted how he really felt to Angie it would change everything. Nothing could ever be the same. There was a time to be silent and a time to speak. Love was worth whatever it cost. Sometimes you had to pay the price.

It was a dilemma and he would be damning himself either way. Looking into her eyes, Mack knew what he had to say.

# CHAPTER 29

**The Nitty Gritty – Shirley Ellis (London American HL 9823S – 1963)**

*Saturday 25 February 1967*

*Late evening. – Manchester.*

They met Silvers and his business associate at the Wimpy in Piccadilly Plaza. It was a popular rendezvous point for many before heading on to The Twisted Wheel. Chris Farlowe and The Thunderbirds were appearing and they were keen to see him live. Mack sat squeezed between Angie and Effy. He and Angie agreed to keep their suspicions regarding Nate to themselves. How it played out depended on what was said. Any mention of dealing would be an automatic out. Angie had wanted to cut all involvement with Silvers at once. Mack was less keen. They needed to be wary of Silvers, never forgetting his scary side. If there was legit work to be had they should take it, but only if it was legit.

Effy could see Angie was tense and distracted, so much so she was clinging to Mack. He had to know she was overstepping the boundaries of friendship with such close physical contact. Yet he was doing nothing to discourage her. Instead, smiling and relaxed, he was making small inconsequential jokey chat. Angie had always avoided touching Mack in any way that Effy could construe as untoward. Now Effy was mystified and uncomfortable with her friend's strange behaviour but surprisingly neither annoyed nor resentful. Not even in the slightest and that too was bizarre and inexplicable. Something wasn't right. It was so unlike Angie. They were keeping whatever it was from her. Ever since the New Year Mack had become reluctant to share his worries. It was as though these worries and problems were kept from her for her own good. It all appeared to stem from their first encounter with Nate Silvers. What on earth was going on?

Angie had been fine when she'd met her during the lunch break. When they parted she'd been cheerful, smiley, looking forward to them going to The Twisted Wheel. Something had happened in the intervening hours.

Nate Silvers arrived with someone he introduced as Manny. Manny was older, in his late twenties, smart and suited but no Mod. The conversation swiftly turned to business.

It was peculiar watching Mack. Before her eyes he transformed into a professional negotiator as though it was the norm. "I want to make it clear from the off, we're only interested in legit business dealings. Anything remotely shady and you can count us out. I hope that's clear."

Nate was momentarily surprised by Mack's remarks. It was clear it was unexpected.

Mack continued. "So, on a business basis the girls and myself are going to operate as two separate but linked partnerships. We're setting up our own modelling agency and a separate fashion design partnership. As we're all under twenty-one and therefore under adult age our dealings will be overseen by my father who will act as an administrative partner in both. He's a bank manager. Hope that's okay?"

Nate's expression flickered in further surprise.

"I don't see a problem with that, Mack. Manny here manages the day-to-day running of Silvers Fashions for my father. Okay. If that's how you want to go about it I see no problem."

"Business is business as my father keeps telling me. He's the money expert, and I'm a fast learner. So let's get down to the real nitty gritty. Tell us what you want, Nate."

Effy looked across at Angie, trying not to look astonished. What was going on? Angie was giving nothing away. Effy tuned back to the three-way conversation between Mack, Nate and Manny. Silvers Fashions wanted to launch a separate young women's range. These would be their takes on popular designs by the likes of Mary Quant but far more affordable for the average working girl. They needed their own portfolio of photographs to do the selling and advertising. They were willing to give Mack and the girls an opportunity to bring something fresh to their marketing. The conversation then switched to Effy's designs. Nate's father was impressed and keen to use her talent and designs.

If they were willing to go ahead they could meet with Alex Silvers to discuss matters further.

Mack turned to Effy. "What do you think? Do you want to see your designs with your own label on sale?"

"We're opening one of our boutiques in London." Nate turned his attention fully on her. "In Chelsea, down the King's Road to be exact. We're

148

talking up-market fashions with up-market price tags. We'd like to use your designs."

"I don't have the time to make them myself…"

"You wouldn't need to. My family have the workshops right here in Manchester. We'd make them up to your spec and pay you per dress made and sold. You could have your name on your dress label like Mary Quant or Barbara Hulanicki. How does that grab you? It's a win-win situation for all of us."

"I'll need to discuss the fine detail with my partners," Effy replied, trying to sound non-committal while experiencing mixed emotions.

"Look, you three, I'll put it all in writing and get our secretary to mail you the details. That'll give you a chance to decide if you want to go ahead. I want to add that my father is as serious and as keen as I've ever seen him. He wants to make use of your designs and you girls as models. Since he saw Mack's photographs, your designs and you girls he's been blown away, like me. We believe this could be of mutual benefit. If you believe we can do business we'll arrange a meeting with my father. In the meantime…" Nate produced three tickets and handed one to each of them, "these'll get you in to The Wheel tonight. They're on me. I'll catch up with you in the early hours. It'll give you the chance to talk it over."

They watched him leave without saying a word.

"Okay, Mack. Start talking – you too, Angie," Effy snapped. "What the hell's going on? And don't spin me any fairy tales. I want the truth if it's not too much to ask."

"So there you have it, Effy. Bottom line. We don't entirely trust him. There's no evidence, just a case of two plus two not adding up like it should." Mack looked her straight in the eyes as he used her choice of arithmetic logic: a choice that wasn't lost on her. "That's why I made up the partnerships on the spur of the moment. I thought if we made it clear we were only in if it was legit it might end up as four. You know the old saying. Everything that glitters isn't gold. Sometimes it's only silver and that tarnishes if it's not kept clean. Now we have to work out how much he's tarnished."

There he was playing clever again. The analogy wasn't lost on her.

"Honest, Effy. Even I didn't know what Mack was going to say. When he and Check told me they suspected Silvers was behind the pill pushing, it scared me and I don't scare easily. I'd heard rumours he was involved with local villains but I didn't believe or want to believe."

"Angie didn't want any more to do with him," Mack added, having edited out Sykes's kidnapping. "I thought we'd test him. See if the legit side of the family business was real and his offers genuine."

"Are you serious, Mack? You want us to get involved with him? After what you've just told me? I'd have thought you'd have more sense." Effy's response was cool rather than angry.

"If the offer of selling your designs and getting you and your sisters modelling jobs are legit why knock it? It's what you want, isn't it? To become a designer?"

"Not if we can't trust him. Don't forget, he who sups with the devil should use a long spoon. Do we really want to sign deals with him if he's so dodgy? Keeping our distance might be a sound idea. What do you think, Angie?"

"I'm in two minds, Eff. What if he can do what he says? Being a model is a good earner. If it pays like it did and it's legit, what do we have to lose? It may be our only way to fame and fortune. Besides, I'd love to see your designs selling in Chelsea. You have a real knack when it comes to clothes. From the conversation I think the deal would be with his father and that's definitely a reputable business. Their clothes are sold by a lot of the catalogue companies. Let's see what deals he comes up with first. We can always kick it into touch if it stinks."

Angie had a point. If she had a future as a designer this might be her one chance. Turning to Mack, her green eyes flashing serious intent, she said, "I won't consider doing anything unless your dad approves and unless he's involved. Like you said, we're all under twenty-one. If I decide to go along with it, and it's a big 'if' at the moment, it all has to be legal and above board."

# CHAPTER 30

**Get on the Right Track – Georgie Fame (EP Columbia SEG 8393 – 1965)**

*Tuesday 28 February 1967*

"How was Jersey?"

Mack removed his parka. "If he follows all the tips I gave him tonight he should smarten up nicely. How did it go with Chloe breaking up with Tim?"

"Not well." Effy kissed him on the cheek as he turned from hanging up his parka and stowing his helmet in the understairs cloakroom. "She said she was fine once she told him. He said some nasty things to her after he failed to make her change her mind."

"I didn't think he'll take it well. He's not the type. When he finds out about Chloe dating Jersey I can't imagine what'll happen. Could end up in a punch-up."

"He should have treated Chloe better. Some of the things he used to say to her were plain nasty. She's better off without him." Effy caressed his hair, running her fingers through it with the softest touch. Looking him in the eyes, she whispered, "I do love you, James MacKinnon."

Hugging her to him, his lips found hers.

"Is that you, James?" His mum's voice broke the kiss and the spell.

"Yes, I'm back."

"Put the kettle on."

"No, Mum, I keep telling you, it doesn't suit me," he joked, using his dad's favourite line. "But I'll make a pot of tea, howzat?"

As they made the tea Effy asked, giggling in a mock cockney accent, "So how did your 'Enery 'Iggins act go? Do you think you can make a my fair gent out of Jersey?"

"I gave him the low down on personal grooming. Hope he wasn't too embarrassed by the tips. I'd like to believe he appreciated them. The Clearasil I gave him was well received. Should help keep the blackheads and spots under control. The new haircut's smartened him up no end. While I was at it I showed him how to tie a proper Windsor knot and how to put a razor-sharp crease in his trousers. Nobody ever taught him do either. All in all, he's coming along a treat."

151

"No matter how hard you try he'll never look as attractive as Audrey Hepburn."

"Chloe might be more appreciative of the new and improved Jersey after my 'Enery 'Iggins tutoring."

Following the all-nighter she'd behaved with unpremeditated coolness. Afterwards she'd felt awful, realising the effect it was having on him. Her coolness had hurt, not that Mack had said anything. The last thing she wanted was to make him feel she loved him less when she loved him more. His response had been stoical. "You can learn nothing from being unhappy. Unhappiness teaches you nothing. I believe in the end things will work out for the best."

Thinking it all through, she'd come round to his and Angie's thinking. Why pass up what might be their best possible and perhaps only chance of the big time? Could she afford to say no to her dreams? She became her old self again, affectionate and loving towards him.

In her softest voice, bordering on a whisper, she said, "Your dad spoke with me while you were out."

Mack sighed. Nothing she told him came as a surprise. The modelling was nothing compared to the setting up of a design business. In short, his father had expressed serious reservations. It might impact on both their futures. Since Effy's parents were not here he had to act in their best interest and speak as they would. Mack grimaced. He and Effy had discussed the probable reactions beforehand. It was understandable, predictable and, knowing his father, expected.

The conversation with his father didn't go as well as it should have done. At least it never became heated during what was a frank two-way exchange. Mack knew the buttons he could push to annoy his father if he'd wanted. Adolescent aggravation was pointless and self-defeating. He'd watched Tom going at it with his Uncle Phil. The resultant ill feeling between them lasted for days and achieved nothing. When it came to tough-mindedness Robert MacKinnon was not someone to annoy. He was resolute and didn't buckle. Mack was too wily to fall into the typical angry resentful teenage trap of hot-tempered outbursts. The only way to tackle his dad was to employ tactical cunning in an overall strategy. His father responded to cold logic, not tantrums. This lesson had been lost on his older brother when he'd lived at home. Mack had learned from Adam's mistakes.

"An agency's job is to find work for its clients. That's how a modelling agency functions, James. A design agency would function in much

152

the same way. How exactly do you envisage persuading advertisers and retailers to take you and the girls with any seriousness? More to the point, have you even thought of how to market models and dress designs? Knowing you no doubt you'd have some ideas on the subjects. Be that as it may, there's more to it than would meet your eye."

"We're only thinking of it as a temporary move. It's just so we can deal legitimately with Silver's Fashions. It's an adult world and none of us are legally adults."

Mack provided the right responses but his father remained unconvinced. The fact of the matter was they were all too young and inexperienced. They needed his father's expertise. Then came the spanner in the works.

"You appear to miss the one important vital point. Technically I could act on your behalf as your father. I could not do so for the girls. In Effy's case I would need the consent of her parents and it would have to be legally agreed beforehand. The same would apply for your friend Angie who would be in the same boat."

"You could adopt them." Mack tried to lighten what had become an intense discussion. "I'm sure they wouldn't mind."

The laughter lines on his father's face responded. "I'm not sure their parents would be too pleased with the idea. I suspect your mother, on the other hand, would be delighted."

Mack was unwilling to be rebuffed and pushed ahead with fresh ammunition. "We're not expecting to hit the big time. It could at least help us to earn some money. And let's face it, dad. Effy, Ellen and Grace could do with some money. They may not be eligible for much of a student grant. Don't think I don't know how much money it's costing Ma and Da Halloran to keep Deidre in medical school. Chances are they won't be able to afford to give much towards Ellen and probably nothing for Effy and Grace. For Effy it might rest on getting a scholarship. And the fact is I'd not get much of a grant either if I qualified for university or college. You earn too much."

"I would support you if you were to go on to higher education. You have your job with Benny for the time being."

"Dad. I don't want to be supported."

"I dare say but as your father that's my responsibility."

"Let's not forget you're guaranteeing Adam's business venture with the Jenkins, not forgetting another mouth to feed when the baby's born."

"And what if you damage Effy's chance of gaining a scholarship? How do you think she would feel in the long run about a lost scholarship? I'm promising nothing. I will look into the offer the Silvers make. Selling a few photographs may be one thing. Establishing agencies are another. Having a hobby is one thing, having a business is another matter."

It ended in an impasse.

Mack knew he'd made points that would niggle his dad into thinking again. *Softly, softly, catchee monkey* emerged from his mental recesses. Patience would win the day. If it didn't at least he'd given it his best try. Somehow he and the girls would find a way to make money. What his father had said did concern him. Suppose they ended blowing Effy's chances of a scholarship?

"And?"

"Nothing. Best we can do is to leave my dad to mull it over. Let's see what's in Nate's offer."

Effy sighed. "I suppose you're right. We can always hope."

Hugging him, she whispered, her warm breath creating a tickling sensation in his ear, "Go up to my room in a couple of minutes. There's something I have to show you."

While Grace and his parents were in the lounge watching television, he sneaked up the stairs, avoiding the two creaking steps. Effy had left the bedroom door open to avoid making another creaking sound. Her left index finger was on her lips. In her right hand was a pink box. He made out the words Ortho-Novin in purple script on a white band. It also read 2Mg. Silently she opened it up, producing a grey dial-like display of pills in blister packaging.

"I've got a six-month supply. There's twenty-one for each month. I'm supposed to take one at the same time each day."

"Are you sure you want to take them?"

"I've already started. So, you can have your wicked way with me."

"Chance would be a fine thing."

Effy had that slight mischievous smile he loved. "Why not tomorrow? Pick me up from school. We can stop off at Whites Terrace and snuggle up in my old room before coming home."

The physical attraction captivating her was not just his overpowering sexuality. Mack was handsome but he was also addictive in other ways. Even when she'd first met him he'd possessed a strangely mature physicality and personality. Yet it was his mind that also held her enraptured, that engaged and intrigued her. He was not without flaws. No one was flawless. Yet in her mind he seemed near flawless. For all his physical and mental toughness Mack possessed depths of romantic tenderness, kindness, sensitivity, loyalty and understanding that made him spellbinding. He was always there, protective and looking out for her, ready to prevent anything hurtful happening. When Angie had described him in the past as Sir Galahad she was right. He was emotional gold, enriching and completing her with his love. Together they could face anything, achieve anything, and overcome anything. Mack was the tower of strength at the centre of her life. She was his now and forever, no matter what the future held. She would do anything rather than ever give him up. No matter what that might be.

# CHAPTER 31

**Touch Me, Kiss Me, Hold Me – The Inspirations (Polydor 56730 – 1967)**

*Wednesday 1 March 1967*

Satisfying her sexual needs was like satisfying hunger pangs. Effy felt starved. When he smoothly slipped her pink lace briefs down her thighs the sensation was delicious, leaving her languorous yet afire with expectation. The sensation was akin to anticipating the satiating taste of food satisfying hunger cravings. She revelled in the way he spread her unresisting legs wide, preparing her for penetration. The deft touch of his exploring fingers aroused her further, expediting wetness. Now came the physical reality. She wanted him inside her. The friction and accommodating expansion became both pleasurable and painful. Pleasure and pain co-existed side by side, almost indivisible. Penetration brought this throbbing desire between her thighs to a relieving conclusion. His exertions made her cry out. She writhed in ecstasy, experiencing a heightened exulting joy as he came to a climax. Her own climax rippled like an intense series of waves spreading through her body. A sense of fulfilled accomplishment flooded her. Effy was delighted knowing she had given and received orgasmic pleasure. With reluctance she relaxed her hold on him as he withdrew from her with exhausted yet tender slowness.

"Wow," Effy heard him exclaim. "Your fingernails must have left puncture marks all over my back."

Pulling him towards her again, they exchanged a long kiss before she replied, giggling, "With the pleasure comes the pain. Didn't you know? Love hurts. Turn over and let me have a look."

Then she gasped. "I'm so, so sorry, Mack. It's worse than I could've imagined. I must've dug my nails in so hard when we got carried away. I've taken the skin off in places and made it bleed."

"What? You're joking? Has your wardrobe got a mirror?"

Effy burst out laughing as he tried to find ways of looking at his back. "Don't be soft, James MacKinnon! I was having you on! But I do apologise for the teeny weeny little nail mark impressions I've given you."

Massaging his back, she left the softest kisses scattered on it. Pressing her breasts into his back, she began nuzzling his ear from behind.

"That was the best sex yet. Next time I want to try a different position."

"Go on?"

"I saw something in the copy of the Kama Sutra you gave me."

"Go on."

"I want to try it with my ankles on your shoulders."

There was a tap on the door. They froze.

"Make yourselves decent. I need to come in." It was Grace.

"You two must think everyone's stupid." Grace tried not to snigger. "I've known for a while what you two get up to when no one's around. I should be shocked but I'm not. Actually, I was more shocked when I caught Tom and Ellen at it. Seems like all my sisters except Aileen like to drop their drawers."

"Don't be vulgar, Grace." Hearing Effy sound prissy was peculiar.

"Ooh, get you. A bit late to be Miss Modesty, don't you think?"

"How did you find out?" She asked mystified.

"Walls have ears, sis. I overheard Adam and Caitlin worrying about you two having sex and you getting pregnant. But the real giveaway came when I found those Durex you thought you'd hidden."

"Were you going through my things?" Effy became annoyed.

Grace's sardonic smile said it all. "It was unintentional, sis. I wasn't hunting for evidence, if that's what you're thinking. I was trying to find something. Anyway, I suspect pretty much everyone is either in the know or too polite to say anything."

"What do you mean... suspect? Who are 'they'?" Mack sounded serious.

Grace rolled her eyes. "Your mum and dad, who else?"

Effy blanched. "Why? What have you heard?"

"I don't want Effy ending up like Caitlin. They're both so young and so taken up with each other, etcetera. I'm worried they'll go too far if they haven't already. You get the idea? At least words pretty much on those lines."

Effy let out a long heartfelt sigh, stared at Mack and bit on her lower lip. Mack shrugged. "We'll have to keep pretending nothing's going on."

"Give your parents a bit more credit. Anyway, I overheard your dad say to your mum he would need to have a 'man to man' chat with you." Grace started giggling. After a moment or so she continued. "God, that's one conversation I'd love to earwig."

157

Effy found it amusing hearing about Mack's discomfort. It made her smile and verge on laughing aloud. He'd gone red, flushing with embarrassment listening to his father. Their man-to-man heart-to-heart had turned into instructions on how to use condoms. It had been delivered *Senior Service* style. The way Mack imagined his dad had instructed raw naval ratings during the war. At the end he'd handed him a packet of three, just in case things became "too heated". Chuckling about it, Mack claimed he'd found himself standing to rigid attention listening to the instructions. His father had even told him to stand at ease.

Effy had giggled at this description but remained silent about her own secretive chat with his mum. It hadn't been an easy listen, either. Jane MacKinnon always treated her as if she was her own. Knowing what a compassionate friend she was to her mother meant a great deal. Like a good daughter, Effy had shown real respect. She'd listened. She'd blushed. She'd said nothing contradictory in reply. Like any caring foster mother, Jane had left her with much to think on. Sharing their woman-to-woman heart-to-heart with Mack would serve no purpose other than causing unnecessary upset.

# CHAPTER 32

**Stay – Virginia Wolves (Stateside SS 563 – 1966)**

*Saturday 11 March 1967*

Effy's response staggered Mack. They'd been taking a look at a year-old edition of *Vogue*, featuring Edie Sedgwick. The model was seated with legs spread in an angular, provocative fashion.

She was wearing a purple body garment like a one-piece bra and corset. The intention was clearly sexual. Bizarre-looking thigh-high studded stockings added to the eroticism.

"Really? You'd do the same pose for a magazine?"

"Yes. Why not? She's not naked. I'd be happy to pose for you in much the same."

He searched her face for the usual teasing smile signalling a come-on. There wasn't one. Effy was serious. "It's not as if I'd be naked displaying my intimate parts. It's only underwear, for heaven's sake. I've had enough of this false modesty crap they try to fill our heads with at school. On second thoughts, I'll let you into a little secret. Ellen got asked if she would consider doing some bra adverts."

"Oh, and when did she get asked this? I supposed you've been asked too, have you?"

"No. Nate told the rest of us we weren't the right size."

"Oh, aye?"

She giggled. "He's left the decision up to her. You don't know the best bit yet."

"And what's that?" The suspicion in his voice rang clear.

The giggling got worse.

"Go on."

"Nate wants you to do the photography," she spluttered. "He thinks it'll be less upsetting for Tom if you're the photographer. Don't say anything to anyone yet. Ellen asked me to have a word with you first. She felt awkward about asking."

"I hope you're not expecting me to ask Tom if it's okay to snap Ellen wearing a bra?"

159

"No. Actually, not just in a bra, he wants her in in several bras *and knickers*."

"Getaway! I'm not so sure about this."

"When the time's right we'll both have a word with him."

"Don't include me in this. You two can sort it out on your own."

Hearing Angie coming down the stairs. Effy put a finger to her lips.

"So? What to do you think of the place?" Angie asked, entering the room. She looked stunning. A simple shift dress in red with a whit band round the hem contrasted with her patterned matching red tights and white box-toed kitten heels. For a moment Mack wondered if it was possible to love two women at once before trying to empty his head of the thought.

"Smart. I didn't think it'd be as nice as this. I think you and Gillian have got yourselves a great spot," Effy answered.

"Are you leaving the scooter here? We can go down to the club in the car. I can bring you both back later."

"Thanks for the offer, Angie, but we've got to get back. It's going to be a busy day for me tomorrow. I've got to go into the scooter workshop at Benny's. Mick Jenkins is going to help me fit a fuel injector to the GT and I need to get it serviced. Then my dad's supposed to be taking me out for a driving lesson. After that I've got a pile of work for school. Effy's got a few designs for Silvers Fashions to complete. As soon as we've seen the Alan Bown Set we'll have to leave."

Mack could see Angie's disappointment.

"Never mind. Another time. Maybe you two can stay over. We could have a laugh together."

"Yes, why not?" Effy answered, a strange glint in her eyes. "The three of us could snuggle up together in your new double bed."

Mack couldn't believe what he'd heard. From Angie's reaction neither could she.

"I'm joking, Angie. Your faces were a treat," Effy teased

"That wasn't funny, Effy." Angie became serious.

"No, it wasn't," added Mack.

Neither could fathom why Effy had said it leaning both distinctly uncomfortable.

# CHAPTER 33

**We're Doing Fine – Dee Dee Warwick (Mercury MF867 – 1965)**

*Friday 17 March 1967*

"Every single booking must be written down. You must include all the relevant details: address, telephone number, the time and duration of each modelling session booking you undertake. It's not optional. Garments sent to you for express use in a photographic session must be recorded on arrival and returned undamaged. Finally, ensure there's a release form to cover copyright issues. That works both ways, legally protecting Effy's designs as well as those belonging to Silvers Fashions. It also protects your copyright as the photographer. Next. Detailed book keeping as well as double cross-checking is something I absolutely insist on. Your mother has agreed to help. Accounting is her area of expertise as are taxation matters."

"Taxation matters?" Mack's surprise was evident.

"You have to account for all earnings to the Inland Revenue." Robert MacKinnon peered over his half-frame reading glasses. "You didn't imagine your earnings would be scot-free, did you?"

Both Mack and Effy were taking written notes.

"Any questions so far?"

"What do you think of their offers for my design?" asked Effy.

"They wanted to buy the design outright. I said no. In the end they agreed to let you keep the copyright and pay you a percentage of the retail price. The number of each garment for sale will be strictly limited for up-market high-end clientele in the London shop. You won't make a fortune but the money you earn won't be negligible either. They will pay on a per dress sold basis. Their plan is to limit each design to five but no more than ten garments at quite frankly ridiculous prices. However, they also need you to produce a version of the same design from their choice of fabrics to sell in cheaper 'knockoff' versions to the catalogue firms. Even so with the price they're quoting you should earn some good money for someone of your age. I see this as potentially an excellent deal financially, providing your designs sell. Your garments will carry your name on them. That was a concession they were willing to make."

161

"What about modelling fees?" Asked Mack.

This was where the complexities came to the fore. Silvers Fashions planned to go into competition with established firms like Woburn's. Mack would become one of their freelance photographers. Many of the catalogue firms relied on Woburn's to meet their photographic needs. Silvers Fashions intended to enter the fray in direct competition employing a number of regional freelance photographers. Angie and the sisters would be the models used to target the teen and young women's market together with any other suitable models. Mack's photographic output would be geared to supplying catalogue photos. The high-end outfits had to look exceptional to be featured in magazines like *Nova* and *Petticoat*. Any other photographs he could market as he saw fit. Payments for the catalogue work would be competitive. They were in line with those made by the other studios. Robert MacKinnon rarely gave much away but even he was startled by the rates on offer to the girls. Mack's mother stopped knitting, open-mouthed with disbelief, when she heard.

It took several hours to wade through all the details. In the end it came to the crunch.

"If this is to go ahead we need two things. First, you will need parental permission. This I now have following on from a letter I wrote to your mother in Ireland and a subsequent telephone call. She is willing to sign for you and your sisters but with a singular stringent proviso. Namely, you and your two sisters are to continue with your full-time studies. Also, any work undertaken must be fully supervised and only take place at weekends or during school holidays. That's the exact same stipulation I make with James. None of you are to jeopardise your futures over what may turn out as nothing more than a short-lived venture. Your sister Bridget is being asked to oversee all the arrangements along with Jane and myself. She also has access to legal advice through her place of work. We've already consulted with one of the young solicitors, a Gregory Williams. I met with him this lunchtime. Your friend Angie will also require one of her parent's permission in writing and should be submitted to me as soon as possible. Incidentally, Nate Silvers and his father have made a second appointment to see me at the bank this week. They appear incredibly keen to get things underway and, it seems, with some urgency. Needless to say, I found their request for this interview intriguing."

And it was urgent.

Everyone ended up working flat-out to get it all underway.

The following months would prove hectic. Effy would produce a series of designs based on the fabrics supplied by Silvers Fashions. She'd also provide input on the final choice of fabrics for the high-end designs. She'd have to produce autumn designs and then others for winter.

An initial payment proved to be more than a year's pay from her Saturday and holiday jobs. With reluctance she gave up working at Dorothy Perkins immediately. The amount of work they might have to do was going to snowball into an avalanche. Angie, having changed jobs, no longer worked Saturdays and would take her involvement in the new model agency with incredible seriousness. As the only one with a car, she would take charge of deliveries from the Silvers as they arrived at Bowler's studio early on Saturday mornings. A lack of hanging racks and suitable changing facilities proved one of the initial obstacles they faced. Chloe Johnson volunteered to work for free but Mack's mum insisted they should make sure she was put on the "expenses" list and would be paid in due course. She even paid for the three girls to visit a hairdresser whom she knew from the Mothers' Union. Mack had automatically tuned out from the conversations about conditioners and split ends.

He'd never known much about his mum's working life until now. She had worked for an accounting partnership for several years after Adam had gone to school. What he learned about her impressed him. His Aunt Ellen had looked after Tom and himself until his parents had moved away from Halifax. Now, working together, his father and mother had sorted out all the financial aspects of his photographic business and the model agency. It was complicated but he was a quick learner. So were Effy and their other partner Angie.

*Saturday 18 March 1967*

"We could do with a couple of other girls as models beside us." He listened into the three-way conversation between Angie, Ellen and Effy.

"I agree. Got any ideas, Angie?"

"How about Alice?"

"She's certainly tall and skinny," commented Gillian. They were seated in Angie and Gillian's new sparsely furnished home.

"I thought we had long legs, but hers go up to her armpits." Effy's description raised a laugh.

163

"Honestly, she's not much taller than us. I'm five foot six. She's only an inch taller but I feel like a fatty next to her," Angie commented.

"Not with your 33-24-33 figures, you're not." He spoke in a preoccupied voice, trying to clean the mechanism of a second-hand camera he'd acquired cheaply. "Sorry, Ellen. I forgot. You're 35-25-34 and a size eight. I've been asked about the possibility of you modelling bras as you're a bit bustier."

"Stop teasing her." Angie sharpness cut the air. "That's not nice."

Ellen sighed. "Actually, he's not teasing. Nate spoke to me about it too. I don't think I dare tell Tom. Nate would like Mack to take the photos."

"He won't mind, I'm pretty sure." Changing the conversation, he offered an idea. "We should get Alice in front of the lens. She's not plain and she's not beautiful but she's quite pretty."

The four young women stared at him.

"What?" He stared back at them.

"Go on, then." Ellen quizzed him with faint sarcasm, putting him on the spot. "Give us your *professional* opinion. This I want to hear."

Mack looked Ellen in the eyes. After a pensive moment or two he stopped fiddling and put the camera down.

"Okay. She may not be a head-turning beauty but she's pretty and I suspect really photogenic. Here are a few positives in her favour. She has lively eyes that shine. They're naturally large and wide-set. In fact, it's something you two and Grace share. Although it's a pity her left eye is a fraction smaller than her right. It's a minor flaw and one most won't notice. Alice's nose is like Jean Shrimpton's and she's blessed with good cheekbones. She'd be your more quirky Peggy Moffitt type of model but prettier. Lovely even lips and a mouth that's not too wide with a nice set of even teeth. Complexion's not too bad and she isn't riddled with spots and blemishes. Also, she looks attractive with her war paint on. Her hair is in a neat styled bob. It isn't greasy, it shines and I'm betting it's dandruff free. All in all, everything about her shows she cares about her appearance. Those long slender arms and ultra-long legs could be her big plus. Her hands have long elegant fingers but she could do a better job of manicuring her nails. Luckily she doesn't have Sandie Shaw size feet. I'm guessing size six or six and a half. And she has decent ankles too, not too thick."

Ellen was speechless, taken aback by Mack's observations.

Angie's sister broke the silence laughing.

"God, Eff. Did I imagine what I thought I heard?" Ellen was staggered.

"Next you'll be telling us her measurements." Gillian chuckled.

"I'm guessing she's about the same size as Effy and Angie, 33-24-33, but I'm probably wrong. Her bust size is a bit of a guess but on the tiny to small size. Borderline A/B cup probably, almost flat chested in proportion to her height. I'd bet she'd fit a size six frock no problem. Put it this way, a mini skirt or frock could be at least an inch shorter on her than it would on you three."

"I told you'd have to watch him," Ellen muttered to Effy, adding, "That was creepy and can you stop him calling dresses frocks."

"No," Effy replied. "I've tried. He's averse to calling them dresses. As for the other, nothing much gets past him. You ought to know by now. Tom and Adam used to call him Lockhart after the TV detective. Now you can see why. James, I'm keeping more of an eye on you in future. I'm not sure I like you looking at other girls so closely."

"Now that's creepy, Eff. You just sounded like my mum." That brought more laughter from Gillian and Angie. "Yeah. Let's see if we can get her interested."

"What about Effy's friend Chloe?" Ellen asked.

Mack's response was tactful but truthful.

"Chloe has an undeniably pretty face with attractive features. No doubt about it in my eyes. Unfortunately, she's five foot three and that's probably too much on the short side for a clothes model. Not just that but her legs are short relative to her trunk to legs ratio. She's not got the proportions advertisers are wanting in photo models. At least going by all the models I've been looking at."

"Mack's right," Effy confirmed. "She's told me modelling is not her bag Acting is what she has her heart set on doing."

"How do you know all this?" Ellen seemed almost annoyed with him. "How come you're such an expert on what models should look like?"

"Stands to reason. You only have to look at the models in magazines. That's what I've done a lot of with Eff. Aside from which it's all to do with clothes sizes and figure measurements, according to Effy and Grace. The golden ratio 1.618 determines the golden number, doesn't it, Effy?"

"I rest my case, girls." Effy smiled

Gillian joined in. "I can't get over what you've observed about Alice. She came to see Angie here last week and your observations about her are uncanny. When Angie told me you picked up things real fast I did wonder. You've proved it to me. I hope for your sake Effy's not the jealous type. If I had a boyfriend like you I probably would be, with your eye for women."

"Effy's got nothing to worry about on that score. It's purely professional and that's what we have to be if we're going to be successful." Mack's response went down with silent approval. They knew he was right.

"What are we going to tell Nate about going down to London for the Easter weekend? If we go we'll miss seeing The Drifters on the Monday down The Plebs. Is anyone bothered?" asked Angie. There was a long pause. "We have to let him know."

"I wish I could go." Ellen sounded miserable. "I can't afford to take the time out from revising. Although I could get tempted to go down the club to see The Drifter with Tom."

"So if you don't go to London with us, I take it Tom won't." Mack slumped back on the sofa.

Ellen confirmed with a nod. "Besides, that London flat doesn't sound big enough for us all."

That would just leave Effy, Angie and himself. It could get awkward.

"I want to go." Effy was categorical. "I've never been to London. I can't pass up an opportunity like this. Not with free accommodation thrown in and getting paid for some live modelling. It's a chance to see the shop where they'll be selling my designs. We can go down Carnaby Street, visit Biba, Oxford Street and do Portobello Market. We have to go."

"And we could go to The Flamingo or The Marquee at night," added Angie, becoming excited. "Maybe both. You never know who we might get to see there. You're right. We definitely have to go if only to do some window-shopping after the modelling. Grace will absolutely love it too."

"There's no way my mum and dad will let Grace go. I don't think they'll be too thrilled about Effy and myself going." Mack grinned, pausing for effect. "But I doubt they'll stop us."

"That leaves the three of us?" Angie gave him a strange look. "What about you, Gillian?"

"Oh, no. Count me out. I have other plans."

In the end it was only the three of them.

# CHAPTER 34

### A Touch of Velvet a Sting of Brass – The Moods Mosaic
### (Columbia DB7801 – 1966)

*Saturday 25 March 1967*

"On Monday you two dedicated followers of fashion can do the rounds of the boutiques. I want to try and hunt out some records while I'm here. We can get up early Sunday morning to do a mini photo shoot if the weather holds up. Once we've got tomorrow out of the way we might have some time to go to the clubs at night."

Angie had been looking forward to driving down on Friday. When they finally found the flat she was completely done in from the hours of driving and it was late. Mack had expected them to end up in some seedy rundown bedsit. They were delighted to find it was somewhere plush.

The one-bedroom Mayfair flat was in Grosvenor Street close to Bond Street station with easy access to the heart of the city. It was located on the second floor of a red brick mansion block. They obtained the keys from the porter who took them up in the lift. Dropping the suitcases and bags, they took in their temporary weekend home. Angie flopped onto the settee while Effy checked the kitchen to discover it was well stocked with tea and coffee.

A scribbled note was on the kitchen table informing them that there were two pints of milk in the fridge. The porter had been instructed to leave it along with a few groceries delivered earlier that afternoon. Someone called Caroline A-B from Silvers Fashions had dropped off a packet of cornflakes, a large sliced white loaf, butter, jam and marmalade for breakfast. No one was hungry. They'd stopped off at a motorway service station for a break and had shared the sandwiches and fruit Mack's mum had packed.

The flat even had a telephone. Mack rang home to let his parents know they'd arrived. The call was brief. Then they sat in silence taking in the surroundings. "All the comforts of home." Angie stretched and yawned.

"You look shattered, Angie. That drive's got you beat. We've a real early start tomorrow. I suggest we get our heads down for some zeds. I'll get some tea on."

"Mack's right," added Effy, testing the mattress. "The double bed is already made up and it feels comfy. Looks like we're getting five-star treatment courtesy of Nate and his dad."

"You two should have the bed," Angie offered.

"Don't be daft," Mack replied. "I'll tuck myself up in the sleeping bag on the settee. Effy can share the bed with you. The settee's too small for two and the wooden floor may look swish but it'll be bone-achingly hard. Besides, you two need to look your rested best in the morning when I have to do the snapping."

They didn't disagree. He disappeared into the kitchen.

Angie looked embarrassed blurting out, "You don't mind sleeping in the same bed, do you?"

"No. I'm used to sharing with my sisters. When Ellen stops with us at Mack's she gets into either mine or Grace's and they're single beds. Don't worry. I won't have my wicked way with you. At least not tonight, I'm too shattered."

Angie stuck her tongue out. "I'm so knackered, I probably wouldn't notice if you did. Anyway, I don't think I'm your type."

Mack guffawed, listening to their banter while making tea in the kitchen. "You two are the last ones I could ever imagine being that way out," he called out.

Carrying in a tray he stopped dead in his tracks for a jaw-dropping episode. Effy and Angie were wrapped round each other, cheek to cheek, looking at him as he came in. Letting go of each other, they exchanged grins and giggles.

"Priceless, Eff. Priceless."

"What a treat. I've never seen him look so gone out." Effy giggled.

"Don't let me stop you two. I'll just sit down with my cup of char and watch you in action."

Angie rolled her eyes. "Dream on, MacKinnon. I'm not into girls but if I was I imagine I could fancy her."

"Oh, that's a shame. For a second there I thought we were up for a kinky weekend."

Effy came over and took the tray from him. She put it down on the small coffee table and then placed her hands on his shoulders. Her face was an expressionless mask and her voice flat. "Be careful what you wish for."

"Stop teasing." Mack planted a kiss on her lips. "Angie might start taking you seriously and get properly worried."

168

"Yes, Eff, don't give him ideas. Anyway, he'd never cope with two of us."

"He might die happy though." She beamed a smile that said everything and nothing.

Angie gave him a strange look as she took one of the cups and went past them. "I'll let you know when I'm out of the bathroom."

*****

Scrunched on the two-seater settee he passed an uncomfortable night. When the travelling alarm clock went off it came as a relief. He stared, bleary-eyed, at the luminous dial face of the clock glowing seven. Attempting to unzip the sleeping bag, he lost his balance. Crashing to the floor he was wide-awake in an instant. Free of the sleeping bag, he stretched before heading for the bathroom.

Once he'd done he gave a couple of gentle taps on the bedroom door to see if the girls were awake. There was no response. The door was ajar so he looked in. Effy and Angie were sleeping back to back. He decided to let them sleep a little bit longer while he had breakfast.

There was a knock on the door as he swallowed the last piece of toast. It was seven thirty. Joe Silvers' appearance surprised Mack. Nate's older brother had to be a few years older but there was no mistaking the family resemblance.

"You and your brother look alike. Pleased to meet you." Mack held out his hand. After a long pause, Joe reluctantly shook it. He gripped it with unwarranted pressure. Mack didn't flinch and returned the same. Nate had forewarned him about his brother Joe who handled the firm's business in London. He remembered Nate's words. "My brother Joe can be an arsehole. Don't give him an inch because he won't just walk over you. He'll trample over you."

Breezing into the living room, Silvers looked round. "So you're the new hot shot photographer Nate thinks he's found? Where is she, this super new cool designer chick cum model?"

"Still getting her beauty zeds."

"Get her up. I need her and the other one down with the hairstylist and make-up artist no later than nine. They'd better be as good as Nate claims. I hope you have your box brownie in working order." The sneering dismissiveness was as obvious as his Mancunian accent.

"Both cameras." Mack's response was cool, concealing the fast-developing seething dislike of this man. "And a Leica, too, loaded and ready

169

to snap. Hope you have decent lighting and backdrops in the shop. The other model has a name, by the way. Angie Thornton."

"Nate thinks highly of you and your girlfriends. To me you're just kids playing at it."

"We're the same age as Twiggy."

"Your point is?"

"Well, *old man*, I prefer to think of us as smart, sharp, cool and stylish young people. And by smart and sharp I'm not just talking appearances. After all, beauty is only skin deep."

"Got a smart-arse gob too."

"You'd better believe it and then some, *Mister* Silvers."

Silvers's dark eyes studied him closely for several moments. "Definitely a smart arse, MacKinnon. You'd better be as great as you've been cracked up to be. A cab will collect you three at quarter to nine sharp. Don't keep the cabbie waiting. His time is our money. I want you down in the lobby ready. We can't keep Vidal waiting; he's a busy man. Oh, and tell your fillies not to bother painting on their smiley faces. We've a pro for that."

"As in Sassoon?" Mack raised an eyebrow.

"Do you know another?"

"Who's paying for him to do their hair? He charges an absolute fortune."

"Seems my father places a lot of faith in theses fillies to deliver. No expense is to be spared in promoting this new range. They can thank him. They'd better be worth it. Girls with no real modelling experience? Can't imagine what he and Nate were thinking. It had better not be a shambles."

The cab arrived on time. Neither Effy nor Angie looked pleased at being ordered not to wear make-up; they kicked up a fuss about it. To Mack they still looked beautiful without any. He deliberately neglected to mention who'd be doing their hair. It would make the girls' day when they found out. Before getting up, Mack had ironed a shirt and his suit trousers, having found an iron in one of the fitted kitchen cupboards.

The suit was new in midnight-blue mohair wool. The three-button three-pocket jacket had narrow notch lapels. Fitted at the waist, it sported a single fifteen-inch centre vent. The shirt had been a find. Pale blue in a silk finish, it had a spear collar. To match the jacket's burgundy lining Mack wore a burgundy tie and top pocket hanky. They had been handmade from the same material by Grace using remnants obtained from his tailor. The tie

170

had been Grace's sewing challenge: one she'd accomplished with aplomb. A gold tiepin and plain gold cufflinks enriched the appearance. The trousers were slim-fit parallels. Dark blue leather brogues with red laces completed the look.

Effy and Angie were wearing identical tent dresses, different only in pattern and colour. Effy wore a striking narrow chevron green and black pattern, Angie the same except in red and black. The square décolleté neckline had an empire waistline with the central topmost full chevron pointing between each breast. Short keyhole sleeves added a further feminine touch. Both wore shimmering pale glitter tights.

"Do you think you could have made the hemline a bit shorter?" Mack joked, eying the six or seven inches of exposed thighs. These dresses were the shortest he'd ever seen either of them wear.

Effy gave him one of her wicked glints: the kind just before they got down to sex. "I'm designing these kinds of dresses for women who want their men to take them off. I bet you'd like to take this one off." They heard the cabbie chuckle on hearing her words.

The journey from the flat to the King's Road boutique took just over ten minutes at this time in morning. Mack kept a tight rein on himself, acting as though it were an everyday occurrence. Effy and Angie's behaviour was the opposite. Excited by the sights, they were bubbly and bouncing in their seats. No sooner had they passed through Sloane Square and onto the King's Road itself than their levels of excitement went up even higher. Passing Lincoln Street the cab slowed. They found themselves outside their destination: Moods Mosaic. Effy let out a whoop as she saw two of her designs in the window. "They look fantastic!"

Vanity cases in hands, the two girls rushed to the window. Their excitement was infectious. Mack found himself grinning as they threw their arms around him and one another in delight. It was all he could do to stop Effy from jumping up and down; he kept a tight grip on his camera bag. His personal bombshell came on entering the boutique. A life-size blow-up poster of Effy, Angie and Ellen confronted him on the wall. It was one of the first original snaps from the parish hall. Blown up to almost full size, it looked amazing.

"Listen, you two, make it happen. Be yourselves, be natural and smiley and don't act. You're both gorgeous and you can knock them dead today. Effy, don't get shy. Angie, don't give anyone any lip. It's going to be

171

great. Here endeth the pep talk." He kissed each in turn on the cheek. "Okay, ladies, lights, action, let's roll."

Joe Silvers was waiting inside. Ignoring Mack, he instructed a young woman to take the girls upstairs to get ready. Literally seconds later Vidal Sassoon appeared with his assistant carrying his bags. Mack watched speechlessly as the hairdresser was ushered through. Joe Silvers escorted him, appearing to be on genuinely friendly terms with the stylist.

"The boutique's not open yet." Mack turned to find an attractive young blonde shop assistant. "We'll be open for customers next week. Today is for private showing only. Do you have an invite?"

"Do I need one?" His cheeky answer failed to impress.

"It's for invited guests only today." The response was delivered in home counties cut glass frosty-cold posh.

"I'm not an invited guest but I am definitely invited."

An unimpressed look crossed her face. "In what capacity?"

His friendly winning smile died and he assumed the icy look he usually employed split seconds before delivering a well-aimed Glasgow kiss. "See this big poster on the wall? The gorgeous model on the left is Effy Halloran. The same Effy Halloran who's the fashion designer you're showcasing today in this boutique. The model on the left is her sister Ellen. You can see the family resemblance. Effy's best friend is the dark-haired model in the centre. That's Angie Thornton whom you've taken to see Mr Sassoon. Effy is my long-time girlfriend. Together with Angie, the three of us are partners in a modelling agency headed by my father. I'm also the guy who snapped this photo. I'm here to snap a few more."

"So *you're* James MacKinnon? But you're so…"

"Young? Everyone keeps saying that."

The apologies flowed profusely. Twenty-year-old Caroline Anstruther-Browne, the newly appointed manageress of Moods Mosaic, was no sales assistant. As Joe Silvers's ex-Rodean main squeeze, she'd probably got the job because she was his entre into Swinging London society. Her chatter proved revealing. Joe knew everyone who was anyone. London's fashion conscious celebrity society would be attending. Journalists like *The Daily Mirror*'s Felicity Green were expected with others from *Petticoat*, *Nova* and *Queen*. They could expect to see some well-known faces from the pop and acting worlds along with politicians, aristocracy and the wealthy, both foreign and domestic. Today's events would change their futures.

# CHAPTER 35

### Here She Comes – The Tymes (Cameo Parkway P.924 – 1964)

*Saturday 25 March 1967*

*Late evening*

Attending the party hadn't been in their plans. Mack and Angie had wanted to go down The Flamingo in Wardour Street. Instead they found themselves in The Cromwellian before ending up in Joe Silvers's Mayfair penthouse. This was in the same building as their flat. The difference was the size. It was huge. The lounge area was the size of the small flat.

It had been a stupendous day made more stupendous by Vidal Sassoon. Styling Effy's hair into a chic shoulder-length bob, he'd given her a sophisticated grown-up look. She hadn't been able to stop admiring her appearance in the mirror. Mack loved it too. She could tell by the compliments and the way he kept looking at her with approving nods of the head.

They found they were wearing not only her designs but also some by others designers. During the better part of the day Mack became the invisible man. She caught occasional glimpses of him with his camera and its strange new long lens attachment he'd borrowed from Ted Bowler. A number of press photographers were present, snapping away beside him. By the time the boutique emptied they were relieved. It had been marvellous but it had also been arduous and draining. Slumped on a comfortable sofa in an elegantly furnished top-floor room above the main shop, the girls relaxed. This, they were told, was for celebrities requiring private viewings and fittings. Then the day's exciting experience began to spoil.

Two other models had been employed beside Angie and Effy. They had left as soon as the showings were over. Throughout the day Joe Silvers's attention seemed to focus on Effy. She was the object under scrutiny and it was unsettling. At first she thought nothing of it, wondering why Angie kept giving her forced strange looks. Now they were resting, it began to become clear. Joe Silvers laid on the charm.

He was the epitome of tall, dark and handsome: a stereotypical good-looking older man. He told them he was twenty-six when Angie asked his age. Whenever his assistant Caroline walked into the room he became business-like in an instant. It was like throwing a light switch on and off. As soon as she left the oozing charm returned and the flattery continued. To begin with Effy felt delighted, flattered and charmed. The propositioning followed. How beautiful her eyes were, what a perfect figure she had, how beautiful her hair looked now it had been styled. She should come to live in London. He would find a place for them both. They should ditch their amateurish agency and become real fashion models in London. He would introduce them to the top photographers like Bailey and Donovan. Effy and Angie had the right looks and were breath-takingly beautiful young women. They could have their hair done by Sassoon all the time. He would put them up in his place until they got their own pads. Imagine going to all the best clubs where the pop and film stars hung out. *She* would soon be a star herself, he said. Effy noted how *they* had turned into *she*. *She* should see where he lived. They should come tonight to the party he was holding, to get to know some of London's top people.

It had begun to go to her head. The idea she might be famous if she did as he suggested. It was all so smooth and for a brief few minutes the fairy-tale was believable. When Angie heard that Mack was not invited the dream crumbled. Angie took immediate umbrage, her words tinged with anger. If Mack didn't go with his girlfriend she wouldn't go either; she added there was no way she would let Effy go on her own. The soft-soaping followed. It would be fine. There would be nothing to worry about. Caroline, his assistant, would act as chaperone. Angie's eyes narrowed into slits, her lips pressed together. Effy took immediate note.

How could she be so foolish, so stupid? It had never occurred to her to ask why Joe Silvers didn't want Mack to come. Closing her eyes, she took a deep breath. She'd behaved like a naïve little schoolgirl accepting sweets without question from a stranger right before he abducted her. All this attention, all these compliments, the flattery; she had wallowed in it for the last few minutes. It was a chat-up line, nothing more. She should have had the gumption to recognise it for what it was. He was trying to seduce her. That's why he didn't want Mack around at the party.

Mack was the only boy she'd ever known. She'd always brushed off attempts from other young men. Compared to him they'd lacked maturity and charm, and his charm was real. Mack was a natural gentleman who'd always known how to treat her right. There was a sudden powerful reality rush. Joe Silvers's charm was superficial and motivated by one thing. He was trying to impress his way into her pants. That's what Angie had tried to communicate with silent signals. She felt herself blush. Joe Silvers mistook it for the effectiveness of his charms rather than her annoyed embarrassment with her own foolishness.

It was the all too obvious tell tale gestures, the saccharine words that alarmed her further. Sitting next to her he'd placed his hand on her knee. Instinctively she moved her leg away, crossing in the opposite direction. He persisted and persisted, touching her arm, her hand, her shoulder, even using his hand to gently sweep her hair to one side in an attempt to caress her face. All the while he continued to ladle out his syrupy, seductive patter. In the end she'd had enough of his pawing. Standing up, she'd moved to sit on Angie's armrest out of reach of his hands.

Changing tack, he told her how important it was for Moods Mosaic that they should attend. How his father expected them to mix with potential clients. In the end she and Angie agreed to go but they were unhappy and full of misgivings. They'd made one single non-negotiable condition: Mack came along or it was no go. Angie backed Effy to the hilt, insisting on Mack attending. Making no headway Joe gave in to their obstinacy. The sugary soft words turned into an irritated sharpness they'd not heard before.

Effy recalled the hushed conversation with Angie while Mack was taking a bath.

"God, Effy, Nate's brother has more front than Blackpool and all the charm of a snake oil salesman. I can't believe it took you so long to twig. He thinks he's some kind of smooth big-time operator who can sweet-talk any girl into bed. My first boyfriend was like him. I was fourteen, still at school and so stupid. He was in his early twenties. Boy, did I get suckered. He was slick and I skidded into the sack with him to learn the name of the game the hard way. The moment Silvers started sweet-talking I had him sussed. Didn't it dawn on you why he didn't want Mack along?"

"I confess I was beginning to get swept up by all the talk of moving to London. I'm so so glad you're here to bring me back down to earth. Where would I be without you?"

"Effy, we may only be young and sometimes a bit naïve but we're not stupid, least of all you. What you lack in experience with men you make up for by being no one's fool. You saw through him, that's the most important thing. He hasn't given up the hunt. He's the type who's going to try to sweet-talk his way into your knickers again tonight you wait and see. We've got to make sure he doesn't piss Mack off. I still remember what he did to the rugby player at the party. He'd probably put him in hospital. I bet he tries to get his mates to split the three of us up at the party so he can get you to himself. What's the betting he'll try to get the three of us drunk? With someone like him we'd better watch he doesn't slip something in our drinks."

"It's as well Mack's teetotal. Should we warn him?"

"What do you think? We don't want our deal soured because Mack plants him one. Let's play Mr Big Time Operator Silvers at his own game. Are you up for some play-acting? Here's what we should do."

# CHAPTER 36

(At the) Discotheque – Chubby Checker (Cameo-Parkway P949 – 1965)

*Saturday/Sunday 25/26 March 1967*

The original plan had been a visit to The Flamingo, or go down The Marquee to see the Richard Kent Style. Another possibility was Brixton's Ram Jam Club on Sunday to see Geno Washington. Caroline, Joe Silvers's posh dolly squeeze, suggested they might go down The Cromwellian.

They found themselves signed into the club ending up in the tiny cellar discotheque that was so packed and steamy dancing was no pleasure. They had to be the youngest there and didn't recognise anyone famous or well known. Not that they stayed too long. The three avoided alcoholic drinks even though Silvers tried desperately to ply them with double gins and vodkas. They stuck to soft drinks, Angie watching to make sure nothing was dropped in them.

What seemed to drive Silvers to distraction was the way Angie and Effy linked Mack's arms at every conceivable opportunity. It didn't go unnoticed. People who'd been at Moods Mosaic earlier recognised the girls as the models. They found themselves attracting attention, the way in which they clung to Mack, looking up at him with adoring passion raised eyebrows.

Angie would wait for the right moment. Introducing Mack as their photographer, she followed this up with outrageous comments like, "We're not just his models. We're very, very close, if you get our drift."

"We love sharing, don't we, Angie? And Mack loves sharing us, don't you? He can't get enough of us and we can't get enough of him," Effy would ad lib with a wink.

Mack played along, wondering how the hell to add to their comments. Smiling, he opted to let the girls do all the work while he put on an enigmatic air. None of it felt weird, not even when Angie squeezed his behind, knowing Silvers was looking. Effy kept nuzzling his ear with her nose. He was rock-hard from their attention and didn't care if anyone noticed the bulge in his trousers. At least it was convincing if nothing else.

Watching the provocative way in which both girls draped themselves round Mack had Silvers gritting his teeth.

177

When they finally arrived at his penthouse the party was already underway. A steady flow of guests kept arriving. Angie was right. Their performance hadn't dissuaded their host.

On the pretext of speaking to her in private about her designs he took her aside. He tried to persuade her to go into another room. Effy politely refused. Unless her boyfriend, as her business partner, was with her, there was nothing to discuss. Silvers became even more insistent.

"Now be reasonable, Effy" The blandishments began to flow as he did his utmost to coax her. "The money you earned today is a pittance compared to what you will earn if you're here all the time. You need to think seriously about your own future, not your boyfriend's or Angie's. Photographers in London are two a penny. Only a few ever make the big time. He has no chance and so no real future. It's too competitive for Northern boys wet behind the ears. You have to be local to know the ropes. If you ditch him now it'll be the best thing you could do for yourself, your career and long-term future."

How interesting that he'd dropped Angie as well!

"Let me be your manager. When they go back to Yorkshire, stay here. I can put you up. I can be the key that unlocks the door to your success. In London it's who you know, not what you know."

"Joe, you're sweet. The truth is, you're only interested in unlocking my legs to get inside my knickers. And I'm not interested in letting you do that. You're just not my type."

A year ago, she wouldn't have dared utter words like those. Thanks to the love of her life and her best friend she'd grown in self-confidence.

Glancing across the room as champagne corks popped she searched for Mack. A couple of hired waitresses were going around with trays of glasses. Silvers attempted to block her view, moving in front of her line of vision. She had to forcibly look around him to catch sight of Mack. He was nursing a glass of champagne he had no intention of drinking. Silvers blocked her view again.

"You need to reconsider. Do you want your designs to sell? Do you want to be successful as a model? Turn me down and you can kiss it goodbye. I'll make sure all the doors are closed in your face. You'll have no future. No one will know you, your designs or your modelling."

"And here was me thinking it was just his brother Nate who was a total bastard." Angie appeared with magical suddenness at Effy's side. For a moment he appeared taken by surprise.

178

Effy looked him in the eyes. "I wonder what Nate will say when I tell him about your offer?"

"Nothing. I can cancel sale of your designs as simple as this." He clicked his fingers.

"What? Stop all those big catalogue company orders to Silvers Fashions? Pull the other one." Effy dismissed the notion with a wave of her hand.

Mack stood silently behind Silvers, listening to the last part of the conversation.

"No disrespect intended, Joe." He slapped a heavy palm down in fake friendliness on Joe's shoulder, making him jump. "I think you're full of crap. Nate warned me before I came down. He told me you'd probably act like a complete twat. Told me to get in touch with him if you did. So I did. Having the phone in the flat is convenient. Apparently your dad wasn't too pleased, either. You paid the girls a paltry ten pounds for today's work. The agreed sum was fifteen guineas each, not a tenner apiece. Anyhow your dad and Nate are on the way down. My Dad has the original agreement paperwork, as does Nate and your dad. You can explain to him and your dad why you underpaid them."

"Coming down?" Joe Silvers frowned. "When?"

"He didn't say." Mack looked him squarely in the eyes with what he hoped was complete smugness. The smugness broadened into a grin as he detected low-level panic. "But he did tell me your dad wasn't chuffed."

"It was a mistake. I must have misheard the amount," Silvers stammered.

"What?" Angie pretended shock. "When you had it in writing? I gave it to your assistant Caroline and watched when she showed you it. Were you trying to read it with your ears?"

Effy wanted to burst out laughing. She almost managed to stop by burying her face in Mack's shoulder, her body shaking as she choked back the laughter.

Angie continued. "Just because we're young doesn't make us stupid, Mr Big Shot. Effy's not just some gorgeous air-headed dolly bird you can con into having sex. She's an Oxford or Cambridge candidate after her A levels. As for Mack, he's so sharp he makes a cutthroat razor look blunt. Nothing much gets past him. Don't be fooled by his looks. He's kicked bigger blokes than you into touch. And it takes us two girls to keep him satisfied."

179

"Eff, you and Angie go and do some last-minute mingling together. Joe and I need an understanding before we say goodnight." Mack was almost in stiches hearing Angie's words.

"What understanding?"

Mack waited until they were out of earshot.

"I'm not going to hold it against you, at least not this time. Nate warned me you're one for shagging anything in a skirt. I'm just glad I wasn't wearing my tartan kilt today."

"Very funny."

"Joe, let me put this it way. London's got enough dolly birds with not too much between the ears to keep your dick active for years. Next time you try to seduce one, make an effort to remember they're women. Women with feelings and emotions like your mum, or your sister if you've got one. They're not just containers for you to dump your spunk the next time you're horny."

"Fuck me. Who do you think you are, lecturing me? A bleeding vicar?"

"I can't blame you for wanting to bed Effy. Or Angie, come to that." Mack's smile evaporated. "They're gorgeous young women in every way you want to imagine. So I'll say this once. Consider my two lovelies off limits. Try it on again with Effy or Angie and I'll make purses out of your balls for them."

"Hard man too," Joe sneered. It was the look in Mack's eyes that he found troubling.

"Ask Nate. You know your brother's rep. He'll confirm what I'm going to say next. I'm hands on and I don't use hired thugs to do my dirty work. If I do say so myself I'm rather good at dishing out the damage. I wouldn't recommend finding yourself on the receiving end."

"I can't believe a seventeen-year-old is threatening me!"

"Ask yourself this, Joe. When is a threat not a threat?"

"I'm sure you're going to tell me."

"When it's a promise, Joe, when it's a promise. Now look at me. Behind this smile is everything someone like you will never understand."

"And what's that?"

"I keep my promises."

# CHAPTER 37

**Girls Are Out to Get You – The Fascinations (Stateside SS 594 – 1967)**

*Sunday 26 March 1967 – 2 a.m.*

"We've decided you should sleep in the bed tonight," Effy announced.

"So which one of you is planning to sleep on the sofa and who's in the bath?"

"Neither of us," came Angie's cool response.

"The three of us," Effy answered. "Angie and I talked it over."

"Don't get any funny ideas," Angie shot back straightaway.

"I'll be in the middle," Effy explained.

"And no messing about, you two," added Angie.

"I don't know what you mean." Effy pretended to be shocked.

"You had me going there for a moment. I thought we were going to have a kinky threesome," Mack joked. "Especially after the way you two carried on at The Cromwellian."

"Be careful what you wish for." Effy repeated it with the same mysterious smile, suggesting something yet saying nothing. Why? What was going on inside her head? He needed to have a talk with her.

Changing the conversation, he became flippant. "Angie, you do know I sleep naked?"

"I don't mind if Effy doesn't. I promise not to ogle you longer than a couple of minutes." Angie yawned. "But Effy has to wear her nighty if I'm sleeping next to her."

"You really don't mind me sharing the bed?"

"God, you're a bit slow tonight. We've just said you can. Do you want it in writing?" Angie yawned again. "We'll go in the bathroom first and get our make-up off. You can go in last. If the lights are off when you come to bed I'm sleeping near the windows so get in the door side. That's Effy's side."

"I hope you don't snore, Angie," he quipped.

Angie stuck her tongue out as the two girls disappeared into the bathroom. "Don't bother to wake me and tell me if I do."

There was enough room for the three of them providing they slept on their sides. Effy put her arm round Mack, mumbling something inaudible when he slipped in beside her. He could tell from the girls' breathing they had both fallen asleep straightaway. Sharing a bed with Effy and Angie didn't feel as crazy as he thought it would. His thoughts kept him awake as he tried to work out what Effy meant. *Be careful what you wish for.* What was she saying to him? There was no way Angie would have said anything to Effy about their indiscretion. In spite of all their reassurances, was she still harbouring suspicions? And if so, why? He had given her no cause. Nor, to his knowledge, had Angie. What was he supposed to be wishing for? Then he remembered. When they'd visited Angie and her sister, Effy had made a comment. It had sounded embarrassing and strange at the time. She had suggested the three of them sharing Angie's new double bed if they stayed over one weekend. Whose idea had it been to suggest using this bed? He couldn't imagine it was Angie's. In which case what was Effy thinking? As he drifted into the zeds he felt the softness of her breasts in his back. Her small hand rested on his beating heart. Was she serious thinking what he thought she was thinking?

As for Joe Silvers, he was in for an even bigger surprise when his father and Nate arrived. But that was going to be a family affair. He'd done his bit of espionage for Nate and his father Alex Silvers.

182

# CHAPTER 38

**We've Got Everything Going for Us – Kiki Dee (Fontana TF 792 –1967)**

*Sunday 26 March 1967 – Morning*

"What do you think makes us such a good team?" Angie's dark brown eyes studied him with that familiar intensity he knew so well. They were sitting in a coffee bar a short throw from Carnaby Street drinking espressos.

"It's simple. We know each other and we trust each other. To me that's so important. As the guy snapping, I want you to look great because we're all close. I don't want to let either of you down. You don't want to let me down. I want you to look stunning and fab, you want to help me make sure I can do that. I also think you make great models because you don't take it too seriously, you treat it as fun and you enjoy it. You're amazing, relaxed and natural in front of the camera lens. How you'd be with one of these top photographers down here I don't know."

"I can see that." Effy took a quick sip of her espresso and wiped the froth from her lips. "I don't mind it in front of the camera but I'm not as keen on the live modelling we did yesterday. I found it uncomfortable and nerve-wracking, getting stared at by all those people. But I'll do it again. Like anything, I guess I can get used to be being stared at; after all, being a walking mannequin is what a model is."

"What about you, Angie?"

"It was okay. I can understand where Effy's at. She gets shy when she's stared at. Me, I'm used to it. Fellas are always eying me up and giving it with the wolf whistles."

"Do you mind it?" Mack leaned forward, looking her in the eyes.

"Do I mind? Do I heck. It's great, it's flattering, and it makes my day when some fella likes what he sees. As long as that's all it is. If men weren't giving me the eye now while I'm young I'd worry there was something wrong with me. I want to know men find me attractive. It's one of the things I like about being a woman. God, I wouldn't want to be a man for all the diamonds in South Africa. For a start they can't wear pretty clothes and jewellery like us and look cute."

"And they're not supposed to show their emotions, either. Got to be stiff upper lip at all times because it's not what's expected," mocked Effy.

"And they can't have a good cry when they're down like we can," Angie teased.

"Yeah, and when the ship's sinking it's women and children first for the life boats." Keeping a straight face, Mack added after a moment's pause, "Notice the word women comes before children."

"Trust you to think of that, MacKinnon." Effy grinned, nudging him. "It's *and*, not second. It means women and children together."

"As a supporter of women's emancipation and the grandson of a suffragette I want to go on record. If true equality is women's goal you should be ready to take your chances along with the men when it comes to lifeboats."

"Your gran was a suffragette?"

"Still is, according to her."

"Wow." Leaning across the table Angie spoke in a low voice, while staring past him. "Don't look now but there's a fella with a copy of The News of the Screws. He's been staring at us. He looks a bit gob-smacked. Oh, God, he's coming over."

Politely yet diffidently, the thirty-something man in the light grey gabardine coat asked, "Please excuse me for interrupting you but are you the three in this photo?"

Spreading the newspaper on the table, he pointed to a photograph. It was of the three of them leaving The Cromwellian in the early hours. They had been standing outside waiting for a cab when some photographer must have snapped them. Effy and Angie stared, open-mouthed in shock. Wrapped round Mack the two girls exuded pure eroticism. Effy was in the foreground. Her hand was on his shoulder and her right leg was raised across Mack's body in a suggestive way. The seductive look on her face was stunning. The hem of her dress had risen to almost the top of her outer thigh. Angie had her cheek pressed against Mack's. Behind them and only just visible stood a disgruntled Joe Silvers. It was quite something to take in all at once.

"If you'd raised your knee another inch higher it would have been one hell of a cheeky shot," gasped Angie. "Thank heavens for tights."

"I have to admit our dresses look shorter and more daring than I imagined," Effy mused. "Pity it's a black-and-white snap. Even so I think my designs looks amazing if I say so myself. What do you think, Mack?"

184

Effy had worn another tent dress. This one was sleeveless and cut in an ultra-feminine way, in a shimmering and glittering sky-blue fabric. A single central inverted pleat ended at a round neck piped with a contrasting fine white band. Angie's collarless dress was also short-sleeved with a round neckline meeting a V-shaped yoke. Like Effy's dress, the amethyst purple material sparkled and the photographer had captured its flow and ripple.

"I designed this tent dress with you in mind." With casual unexpected coolness, Effy continued, locking eyes with Mack. "So you could easily undress me by slipping it up over my head. Or you could just pull it right up if you were in a real rush."

Angie's was open-mouthed as she gasped out a shocked titter.

Mack felt himself go red. He liked to think he couldn't embarrass easily. Effy went into a fit of nervous giggles, running her hand through his hair and giving him a peck on his reddened cheek. The man looked on in silence, wondering if his ears had deceived him.

"What does it say? Go on. Read it," Angie ordered Mack, tilting her head as she tried to make out the words.

"'Swinging London's bright young hedonists. Making the scene at The Cromwellian last night were Effie Halloran and Angela Thornton with an unknown young man. The teenage models were the stars of the Kings Road's newest boutique Moods Mosaic yesterday. Last night they joined celebrity revellers partying in the club's discotheque.'"

"They've spelled Effy 'Effie'." She was unable to take her eyes from the newspaper.

"I thought I recognised you," said the man with obvious delight. "Could I trouble you young ladies to autograph the photo for me?"

Angie and Effy looked at him in astonishment.

"You don't mind, do you? I've never met any famous fashion models before."

They obliged, borrowing a biro from the girl behind the coffee-bar counter. Afterwards they went out and bought three copies of the paper.

Mack was rubbing his chin, puzzling over the photo. "I have no memory whatsoever of a camera flash when we came out of the club. We must have been too busy play-acting as we rolled out of the place. It's an angled shot and my head's turned, so I may not even have noticed it. Do you remember anything?"

185

Angie 's brow furrowed. "Something flashed but I didn't take any notice. Never even thought about it. We were all on a high mucking about making Joe Silvers jealous."

"Do you think we should check out the other papers like *The People* and *Sunday Mirror* to see if there's anything in them?" Effy suggested. "I'm glad your mum and dad read the *Sunday Telegraph* and *Observer*. I can't imagine it'll be in any of them. I'd dread to think what your mum might say if she saw us."

"My dad reads the News of the Screws." Angie laughed. "That photo should wind him up to the top of the tree."

"Might be as well to check out the fashion pages. There were a lot of press photographers snapping away at the shop yesterday. I wouldn't be surprised if they found their way into some of the papers. I was going to buy the Monday morning dailies to see if they'd printed anything." The full impact of the threesome's press debut struck Mack with serious concern.

"What's the matter?" Effy noticed his eyes narrowing and his eyebrows furrowing.

"I'm just wondering how this will all go down. It's bound to leak out. I'll be getting some stick from the guys at school. As for you two... think about it? What are your teachers and classmates going to say, Eff? And Angie, aren't you supposed to be a bit prim and business-like as a solicitor's receptionist? How are they going to take it?"

Effy thrust her arms into the air jubilantly, grinning as she reacted to his words. "I can't wait! It's just what they need in my Sixth Form, shaking up and bringing into the Sixties. Mack, the guys at your place won't give you any stick. They'll be greener with envy than a pub full of Irishmen on St. Patrick's Day. Think about it. One look at that photo and they'll all be thinking you're shagging the pair of us."

"Effy!" Angie found herself open-mouthed. "Mack, I can't believe I just heard her say that!"

"I can't either," he replied, wide-eyed. "Shagging? It doesn't sound right coming from you."

Effy put her arm around his waist and rested her head against his shoulder, smiling. "It's time I was more like you, Angie, confident and daring. Anyway..." She looked up at him, her emerald eyes glowing. "You've got to admit what I said is true. When they look at that picture that's what they'll be thinking. You'll be looked on as a stud. Tell me you don't like the idea and I know you'll be lying. Every man wants to think he's a

186

Casanova. And I happen to know you are one. Admit it. You'll be basking in the limelight."

"Effy, Angie's embarrassed." He couldn't remember Angie blushing. Her pale complexion rarely coloured. But now she was blushing and staring down at the pavement. "I don't want Angie upset and uncomfortable or feeling a bit of a gooseberry this weekend. Remember what we agreed. She's our friend and we're not going to make her feel like a third wheel this weekend."

"It's only Effy joking, Mack. Don't go making something out of nothing." Angie was trying to remain cheerful but clearly she was upset. "I know it's an important weekend for all three of us. I know it can't be easy having me tagging along. I should go for a walk this afternoon and give you two some time together."

Effy let go of Mack and hugged her. "No, Angie, no! I'm so, so, so sorry. No. I don't want you to do that. The three of us are very special to each other and not because of this modelling thing. I don't ever want to lose you as a friend."

The words that tumbled from her lips next left them silent.

"Sometimes I wish the three of us could be like a family. I'd rather share the two of you than lose either of you."

"We are like a family already, Effy. Don't worry. I'll always be your friend. To the both of you." Angie broke into tears. "I won't let anything come between the three of us. We already share so much that's so special."

Mack understood Effy's words in a different way from Angie. He wasn't sure what to make of them. Yet it made crazy sense when he thought about it. Was his girlfriend suggesting a three-way intimate relationship? How could Effy love him and expect him to share what he had with her with Angie? He tried to dismiss it but the idea continued to prey on his mind. Angie loved him like Effy did. She'd confessed it to him that day in The Pack Horse. He'd be lying if he denied feeling the same about her. How could he love them both?

# CHAPTER 39

**You're Ready Now – Frankie Valli (Philips BF1512 – 1966)**

*Easter Sunday, 26 March 1967 – Later*

They bought copies of the Sunday tabloids, finding further surprises. Making their way into Soho they sought out another espresso coffee bar.

"The *Sunday Mirror* has a brief feature about the boutique and two photos of me and Angie. Goodness, Angie, you do look glamorous. Take a peek at this." Effy passed the newspaper over to her.

"The *Mail* has pictures of you two and the other models. There's a photo of the shop front with your designs, too." Mack read aloud. "'Moods Mosaic is yet another boutique springing up on the King's Road. Catering for the discriminating up-market buyer, they will carry exclusive designs only. The stars of the grand opening stealing the show on Saturday were models Effie Halloran (17) and Angela Thornton (18). As fresh teen faces they moved with the assured confidence of the swinging Sixties Mod generation. A further surprise came when the designer of the outfits was revealed to be none other than young Miss Halloran, the model. London designers will have to look over their shoulders from now on. They face serious competition in the future.'"

"Wow. That's just brilliant, Effy! You're a star!" Angie snatched the paper from Mack in a single swift motion, turning it so they could both read it.

Mack couldn't help smiling at their excited faces. The girls gave further delighted squeals as they found items in other newspapers.

"Oh, Mack. There's nothing about you in any of the papers." Angie looked disappointed.

"That's okay. Watch this space," he replied with an air of mystery. "My turn will be coming."

Effy was puzzled. "What do you mean... your turn will be coming?"

"Patience. As soon as I know something definite I'll tell you. Meantime we should check out Carnaby Street and let me get some more photos of you down there."

"Can we try and get some extra copies of the papers first? We'll need one each, won't we, Angie? Gillian's going to love them. I want to show my sisters too though Ellen is going to be upset when she sees and hears what we've been up to."

"So is Grace," Mack added. "That's not going to be fun. Still, her moment of fame is yet to come. Wait till she's showing herself off in the catalogues to all her friends."

"There'll be no living with her." Effy grinned.

"Let's get these newspapers back to the flat and then head to Soho before we lose the good light."

Mack didn't know what to expect but Carnaby Street proved a bit of an anti-climax. The narrow street was probably no more than two hundred yards long. There were more people around than he had anticipated for a Sunday. Quite a few foreign tourists were snapping pictures and gaping at the shop windows. They took a look at most of the shops: *Lord John* and *Lady Jane, Mates, Aristos, Merc* and some others. *I Was Lord Kitchener's Valet* gave them the biggest laugh. When Angie and Effy suggested he should buy a cape, a red military jacket and some bell-bottom trousers they fell about laughing at the way he recoiled. Under no circumstances would he be seen dead in anything so outlandish. He snapped the two girls giggling outside the shop, little realising that in time the photo would become an iconic Sixties image. There were a quite few Lambretta and Vespa scooters parked near *Toppers*, their Mod owners standing about chatting. Catcalls and wolf whistles made Effy blush. Mack had the cheek to ask if he could take shots of the girls posing by the best scooters. Some classic snaps would emerge from this impromptu shoot, too, and would find their way into magazines.

Eventually they found somewhere cheap to eat. A tiny Greek Cypriot place was open with basic dishes on the menu. The girls settled for egg and chips, Mack opted for bangers and mash. They decided to return on Monday to try the exotic-sounding moussaka on offer. Afterwards they made their way to Piccadilly Circus but it was too busy for any decent pictures. Trafalgar Square wasn't much better. The girls' feet began to hurt so they called it an afternoon and headed back to the flat. Mack suggested they should get up early and try to shoot in nearby Grosvenor Square.

Three sealed envelopes with their names were waiting for them.

Angie counted the notes. "I've got another tenner."

"So have I." Effy looked over to Mack. "It's more than we're owed."

Mack finished reading the note in his envelope. "Mr Silvers Sr. apologises for the under payment yesterday. He and Nate are up in North London tonight with Joe visiting relatives. He would like to see us tomorrow here at the flat at ten o'clock."

"I wonder what he wants to see us about?" Angie asked.

"Dare say we'll find out. Don't think it'll anything to worry about. Got another note here from Joe Silvers. He's organised a cab to take us to the Ram Jam Club in Brixton tonight to see Geno Washington."

"Is it his way of apologising for the way he behaved at the party?" suggested Effy.

"More likely for trying to con us out of our earnings. What do you think, Mack?"

"Call me suspicious. He doesn't strike me as someone who does anything for nothing unless it suits him. Joe Silvers is another Scooby. Smarter, slicker, less of a psycho, but still a piece of work."

"We could always take my car?" Angie proposed.

"Or we could take the tube," contributed Effy.

"No offence, Angie, but it was hard enough finding our way through London to get here. It's too easy to get lost when you don't know your way around. We could take the underground but I don't know when it stops running at night or how we get to Brixton on it. We'd probably have to get a cab back in any case."

They decided to go. Mack was to prove right. Joe Silvers had his reasons.

# CHAPTER 40

**Last Night – The Mar-Keys (London HLK-9399 – 1961)**

*Easter Monday, 27 March 1967*

Angie opened the flat door to admit Nate, Joe and their father. Alex Silvers, short, tanned and broad in build, wore a light grey suit that matched his thick thatch of grey hair.

"You must be the dark-haired beauty, Angela." His eyes twinkled, and his chubby face widened into a smile. "What a pleasure to finally meet you. Your photos don't do you justice. Nate was right. Now I meet you in person, I can see you are the kind of model we've been looking to find."

Taking Angie's hand, he kissed it.

Turning to Nate, with approval writ large in his smile, he said, "A shame the young lady is not available for courting."

Angie lit up a bright smile as she led them into the living room. Effy was standing by the settee. There was no sign of Mack.

"And you are our genius girl designer." He took her hand. Effy was expecting him to shake it but instead he kissed it in the same manner as he had with Angie.

"Another stunning beauty. Effy with a 'y', I am highly delighted to finally meet you. Photographs are no substitute. Silvers Fashions are lucky indeed to have you as a model but as a designer we are more than doubly blessed. High praise in today's papers for your designs! You must feel a real sense of delight and accomplishment. Your designs are what young women want today. After forty years in the rag trade I know what I'm on about. Where is your young man, Mack?"

The two girls looked straight at Joe shifting about uneasily, his eyes darting round the room. Their radiant smiles disappeared for a brief moment to be replaced by ice-cold glares.

"Do sit down, Mr Silvers. Could I offer you a tea or coffee?"

"No, thank you, Effy. Is he not here?"

The bedroom door opened and Mack appeared, wearing tan-coloured Levi cords and an Aertex top. "Sorry to keep you waiting, Mr Silvers, and a great pleasure to meet you again. I overslept this morning and had to have a bath. I was getting dressed when I heard you come in."

Joe Silvers paled. The pallor was noticeable to everyone except his father.

Mack shook Mr Silvers's hand.

"That's a nasty cut under your left eye," Nate observed

Silvers Senior took a close look. "How did that happen, son?"

Mack smiled directly at Joe Silvers. "It's nothing. A scratch, nothing more, no stitches were needed. It can happen to the best of us. I was careless last night and caught my cheek on something sharp outside the Ram Jam Club. Luckily for me it didn't take my eye out. *I won't be that careless ever again*. I'm a man of my word. *I keep my promises*. Sometimes sooner, sometimes later, usually when it's least expected."

The last comment was aimed straight at Joe. Nate was enjoying watching his brother squirming uncomfortably, staring at the polished wooden floor.

They'd made it to see Geno Washington and the Ram Jam Band. A dynamic high-energy live band, it brought the house down wherever it played. Washington was a showman and knew how to work up an audience to the rafters. The club was capacity-filled, hot, steamy and sweaty. They'd agreed to leave early and had stepped out into Brixton Road. The cold night air hit them. They began to walk, hunting for a cab. Less than thirty yards down the deserted road they found themselves confronted by five Mods. Their leader was a West Indian. Hard Mods was the name bandied about these days to describe this kind. To Mack, Hard Mods were casual dressers into fighting, and part of the growing soccer hooliganism on the football terraces.

"He's the one. I recognise the birds from the newspapers."

They heard more footsteps. Glancing around, they saw three more guys and a girl. Mack's heart sank. Angie recognised him straightaway. Ronnie Sykes.

"Well, well, well, MacKinnon, fancy bumping into you again here of all places? Looks like you're in a spot of bother. Tivoli Boys looking to cut you up?"

"When we've crunched this one we'll kick your fuckin' heads in, you Peckham wankers. We'll do you for free for coming on our turf."

"Listen, Yardie Boy, go ahead, knock yourself out. We'll visit you and your mates in hospital with grapes and flowers after he's done you."

"You staying out of this, Sykes?" Mack glanced at him, keeping one eye on the other lot.

"We'll just watch the show. Good odds, five to one in your favour."

Angie and Effy were struggling to come in front of him to try and form a shield. He was struggling to hold them back. Had his arms been where they should have been it would never have happened. Yardie Boy's flick-knife blade opened up as he jabbed at Mack's cheek. He wasn't quite quick enough to avoid the tip of the blade scoring him under his eye. Mack resorted to the one move *30 seconds Lenny* had warned him to avoid using unless it was life and death.

The Tivoli Boy over-extended his knife arm. Mack delivered an edge of the palm karate-style blow to the windpipe. A crushed windpipe could kill a man. Delivered with whiplash speed, it felled his opponent. Yardie Boy stumbled backwards. Still clutching the flick knife, he crashed to the ground like a sack of coal dropped off a lorry, gasping for air. Mack took the second close-cropped blond-haired assailant with a vicious snap kick to the knee. Catching him with a vicious elbow to the head, he grabbed the guy's Harrington collar ends. Reeling him in front of the next assailant he used him as a momentary barrier. Slowing down this opponent he glimpsed Sykes and his mates joining the fray. It wasn't him they were attacking. It was the so-called Tivoli Boys. Mack kneed the one he was using as a shield. Shoving him backwards into the other one he caused a collision, sending them sprawling off balance. Delivering an almighty stinging slap to the side of the head he disorientated the last one. Grabbing him by the neck, he kneed him with massive force in the gut and felled him. At this point Sykes's friends proceeded to hit and kick seven shades out of the others. Mack watched as Yardie Boy tried to sit up, still clutching the flick knife. Mack did the unthinkable. Dazed from the blow to his windpipe, Yardie Boy struggled to get air back into his lungs; he had no time to react to a clenched fist that broke his nose and laid him out flat. The other Tivoli boys fled as Sykes's mate jeered them down the road. One of the Peckham boys gave the downed youth a final vicious parting kick that brought him round to consciousness. Angie and Effy stood there trembling with shock, horrified at what they'd witnessed. It had happened with such speed, they still couldn't take it in.

Ronnie Sykes turned to Mack, still pumped for violence. Mack was expecting another brawl. But 'Smiler' Sykes grinned, teeth freshly capped. "You are the most fucking dangerous bloke I've ever seen. I knew you could take him and his mates. I wanted to see it for myself."

"So you're not going to have a go at me again?"

"No fucking chance. No way. Anyhow I owe you big time. You saved my life. That bastard Silvers and his guys would have dumped me in the canal but for you sticking up for me. I'm still walking thanks to you. And thanks to you I'm down here in London. Best thing that could have happened. I've got a well-paying job and this gorgeous bird."

The tiny sparrow-like figure put her arm round Ronnie. "Is this 'im?" She looked at Mack in awe.

'That's him. That's 'The Mack'. I owe him big time for knocking some sense into my stupid head and saving my life. Thanks for making me see what a stupid tosser I was hanging around with Scooby."

Mack watched carefully as he and his girlfriend approached. Extending his hand, he said, "Let's put it all in the past."

They shook hands.

"Where can we get a taxi round here?" Effy asked in a trembling voice.

"We'll get you to one if you follow us," chirruped Sykes's girlfriend with a pronounced Cockney twang.

"Just give me a minute, will you, Ronnie?"

"Yeah, but let's not hang about too long. We're on the Tivoli's patch."

Mack bent over Yardie Boy. Grabbing him by the throat, he whispered something in his ear. Effy and Angie didn't hear what was said. Mack grinned and patted Yardie Boy on the cheek. "No hard feelings pal."

Picking up the flick knife where it had fallen he threw it down the nearest pavement drain.

# CHAPTER 41

**Love Is Strange – Betty Everett & Jerry Butler (Fontana TF 528 – 1964)**

*Easter Monday 27 March – Later*

Nate and his father treated them to lunch in a posh restaurant. Joe Silvers cried off. That came as no surprise. Nate and his father laughed, joked, smiled a lot, made small talk and told them about their future projects. They wanted the girls to do the same in their new Manchester boutique but were keen for them to do more in London. They owned several flats in the capital for the use of overseas clients. If they came down with other models, arrangements could be made to house them. Mack was asked if he could find other girls in addition to Effy's sisters. Smiling, he told them that might be possible. He didn't tell them about the connection he'd made on the day. One was with a certain advertising executive and the other with a well-known fashion journalist. Their business cards were in his wallet. When Mack slipped out to visit the toilet Nate went too. Their conversation was quick, to the point and detailed.

Nate said that his father's anger with Joe had reached volcanic levels. Alex Silvers was so furious he was considering throwing Joe out of the family business. He was toying with appointing Manny to run affairs in the City. Nate explained his father was a respected businessman known for honest dealing. Silver Fashions and the goods they produced had a reputation second to none built up over three generations. The firm's future planned expansion depended on that reputation being maintained. Joe's dishonest carrying on could have destroyed it. Mack's information had confirmed his suspected dishonesty.

Nate had given Mack a blunt warning about his brother before coming to London. Joe was a crook flogging all sorts illegally down in Brixton and other London boroughs like Camden and Peckham. Then again, Nate's own activities weren't much better. No matter what Mack thought about his activities, Nate made one thing clear. His activities had no connection to the family business, unlike those of his brother. "I'm doing my own thing for me," was his comment. "There's no way I would dare to ruin Silvers Fashions. My father would never forgive me. It's his whole life and a third-generation business. We're meant to take it over one day. I do what I do for kicks, though now I may have to concentrate more on the family business if he kicks my brother out."

What had most upset Nate's father was discovering Joe passing off fakes as fashion originals. He hadn't specified whose originals but one King's Road big name suggested itself. The fakes were so clever that they fooled most buyers, even down to replicated labels sewn into the garments. Of course Nate expected Mack to treat everything he told him in strict confidence.

Effy would have been terribly upset if she had learned that Joe Silvers had made copies of her designs in London workshops. He'd exceeded the limited number of high-end dresses originally agreed on. During the opening Mack had sneaked into the back and done some counting. There were as many as twenty copies of each dress: at least double the agreed number for three of the designs. As the originals were to be sold for between thirty and fifty guineas, Joe intended to make a killing by defrauding both his father and Effy.

Alex Silvers wanted to ensure Effy had a fair deal and stuck with him. Her designs were going to sell and he was never wrong.

As a good will gesture and by way of an apology Alex Silvers wanted to make her a special one-off additional payment. The hundred and twenty-five pounds payment was an incentive above and beyond her current deal: a sweetener to retain her. Nate persuaded Mack not to disclose the full reasons why. Neither he nor his father wanted to lose her services to rivals. Given the initial press responses to her designs over the weekend it was not surprising.

The planned photo shoot in Grosvenor Square didn't pan out. They stayed in the restaurant far longer than expected. Angie had to be at work in the morning so they needed to get on the road. The Bank Holiday traffic proved a nightmare. They finally made it to Elstree and then onto the recently opened Junction 4. Next time they would get better organised to avoid the traffic jams. Travelling up the M1 at a steady fifty, there was constant talk, some light-hearted and some serious.

The events in Brixton had shocked and terrified the girls. What shocked them even more was when Mack revealed it had been planned. He'd forced Yardie Boy into admitting getting paid to break a few bones. His. Mack hadn't time to extract more information. Joe Silvers was behind it, there was a definite connection. Not that it mattered. All that mattered was how and when he would keep his promise. Joe Silvers would pay a high price for this when the time came. Neither Effy nor Angie mentioned the fight. If he could have read their thoughts they would have surprised him. Secretly each girl admired the way he'd seen off the assailants.

They stopped to refill with petrol and to take a break. Angie's tiredness was clear. Mack volunteered to drive but Angie wouldn't risk it. He hadn't passed his test and she wasn't insured for anyone else. Instead she asked if they would mind staying over at her place since they didn't have to go anywhere in the morning. Travelling on to Bradford would only add to her journey time. It made sense. It made less sense to the usually unflappable Gillian when she discovered they were all going to sleep in the one bed.

"It's okay, Gill." Angie couldn't stop yawning, her eyes closing. "We've already slept together in one bed down in London. Not like that, so stop having dirty thoughts."

Turning to Mack she added, "If you want to spend the day here and wait until I get back from work, I'll drive you over with your suitcases and bags. It'll be much easier than catching the bus and trying to cart the suitcases full of clothes. You can have some time alone together. I'll be out at work, and so will Gillian."

Angie's wink to Effy made the latter blush.

"I suppose as we haven't another bed and there's only the second-hand sofa I'll have to be broadminded." Gillian looked at her sister askance. "As long as you're not going to be getting up to anything."

"I'm too cream crackered." Angie stifled another yawn, teasing her older sister. "But the next time who knows. I'm sure Mack would enjoy having it off with both of us. What do you think, Effy?"

Effy blushed again. Realising Angie was winding her sister up, she responded with a wink, saying, "It might be too much for the poor dear, the challenge of the two of us. I don't think he'd cope. But we could always try and find out."

Mack was still absorbing what the two had said when Gill gave him the strangest look, saying, "I hope they're only winding me up and not giving you any ideas."

"When they get together they become a double act, Gill. I'm used to it." He added, "They'd run a mile if I tried. Anyway, they could be right. I would find it hard to handle them both at once."

197

Angie suddenly sat on his lap, giggling, "You won't know until you try." She jumped off just as quickly, laughing. "We're first in the bathroom. Are you coming, Eff?"

When they'd gone upstairs Gillian put the medical textbook down she had been trying to read. "Nothing has happened, has it?" There was a mixture of curious awkwardness in her voice.

"No, Gillian. Nothing. Eff slept in the middle with her back to Angie. I slept with my back to Effy. It was all innocent."

Gillian gave him another peculiar look. "I'm still a bit old-fashioned when it comes to sex, even with the job I do. Things can happen that begin as a bit of fun but can soon destroy friendships and relationships. These days with the Pill available you can have sex without the undue worry of pregnancy. A lot of young people don't realise there's an important emotional side to sex. A loving relationship between a man and a woman is a special bond. Casual sex can irreparably damage such a bond."

It was a not so veiled warning.

"I know they're both on the Pill. I can't understand why Angie's on it. She hasn't got anyone steady and she doesn't look like she's bothered about finding anyone. Keeps saying she hasn't found who she's looking for."

Gillian bit her lip. Averting her eyes, she withdrew into a brief silence. When she spoke, it was in a flat voice and she avoided his gaze.

"Over a year ago Angie told me she'd met this wonderful boy down in town. She told me she'd had a one-night fling with him. Told me the usual things: how good-looking he was, how nice he was, how he treated her in such a lovely way. She told me she felt awful about that night because he already had a girlfriend and she'd seduced him. For Angie feeling guilty afterwards wasn't normal. She'd become very hardened after being used and abused in the past. But you know something? She couldn't stop talking about this one boy. Somehow he was so special. Every time she saw him she was in seventh heaven and couldn't wait to tell me all about him. Then there was no more mention of this Romeo on a scooter. Instead she'd become friends with a girl from Bradford whose boyfriend also came from there. I never gave it much thought at the time. I didn't connect the boy and her new friend until I met Effy. When I heard your name, I knew it was you. I did wonder if Angie was only being a friend to Effy to be near you. I still think there might be some of that, although I must admit they are as close as two girls could ever be without being related. And here you are. And there they are. Two girls who dote on you, each filled with a strong love for you because a strong love is what they both have. And you must know the truth of it, surely?"

Mack, head bowed and tight-lipped, refuted nothing. He sighed and in a low hushed voice said, "Effy doesn't know what happened between us. We agreed never to tell her. I'm begging you to do the same. Effy can never know. Knowing would hurt her more now than it might have then. It would wreck everything we three share, our friendships and how we are with each other. I love Effy; she's everything to me. As for Angie, I can't help feeling the same way about her even though we've never given anyone cause to think it. Angie can't help it, neither can I. How do I stop loving someone when I already love another so completely?"

Gillian looked him in the eyes. "I have no idea but I do know this. Nothing will come from my lips. Do right by both these girls. Don't hurt either of them, especially not my Angie. The torch she carries for you blazes brighter than you think. Nor is she as tough and as hard as she likes to make everyone believe. As for Effy, she's much stronger than she thinks and you know. But finding out could break her. I suspect it would break you too. Sex is one thing, but loving someone is something else and it's never simple. Trying to love two would be a hard thing to do. You need to ask yourself if it's even possible. Breaking one heart would be awful. Seeing three broken could leave lifelong scars and regrets."

# CHAPTER 42

**The First Cut Is the Deepest – PP Arnold (Immediate IM047 – 1967)**

*Tuesday 28 March 1967*

Mack didn't expect the reaction they received on returning home. His mother's face was impassive as she greeted the three of them. Angie helped them with their bags. Turning to Effy, she whispered, "I'm off. Best of luck with Mrs MacKinnon, I've an idea it's going to get interesting in a couple of minutes. I'd rather not be here to find out."

Mack's dad appeared, also impassive. "Don't go, Angie. Please stay a few minutes. We'd like a word with the three of you."

"I can't stop, Mr MacKinnon," Angie began to protest. "I've…"

"We won't keep you long."


Angie hadn't woken them when she got out of bed that morning. The alarm had. It sounded loud enough to wake the inhabitants of all the cemeteries within a five-mile radius.

"Sorry, guys, I need it loud," she'd apologised, returning from the bathroom. "Otherwise I'd never get up in time. Mack, shut your eyes while I get my make-up and clothes on. No peeking."

"Yeah, yeah, okay. Those black lacy briefs are cute, so is the matching bra." He still sounded drowsy in his head.

Effy kneed him in the thigh, the hand round his waist shooting up to cover his eyes.

After Angie left for work they got up. They had the whole day ahead of them. As they sat munching on toast and drinking coffee, Mack asked, "What shall we do first? I was thinking we'd take a walk and use up the film from yesterday. Do some outdoor fashion snapping if we can find a decent spot? It's looking like a decent day with good light conditions, not too bright and not too cloudy."

She nuzzled his cheek with her nose before kissing him. "I have a better idea. Before we do that let's go back upstairs. I feel the need for you to make mad passionate love to me. You won't even have to take my pants off.

I've still not put any on. You can spread my legs and satisfy both our needs. I feel the need in me right now."

"I'd never thought you'd ask."

"I want to try that position, you know, the one I told you about."

Afterwards, wrapped in each other's arms, they drowsed in silence.

"I could never live without you," Effy murmured. "Will you always love me?"

"I will always love you."

"Do you promise?"

"I promise with all of my heart and soul."

"Even if you find you love someone else as much as me?"

It was an uncomfortable question. Uncomfortable and so scary it shook him out of his post-intercourse drowsiness. It was too close to the truth.

"That's a strange question to ask."

"Well? Tell me."

"In such a hypothetical situation I would love you as much as ever."

"Are you sure? Really sure?"

"Yes."

"Could you love someone else as much as you love me?"

"Why are you asking? Isn't it enough to know I love you?"

"No reason. We should get up. Those photographs won't take themselves." She rose from the bed, leaving him marvelling at her naked body. "We'd better change the sheets," she said,

The late morning's shooting was productive. The shots he hoped would work best were snaps of Effy posing in an open telephone box. The questions she had asked kept nagging at him, refusing to leave his thoughts. He found himself distracted and disturbed. They took the bus into town.

Effy's behaviour became stranger as the day wore on. They walked round the town centre shops. She seemed to vacillate between an unusual extroverted happiness and moments of intense subdued sadness. Was she still brooding over those questions? Was it tied to their weekend in London? Had something happened to awaken her suspicions again?

Walking up Cheapside from the Victorian market she suggested taking some daytime photos outside The Plebs. So they ventured into the Upper George Yard. Mack wasn't too hopeful but her confidence as a model had increased since the weekend. There was a mysterious elusive quality about her today. He couldn't work out what it was but whatever it was he

201

wanted the camera to capture it. Patiently, he tried to stay focused, realising with each passing moment she was studying him with an unusual and peculiar intensity.

Those questions now plunged dagger-like into his heart with heaviness and dread. He now knew for certain they were linked to her behaviour. If she knew anything, he reasoned, they wouldn't have had such passionate sex. It was only since then the suspicions had surfaced again. Was it something he'd done or said? Her riveting gaze told him everything was not right but he could not work out what had gone wrong or why.

Stopping off at The Beefeater in George's Square they bought coffee and sandwiches. They sat in silence. Effy continued to look at him as though she was seeing him anew. It was unnerving. The question came from nowhere. Without warning, it rooted him to the spot, turning his whole universe upside down, inside out.

"Could you love someone else at the same time as you love me?" Her voice was tremulous, small but determined. She repeated the question again, her emerald eyes searching him for the slightest reaction. Then she seemed to change her mind in an instant. "No, let me start again. No more evasiveness, Mack. I know everything."

"Know what?" His worst fear engulfed him, draining the strength from his body.

"Everything. I know everything. I came down in my stocking feet last night. The door was ajar. I found myself listening to your conversation with Gillian. So no more playing games. Don't try to spare me. No more evasiveness. I know you too well. *I know everything.*"

He felt as though he was dying, a horrible despairing heaviness crushing his heart. The worst he'd imagined happening was happening. The enveloping dread broke him. He fell apart before her eyes.

Effy hadn't foreseen such a devastating reaction. The last thing she expected was to see her tower of strength buckle and collapse before her eyes. The repressed guilt flooded out in heart-rending tears flowing down his face. Pushing aside the cup and plates in front of them, she grasped both his hand. She began to cry too.

She had always seen Mack as strong, tough and emotionally resilient. Seeing him like this, in so much painful distress, vulnerable and reduced to tears, upset her. It was so unlike him and it shook her. In wanting to know the truth she had never expected anything like this. She came and sat down beside him, placing a reassuring forgiving arm around him. As she pressed her cheek to his, their tears mingled.

"Neither of us wanted to hurt you," he confessed. "It's all my fault. It was an unforgiveable thing I did. I'm to blame. I'm the guilty one. You mustn't blame Angie. It was before she knew you. I'm guilty of betraying you and what we had and what we have. How can you ever forgive me? Forgive us? I must look and sound pathetic crying like a little kid but I need you to know I've always loved you. I've never stopped loving you. I still love you more than anything. All I, we, wanted to do was to spare you the hurt."

Two elderly women pensioners were looking on from a nearby table. "Oh dear, they must breaking up," they heard one say.

"I still love you, Mack. Please don't cry. I never thought my knowing would upset you so much. You may find this hard to believe. I lay in bed last night between the two of you and it was all clear to me. Neither you nor Angie wanted to hurt me so you kept it from me. That was the only reason you didn't say anything. You were doing what you thought was right protecting me from feeling the hurt. Looking back, it was a difficult time with a lot of uncertainty for you and me. You were younger then and didn't stop to think about the consequence of what you were doing. I'm not so surprised by what happened. Let's face it Angie's gorgeous, sexy and so much fun. If I'd never gone out with you I'm certain you would have ended up together. By rights I should be furious as hell with the pair of you but I'm not. I can't be. I've always suspected there was more going on between you two. Even the first time I met Angie, when she and Linda came into the square from the Vic Lounge, I had my suspicions."

"So where does that leave you and me, Effy?"

"It leaves you having to be honest with yourself and with me and with Angie. No more self-deception, no more pretending. It's time to come clean and be honest with both Angie and myself. Admit the truth. You love both of us."

203

# CHAPTER 43

### I – Kiki Dee (Fontana TF 833 – 1967)

*Tuesday 28 March 1967*

"Mrs Ellis next door came round with this." Robert Mackinnon showed them the photograph from Sunday paper. It was the infamous one showing them leaving The Cromwellian.

"Seeing this came as quite a shock, I can tell you. Never in my wildest imaginings could I have imagined you three leaving a gambling club wrapped round each other as if you'd been to an orgy."

"We were larking about, Mr MacKinnon. It isn't what it seems." Angie came straight out in their defence. "It was a bit of fun, and it was our misfortune to get snapped like that. You've got to admit it is a good photo."

"What kind of image do you think this will present to the world? And I'm more concerned about you two young ladies and the effect it will have on your reputations." Mack's dad wasn't angry but there was a detectable edge to his words.

"I'm sorry if it's upset you and Jane. It isn't such a big deal, as Mack will tell you. Because of this photo we're going to have more work than we can handle. It's fantastic publicity." Effy put on her most winsome smile. In a conscious act she placed one arm round Mack's waist and the other round Angie's. Angie's hand came to rest on her shoulder.

"Yes, and Silvers Fashions have made Effy a no-strings payment of one hundred and twenty-five pounds as a generous gesture in the hopes she'll keep working for them. That's on top of the modelling fee. They've paid me the same fee and are going to cover my petrol expenses for the journey too." Angie looked over at Mack. "We also got the use of a posh flat that didn't cost us a penny. Nate's dad even treated us to a slap-up meal in a posh restaurant. I'm not sure what Mack got paid."

Their unified defensive wall stumped and confused his father. Mack had expected the worst to come from his mother's lips. Contrary to what he expected, it proved the opposite.

"What did I tell you, Robert? Orgy? Honestly? How could you think such a thing of Effy and Angie? I'm sure nothing untoward went on.

Although youthful larking about like that may not do much for your reputations in the eyes of some. Mrs Ellis was a little surprised, I have to say."

"It seems your mum's relatives in Ireland saw the same syndicated photo in a local newspaper." Robert Mackinnon addressed Effy. "She managed to keep it from your father. It's the kind of thing that could trigger a relapse after the progress he's made. I'm sure you can understand your mother's concern given your father's history of mental disturbance and depression. I've had some interesting chats over the phone with Bridget, too, who was also concerned about possible adverse publicity."

"Do we have any further news of their return?" Effy asked.

"Nothing was mentioned."

Grace appeared at the dining room door, staring at the three of them and grinning with impish delight. "Get you lot, one for all and all for one. That's you three all over. Anyone would think you were joined at the hips."

"You could be right, Grace. Better that way than not at all," Effy replied with a mysterious non-committal smile. As she spoke those words Angie and Mack felt her grip tighten, pulling them closer to her. "You're right, all for one and one for all. That's what friends do, isn't it, stay united in adversity?"

When Angie left Effy followed, making some excuse. Climbing into the Herald she said, "Let's go somewhere. We need to talk. I have something to say you will find shocking, even appalling. I need to say it. I want you to hear it and say nothing until I finish if you value our friendship."

She'd meant to be gone a few minutes. They'd driven away to leave Mack and his parents wondering what was going on. An hour and a half later the car pulled up outside the house. Watching through the window Mack saw the two girls hug one another before Effy waved Angie off.

Later that evening, up in their attic bedroom, Grace was revelling in all the newspaper cuttings. "Oh, how I wish I'd been there! I'll never forgive everyone for not letting me go. I would have loved to model in Moods Mosaic. And Vidal Sassoon styled your hair! God, Eff, I'm so green with envy. How fab is that? Your hair looks gorgeous. Makes you look so grown up. That must have been so far out having him do your hair. Wait till I tell them at school. Did you see any famous film stars or pop stars?"

Effy's mind kept drifting away. As she recalled the weekend's events Grace's words faded into emptiness. The memory of the weekend had fast become a kaleidoscopic jumbled haze. The horrific violence in Brixton kept returning to the fore. It was the sharpest memory continuing to jump out of the jumbled weekend. When she thought about Ronnie Sykes and the strange way worst enemies had reconciled, it made her reflect. Relationships could change over time and circumstance. Mack had been her rock, her anchor, when much of her life had existed in a storm. There was nothing she wouldn't have trusted him with. All Mack had ever done was protect her. Well intentioned as the secret was, it had concealed a greater secret he'd kept even from himself.

Angie? What was she to make of her friend? It was too easy to believe Angie had played her for a fool, ingratiating herself in their life. But that was too simplistic. Angie was a far more complex person, yet in some ways so straightforward. They had become so close, like sisters, but without the hang-up that came with being family. Girls needed other girls as friends to share their lives and Effy was no different, neither was Angie. They had both shared their bottled-up thoughts and feelings with one another. Except for this important one that Angie had kept locked up within herself: she was in love with Mack. It was the single thing Angie hadn't shared and it was understandable. Like Mack, she must have experienced extraordinary guilt over what had happened between them. Unlike herself, Angie had been used and abused by men. She'd never made any secret of the mistreatment she'd suffered. Her reluctance to form romantic liaisons was easy to understand. It was all to do with trust. Effy could understand why Angie had fallen for Mack. He was everything Angie didn't see in other men, young or old.

He was everything that was desirable in a young man. Trustworthy, loyal, strong, dependable, mature, a protector devoted to those he loved. He was a young man among young men who were still boys. Effy recollected how Angie had once described him as a knight in shining armour. She'd been right. Why should she feel surprised that Angie carried a torch for him? Why should she blame her for harbouring feelings for him? It was clear she'd done her best to bury them. There had never been a moment when Angie had shown how she really felt. When they were together she would never talk about him. It must have been a terrible hurt, knowing it could only be a one-way love. Repressing those feelings must have been heart-rending.

Now their lives were becoming so complicated and so entwined. Their futures would bind them closer than ever before. What had happened in the past could not be undone. Severing ties with Angie was unthinkable and too cruel to even consider. Effy was not willing to sacrifice Mack or her friendship with Angie. When she considered it all she found herself wondering why she didn't feel jealous. By rights she should feel angry, resentful, hurt. Instead she felt nothing except incredible sadness thinking how they must feel so torn by their love and friendship. She couldn't abide the thought of the suffering the three of them were experiencing.

Effy blamed herself. She felt like Pandora who'd opened a box unleashing evils into the world. It had torn her apart seeing the damaging impact on Mack. In forcing him to admit he had strong feelings for Angie she had released a genie that wouldn't go back in the bottle. She couldn't turn back the hands of time, no matter how hard she wished to do so. These were the consequences she would have to confront for what she'd done. Knowing how hard and devastating the admission had hit Mack hurt her too.

"Oi! Earth to Planet Eff! Did you hear what I've just said?" Grace shook her arm. "I don't know where you've been the last few minutes but you haven't heard a word I've been saying."

"I'm sorry, Grace. A lot has happened in the last few days. In the words of that song, I've been reviewing the situation. Go on, tell me again."

"I met up with Jean and some friends from school in town today. They've seen quite a few of the newspaper items between them. God, you'd better get yourself ready for a right storm when we get back after the holiday. That photo of you and Angie was so blatant and daring."

"Yes, it was, wasn't it? We had a threesome in bed together later that night. It was awesome." Effy delivered the words in a distracted flat manner. Watching Grace absorb her words was a sight worth the prank. She needed to try and cheer herself up. "Do you know he wore us both out? There was no stopping once he got going. He ravished us in turn with an insatiable animal passion and hunger. It went on like that all night long, he just wouldn't leave us alone and let us sleep… and if you believe that, sis, you've been well and truly had."

Grace slapped her on the arm. "You had me going there, you wicked woman. Mind you, I wouldn't have put it past you three, seeing that photo. It oozes hot sex and smouldering passion. Even Ellen and Tom thought you three were misbehaving. What were you playing at? What made you do it?"

Effy pointed to Joe Silvers in the background. "Him. He was trying to get into my knickers all day Saturday. I couldn't get him to take no for an answer. Mack was busy taking photos and didn't know what was going on until later. Angie suggested we gave him the impression we were both besotted with Mack so he'd leave us alone."

"And did he?"

"No. In the end Mack had to have a word with him. He didn't take it too well and we had some bother, but nothing Mack couldn't sort." Effy's version was a vague and censored account of events in Brixton Road. "All this fuss will be forgotten by the time we get back to school."

But it wasn't.

In the following two days she couldn't avoid the raw emotional turmoil Mack was experiencing. He needed her constant reassurances as though he believed she was about to forsake him. Other things were happening around them, knocking his confidence further. Benny Jenkins had effectively sacked him from his Saturday job by hiring a full-time stores assistant. Benny still wanted Mack to come in on the odd day to help out if they became really busy. An extra pair of hand would always be useful. To show no hard feelings Benny let him know he could still use the workshop. Any repairs, servicing and upgrades to the GT200 could still be done out of hours. They would even let him have parts at trade prices as before. Not even the new fuel injection system seemed to raise his spirits. Effy had never known him so down and it was all her doing. She was responsible for the crisis. When Angie called her, she felt a strange sense of relief. Angie had come to a decision.

Effy made Mack leave his schoolwork and revising, forcing him to take her out on a ride. They didn't go far. Only to Lister Park and to Cartwright Hall where they'd had their first date over two years earlier. Leaving the Lambretta in North Park Road they walked through the gate leading to the hall. She tried to raise his spirits, her arm tightly in his talking about the first time they'd come here. Stopping in the garden area not far from the main entrance he turned to her. She'd never seen him looking so scared. The young man she knew who never showed fear even when confronted with violence was quiet and seemed terrified.

"You haven't brought me here where we began to tell me it's all over, have you?"

Facing him she raised her heels off the ground. Placing her hands tenderly round his neck she gave him the most passionate kiss she could.

Dropping her hands to his shoulders, she pressed herself against him, burying her face in his parka. "Don't be stupid, you soft bugger. Now listen to what you've made me do. Swear. You truly have been a bad influence but I wouldn't have it any other way. If I've been distant since I found out what happened between you and Angie you shouldn't be surprised. Knowing how you both felt about one another and me, I've needed to come to terms with it.

I remember Gillian saying something like: loving two is the hardest thing to do if not downright impossible. None of us can help the way we feel. I know you and I love you. I have never doubted our love because ours is a strong love, rare and precious. I won't give you up. I will fight to keep what we have. There's no escaping from it for you and there's no retreating from it for me. You're like the air I breathe. I couldn't live without you and you'd be the same. Together we can face anything. At the same time I don't want to lose Angie's friendship because it, too, is special for me."

Effy let those words sink in before carrying on.

"We three are not some simple uncomplicated partnership. Our futures are linked and bound. Which is why what I'm going to say next isn't easy for me to say. Nor will it be easy for you to hear. I don't want you misunderstanding what I'm saying next. You may hate me for it afterwards but it's a risk I have to take. I've thought about it long and hard. It's not a spur of the moment decision."

Effy looked up at him for a moment or two. There was a glimmer of panic in his eyes. Taking a big breath, she began. "Okay, here goes nothing. If she wants to sleep with you and is willing to share you with me, loving you like I love you, I'll live with it if that's what it takes. I'm willing to share you with Angie."

"I couldn't…" he began. She stopped him with a long kiss.

"What did I say? You can because I'm saying you can. Accept what I've said. I had my chat with her in the car on Tuesday evening. I said pretty much the same to her as I have to you. I made it clear I loved you and I would never under any circumstances give you up. If we both choose to be with you it could only be because we really loved you and as equals. I made it a take it or leave it choice. It's her and me, or it's only me. We either share you or I keep you all to myself. There can be no other choices. I'm willing to give sharing you a go. I wouldn't do it for anyone else other than Angie. I gave her time to think it through. She gave me her answer."

"And?"

"That's for you two to work out your side of it. You know where I stand. I've made it as clear as I know how. Go over and talk to her. Find out what she wants. If we end up sharing you, you will have to do right by both of us."

"I don't know if I can do this, Effy. I know how I feel about you. How I've always felt since that day we first walked down here from the library. I remember the time we spent inside the art gallery, sheltering from the rain and talking. How could I do this to you? I'd feel as if I was betraying you and being unfaithful after all the things we've shared. Think about it. It all sounds fine when you say something like that. But how are you and she going to feel once you know I'm having sex with both of you? Have you thought about that? How do you know you or Angie won't get jealous? What if you start thinking things like, 'he loves her more than me'? Don't say it couldn't happen because it could and might. We're only human. Then what?"

"If things stay as they are at the moment and we don't work it out, Mack, it'll continue to make the three of us miserable. She does love you. I made her admit it to me. It might be something we have to chance. I'd be lying if I said I wasn't worried about the possibility of jealousy when it came to sex. If I'm honest I don't know how I'd feel, thinking about you two together. At least I'd be sure of one thing."

Mack looked into her emerald eyes shining up at him. "What's that?"

"We'd both be doing it because we loved you."

# CHAPTER 44

**Take Me in Your Arms and Love Me – Gladys Knight & The Pips
(Tamla Motown TMG 604 – 1966)**

*Wednesday 21 December 1967*

Jubilee Road was deserted. Mack slowed the Lambretta as he approached the house. The Triumph Herald parked outside told him she was home at last. A fine misty rain was starting to come down as he brought the scooter to a stop. He let the engine idle for several seconds before turning the ignition off. The fuel injector still wasn't set up quite right. He would need to mess with it until he had a more precise adjustment. It would have to wait. Unclipping the helmet strap, he made for the door.

Angie must have heard him arriving. She was already coming to the door; he saw she was still wearing her office clothes. He remembered her buying the black-and-white houndstooth jacket and matching skirt. Effy had gone with her to help choose it. It was five thirty. She must have been late coming home from work. Angie looked tired, drawn and paler than usual as she invited him in. No sooner was the door closed than she burst into floods of tears. Her arms went around his waist, holding him tightly against her. Her sobbing body pulsed against his. Her head was buried against his chest. It felt strange to hold her so close again, strange yet somehow so normal, so natural. The fragrant scent of her dark hair, indefinable yet so feminine, filled his nostrils, overpowering his senses.

"What have we done, Mack? It's my fault." More uncontrolled sobbing followed as Angie kept repeating over and over, "It's all my fault."

Mack stroked her hair, his touch gentle and, he hoped, reassuring. He said nothing in reply, doing his best to comfort her without words. He'd never seen her like this. Angie had always seemed so strong, so level headed, so self-sufficient. This was a side of her he'd never suspected even existed.

"Let me sit you down," he whispered after a while, "so we can talk. It's not your fault. Don't blame yourself. I'm the one who's caused this mess. If I'd been more of a man and less of a boy I should have stopped you that night."

"If I'd been less of a slut and more of a woman I wouldn't have behaved the way I did."

"Don't use that word. It's not you. It never will be." Removing his parka, he hunted out a clean hanky from his Harrington jacket pocket. Her mascara had run. With tender dabs he dried her tears, trying to remove the smudged mascara.

"I'm late in. I stopped at my mum's to see how she was doing. Gillian is with her this evening. Have you eaten?"

"No. I came over earlier but you weren't home so I stopped off in town for a coffee."

"I'll get us something." She took off her jacket and went into the kitchen. He followed her. "We've not much, I'm afraid. Gill is hopeless at remembering to buy in. There's a beef stew from last night that I cooked. Will that be okay? I'll go and get changed into something else. These two-piece suits are smart for work but not for wearing round the house."


While she was gone he occupied himself looking at the February's issue of *She* magazine. The newsagents had written "G. Thornton" in the right-hand top corner. Mack studied the photo of the blonde model on the front cover. They'd snapped her reclining in what looked like some kind of peculiar yellow deckchair in a garden. He couldn't help thinking what a ridiculous front cover it was. He would have done something better.

Angie returned wearing a plain dark-blue shift dress. Placing her arms around him, she said, "I prefer *Petticoat* magazine." It was to be an omen.

After eating they shared the washing up and drying. There was nothing slovenly about the new home. They hadn't much by way of furnishings but the sisters kept it sparkling clean. The woodwork was polished and dusted and there were a few ornaments here and there. Sitting on the settee, Angie snuggled up to him. "Please just hold me, Mack. I miss being hugged and touched. I miss having someone to hold and comfort me. Let's not talk. I need your arms around me."

So he sat with her in silence, cradling her in his arms. After a time she said, "I can't stop loving you. I've tried and tried and tried. You haunt my heart and my thoughts all the time. They say time is meant to heal but my heart has never healed. I can't help it. I never wanted to hurt Effy or you. She's more than just a friend. After my sister and parents, she is the closest person in my life, like another sister."

"What? Closer than me?" he joked.

212

"You know what I mean. You're the man in my life."

"I'm only seventeen, Angie."

"You're a young man in that case but more of a man than some of the so-called grown men I've come across. Especially that creep Joe Silvers. He gives me the shivers. You're in a different league." Angie gave him a squeeze.

Mack let out a loud sigh. "You asked not so long ago if I was honest enough to admit I loved you. You knew the answer before I gave it. I still do and I can't help it, even though you know how much I love Effy. You have to know I could never ever leave her. Then again it would hurt her and me if you weren't in our lives. I don't know what to make of her idea of me sharing you with her. I don't even know if you could do it. I don't even know if I could do it. All I know is that I can't keep you hurting in a one-way love any longer."

"Effy told me she was serious about it, and I mean serious. I couldn't take it in. Nor could I doubt she meant what she said. She told me she would rather share you with me than risk losing either one of us. Like you, I can't imagine how it could work."

"You and me too." He let out another big sigh. "I'll ask you the same question I asked her.'

Angie's dark brown eyes looked into his. "Okay. Go ahead."

"How are you and she going to feel once I'm having sex with each of you in turn? It's like I pointed out to Effy, theory is one thing and practice is something else. What happens if one or both of you start getting jealous of each other?"

Angie's face lit up and she began to have an attack of the giggles.

"What's so funny? I'm being serious."

"You. You made it sound as if we'd have sex the in same bed." Angie's embarrassed giggles turned to laughter. "I just imagined you flipping a coin. Heads you first, tails you second."

"I didn't mean it like that," he protested, his serious demeanour cracking into a broad grin. "I love that about you, Angie. You just have a knack of making things sound funny. No. I can't imagine the three of us would do something like that."

"Nor me. As close as we are that might be pushing things too far. You're right, though; jealousy is going to be a real risk. It will be down to you to stop it from happening."

"Me. How?"

"You will have to treat us equally and be seen to treat us equally. If Effy saw you treating me better than her it would be wrong. And I wouldn't put up with it in any case. Take that as read. Never forget what an amazing sacrifice she's making by agreeing to let me share you with her. Everything to do with us two girls is going to be down to you. And don't forget, Effy has an enormous advantage in her favour that I will always have to live with."

"What's that?"

"She's living with you and she is your first love. I'm not. I'll always be second but a loving equal if you'll let me. You're bound to spend more time together. We'll not be able to spend as much 'you and me time'. I can live with it as long as we have some time together and I know you love me too. Then there are other problems the three of us are going to face together. Everyone knows Effy's your girl. What's going to happen if I'm seen alone with you? How long do you think it would take Tom and Ellen to rumble what's going on? How will they react? What will happen if your parents know what we were getting up to? Come to think of it, if my dad knew he would go spare. Thank heavens I'm no longer living at home. Oh! I've had a thought. What happens when Ellen moves in? I suppose we'll have that bridge to cross. Sooner or later our threesome is bound to come out. How would we deal with it?"

"So what are you saying? That it's not going to work because it can't or you think we can?"

"First I need to know that you want me to share you with Effy."

"If I say yes…"

"I'll be willing to take a back seat to you and Effy. Look, Mack, I won't expect you to split your time equally between the two of us. It would never work as things are now. After London we're going to be busy and I suspect working together a lot. Not only the three of us. There'll be Ellen and Grace. If we get Alice as a model and anyone else it will become even more complicated. Effy suggested a good idea. After that photograph of us in the papers, we could keep playing up that angle. It would work as a publicity stunt but it could also work as a cover. No one would think any more of it; at least those who knew us. It would also keep wolves the likes of Joe Silvers away from Effy and myself. Your parents would need to know it was an act even if it wasn't. The important thing I'd want from you if you agreed to this relationship would be to treat the two of us with equal respect. More than anything I'd want to know you cared for me and loved me like you love Effy. If anyone could I know you could."

214

"So is this you saying yes?"

"Eff's left it up to you and me. I'm saying yes but I need to know you're really, really sure you want to go ahead having both of us in your life. I want you to be really, really sure, for Effy's sake as well as for mine. I won't do anything to hurt her or you. You do realise once we go ahead nothing can ever be quite the same again between the three of us? It might turn out a complete disaster, wrecking everything we already have. I need you to be one hundred per cent certain before you commit yourself."

"Can we ever be sure?" Mack kissed her on the forehead. "We'll have to cross our fingers and make a leap of faith. I'm ready. I hope with all my heart and soul the three of us are not leaping over an emotional cliff."

"There are a few things we will need to agree on first. We'll have to set some ground rules but the three of us can work those out. You and I could start now if you want but I have my GCE English class at Tech this evening. I have to be there for seven thirty. I can't afford to miss it. I'm sitting the exam soon together with other subjects. And, unfortunately for you, I'm also on my period so we can't seal the deal. But we still have half an hour before I need to get ready to go."

Weird didn't come close to describing how strange it was finding himself locked in a passionate embrace with Angie. Kissing her again with unbelievable intensity was surreal.

# CHAPTER 45

**A Groovy Kind of Love – Wayne Fontana & The Mindbenders
(Fontana TF644 –1965)**

*Saturday 8 April 1967*

A babbling and excited Grace greeted Mack and Effy as they returned home with Angie and Alice Liddell. They'd gone to the studio in Leeds Road to do Alice's test photo shoot.

"Guess what? There's been a phone call. It's important. I had to take it. Your mum and dad were out. You'll never guess who it was from… it's dead exciting."

"Is she always like this?" Alice asked as Grace danced round them like a possessed dervish.

"Yes," they chorused.

"Oh, be like that you lot. I don't think I'll bother telling you."

"Oh, for heaven's sake, Grace." Effy became exasperated. "Act your age."

"I've never been this age so how am I supposed to act?"

"Spill, Gracie, or I'll give your mop my version of a Sassoon crop. It'll be a basin cut, carrot head, so start talking," joked Angie.

Lately Grace had taken even more to Angie. Her eyes shone with admiration whenever she came round. "God, you actually think you're so funny, *Miss* Thornton."

"That's because I am," Angie retorted, "and you know I am."

"So who was it?" Mack asked.

"Someone from *Petticoat* magazine wanted to speak to a *Mister* Mack MacKinnon no less. I did my best secretarial voice and asked what it was about. They want to speak to you early next week. She sounded keen to use some photos you'd done for the Silvers for the catalogues."

"Did you get her telephone number?"

"Oh, no." Grace's face dropped. "I was so excited I forgot to write it down."

"Ignore her, Mack." Angie laughed. "Gracie's taking the wee wee again trying to wind us up."

216

"Trust you to spoil it, Angie. Actually, no, I'm not joking. Seems Mr Alex Silvers has been waving a magic wand with someone down there. And I was kidding. I wrote down the phone number and the name of the person you're supposed to contact. It's their office number."

Effy, Mack and Angie exchanged glances.

"We've not finished choosing the fabrics for all the designs yet, Effy!" The importance of the telephone call struck Grace. "We're going to have to get to work, sis."

"I've made a start but I haven't finalised them. Looks like Grace and myself will be busy tonight. Why don't you and Angie go to The Wheel without me? I saw Mary Wells last weekend and work has to come before pleasure."

"Are you sure?" Mack gave her a quizzical look.

"Yes. Angie can keep you out of trouble and stop you getting into any more fights. Anyway, I'm sure Ben E. King will be on again. Who knows, Nate might want to see you and Angie? You can chaperone her and make sure she behaves herself." Effy beamed at Angie. "I know Mack will make sure nothing untoward happens."

"As long you don't mind me borrowing him for the night." Angie exchanged smiles. "I'll do my best to make sure he behaves himself and doesn't go with any strange girls."

"We can always go down The Plebs and see Root & Jenny Jackson again if you don't fancy trekking over to Manchester," he suggested.

"I saw Ben E. King last November at The Wheel. He was brilliant but you're right. Maybe we should stay closer to home. We can decide later."

"Don't think me rude." Alice had been staring at Mack's hand and then at Effy's and then at Angie's. "I couldn't help noticing those rings you three are wearing. They're the same and look like wedding bands, Can I ask why you wear them?"

"It's something the three of us decided to do," Effy explained. "We wear the same yellow Lucite rings like wedding bands to remind us."

"To remind you of what?"

"That we're wedded to each other and our business as partners. We are our priority." Mack elaborated further. "It's also to keep the guys at bay. Effy and Angie get fed up with blokes trying to chat them up all the time. The rings are meant to act as a deterrent, making blokes think they're married."

"We kind of are," Angie fleshed the tale out a little more. "The three of us take our relationship very seriously."

"Very, very, very seriously." Effy looked at Mack. "Our trust in one another is unshakable and without doubts."

"I see." Alice looked bemused at their explanation. "I hope it doesn't include models working for you?"

"No, Alice. Our relationship is bigamous enough already without growing it into Mack's personal harem." Effy's wicked glint broadened into a smile.

"I tell you, Alice, these three have become so weird since they got back from London. And they're getting weirder." Grace shook her head, playing with her mane of red hair as she spoke. "And that photograph... well... it had my school friends all worked up and talking about it. I pity you, Eff, when you walk back into college on Monday. There's going to be a lot of nosiness."

"I hate to say it but my brother couldn't stop looking at the photo. He said he wished he had one girl looking at him like that let alone two. He was quite envious of you, Mack. He even asked me before I came to ask if you could give him some tips."

"Tell you what, Alice, you can say I'm going to write a book. One of those in the 'Teach Yourself' series and when I do I'll give him a signed copy."

"You see what me and Effy have to put up with, Alice," groaned Angie. "His swollen head."

"Go and get that film developed, we're all keen to see how Alice looks in this morning's shoot." Effy shooed him off. "You too, Grace, since you're the official darkroom assistant."

His mum returned as they headed for the cellar door and the dark room. She looked tired and the bump carrying his as yet unborn sibling seemed even larger today.

"Why didn't you wait until we got home? Effy and I could have gone down the shops."

"James, I'm pregnant, not incapable. I already have Effy and Grace scurrying round after me. Effy's such a godsend. You're lucky to have her as a girlfriend. You two were made for each other."

Her words made him feel awful, sick to his stomach.

Mack told Effy how he felt when she came to his room. They spoke in whispers. He repeated his mother's words to her.

"Your mum's right. You *are* lucky to have me. We *are* made for each other. You're also lucky to have Angie, strange as it sounds coming from me. Gosh, you are insecure. What can I say to reassure you we are alright?"

"I always said I wanted to marry you. I still do even though I've found myself locked in this love triangle. Will you still want to marry me someday, even after what we've started?"

Effy took his head in her hands, cradling him to her breasts. "I said I would, didn't I? Nothing's going to change that. I'll never stop loving or wanting you. I love you even though we're in too deep in this strange threesome. You can only marry one of us. Angie's already told me it will have to be me. Someday she'll explain why it has to be me. I'm happy knowing I still have you. I only wish I had more opportunities to make love to you."

"You know I can hear your heart beating when I'm close to you like this. I can feel you breathing and hear you sighing. It's the sound of your sighing that's upsetting me, as well as thinking about this new side of our lives and what it will involve. Effy, how will we cope?"

"Don't. When you're with her you're with her. Give her all of yourself and for goodness sake don't go thinking of me. That would be unfair to the three of us. When you're with me I want you only thinking of me. I know it'll be hard but remember what we agreed. There's no turning back, we're all in too deep, but I won't have you hurt Angie. Be a man about it like the man we both believe you are. How many men get so lucky? You have two girls so in love with you they are willing to share their love. Now kiss me and go."

Effy had to break off the kiss. "Wow, tiger! Save something in the tank for Angie."

"Before I zoom off, what do you think of the photos of Alice? Did you really like what you saw? You weren't just saying it because she was there?"

"You were right about her. She is photogenic and you've made her look brilliant. She has a kind of quirkiness like you said. We should definitely be serious about using her. I love the way you always manage to catch expressive eyes in all your photos. You do it with all of us. You've done it with Alice too. I like to think you look into a girl's soul when you click the camera button."

"It's not something I'm conscious of doing."

He gave her one last kiss. No matter what she had said to him he still felt terrible as he left the room and headed downstairs.

From the attic bedroom Effy watched him kickstart the scooter into life. He gave the house one last fleeting glance before riding off. She watched him disappear from sight. Grace was talking but Effy wasn't listening. A single tear trickled down her cheek. A single silent sob left her body.

(Book 2 End - To be continued)

NOVEL SOUNDTRACK

The title "Strong Love" was taken from the 1965 Spencer Davis Group recording.

| | |
|---|---|
| 01 Something About You – The Four Tops | Tamla Motown TMG 542 – 1965 |
| 02 Determination – The Contours | Tamla Motown TMG 564 – 1966 |
| 03 He's a Rebel –The Crystals | London HLU 9611 – 1962 |
| 04 He's a Lover – Mary Wells | Stateside SS 439 – 1965 |
| 05 Nothing's Too Good for my Baby – Stevie Wonder | Tamla Motown TMG 558 – 1966 |
| 06 Said I Wasn't Gonna Tell Nobody – Sam & Dave | Atlantic 484047 – 1965 |
| 07 Jingle Bells – Booker T & The MG's | Atlantic 584060 – 1966 |
| 08 Who Could Ever Doubt My Love – The Isley Brothers | Tamla Motown TMG 566 – 1966 |
| 09 He's Just a Playboy – The Drifters | UK Atlantic 4008 B Side 1964 |
| 10 Maybe I Know – Lesley Gore | Mercury MF 829 – 1964 |
| 11 Just A Little Misunderstanding – The Contours | Tamla Motown TMG 564 – 1966 |
| 12 That's What Love Is Made Of – The Miracles | Stateside SS 353 – 1964 |
| 13 Stop Look and Listen – The Chiffons | Stateside SS 550 – 1966 |
| 14 Chain Reaction – The Spellbinders | CBS 202622 -1966 |
| 15 Sweet Thing – Detroit Spinners | Tamla Motown TMG 514 – 1965 |
| 16 Keep Looking – Solomon Burke | Atlantic 584026 – 1966 |
| 17 Sock It to 'Em JB – Rex Garvin & The Mighty Cravers | Atlantic 584-028 – 1966 |
| 18 Shoot Your Shot – Jr. Walker and The All Stars | Tamla Motown TMG 559 – 1966 |
| 19 I Got What It Takes – Brooks & Jerry | Direction 58-3267 – 1967 |
| 20 Aim and Ambition – Jimmy Cliff | Island Records WIP 6004-B – 1967 |
| 21 It Ain't Watcha Do  (It's The way That You Do It)– Little Richard | Sue Records 4015 – 1966 |
| 22 Heart Trouble – The Eyes of Blue | Deram DM 106 – 1966 |
| 23 Born Under a Bad Sign – Albert King | Stax 601015 |
| 24 What a Sad Feeling – Betty Harris | Stateside SS 475 – 1965 |
| 25 Confusion – Lee Dorsey | Stateside SS 552 – 1966 |
| 26 Get on Up – The Esquires | Stateside SS 2048 – 1967 |
| 27 Tell It Like It Is – Geno Washington & The Ram Jam Band | Piccadilly N.35403 – 1967 |
| 28 I'm a Fool to Want You – Ketty Lester | LP London HA – N2455 – 1962 |
| 29 The Nitty Gritty – Shirley Ellis | London HL 9823S – 1963 |
| 30 Get On The Right Track – Georgie Fame | EP Columbia SEG 8393 – 1965 |
| 31 Touch Me, Kiss Me, Hold Me – The Inspirations | Polydor 56730 – 1967 |
| 32 Stay – Virginia Wolves | Stateside SS 563 – 1966 |
| 33 We're Doing Fine – Dee Dee Warwick | Mercury MF867 – 1965 |
| 34 A Touch of Velvet a Sting Of Brass – The Moods Mosaic | Columbia DB7801 – 1966 |
| 35 Here She Comes – The Tymes | Cameo Parkway P.924 – 1964 |
| 36 (At the) Discotheque – Chubby Checker | Cameo-Parkway P949 – 1965 |
| 37 Girls Are Out to Get You – The Fascinations | Stateside SS 594 – 1967 |
| 38 We've Got Everything Going for Us – Kiki Dee | Fontana TF 792 – 1967 |
| 39 You're Ready Now – Frankie Valli | Philips BF1512 – 1966 |
| 40 Last Night – The Mar-Keys | London HLK-9399 – 1961 |
| 41 Love Is Strange – Betty Everett & Jerry Butler | Fontana TF 528 – 1964 |
| 42 The First Cut Is the Deepest – PP Arnold | Immediate IM047 – 1967 |
| 43 I – Kiki Dee | Fontana TF 833 – 1967 |
| 44 Take Me in Your Arms and Love Me – Gladys Knight & The Pips | Tamla Motown TMG 604 – 1966 |
| 45 A Groovy Kind of Love – Wayne Fontana & The Mindbenders | Fontana TF644 – 1965 |

# ACKNOWLEDGEMENTS

I want to thank my wife Julie for being my Beta reader and for providing much needed feedback during the writing of this novel. I must also mention Carl Blackburn and Nigel Deacon, who have been constant in encouraging me to write this sequel along with all the members of my Facebook group: John Knight @ Jimmy Mack.

Without the help I've received from Tony Beesley, Jayne Thomas, Franny O'Brien, Jason Disley, Jason Brummell, Mike Warburton, Nikki and Andy Topp-Walker, Curly and Kendra Waters, Mickey Danby-Foy, Natalie Allen, Lyn Rainford, Vivy Mower, Martin Dransfield, Hilary Magee, Rod Looker, Mark Aldridge, Ana Suy, Joanie Clarke, Richard Newsome, Sean Charlton, Ian Nicol, Steve Burke, and too many others to mention, I doubt I would have reached as many readers as I have. If I've missed mentioning anyone by name please forgive me.

Thanks also to Sarah Quigley for her professional and detailed copy/line edit of the manuscript. Without her attention to detail this novel would not be the best it could be. Finally I have to mention all who bought '*Jimmy Mack – Some Kind of Wonderful*' and have been waiting for this sequel – where would I be without you? I hope this sequel doesn't disappoint.

## About the author

John Knight was born in Halifax, West Yorkshire, in 1949. Now retired and living in Cheshire he divides his time between the UK and Spain. A Mod from the age of sixteen he believes that *once you're a Mod, you're always a Mod*. He is working on a series of novels set in the Sixties following on from *Jimmy Mack* and *Jimmy Mack 1967 – Strong Love (Side A)*. These will have parallel interweaving storylines.

# THE STORY BEHIND THE STORY

What prompted me to push the boundaries of fictional romance and begin to explore the idea of defying the conventional love story?

Answer: Monty Python's famous phrase, "…and now for something completely different."

Well, not quite but joking aside it was there somewhere in the creative mix. I'd started on the sequel to *Jimmy Mack* and was listening to the Soul Children's *I'll be the other woman.* I hadn't heard the song in years but hearing it again I found myself contemplating the lyrics. Before I knew it I had sought out William Bell's *"Trying to love two"* on the same theme. About the same time I also saw the movie *Professor Marston and the Wonder Wome*n dealing with an unusual, if little known, highly controversial domestic arrangement. Now, none of these were directly about the idea fermenting in my head. Recollecting a memory from my teenage years triggered further speculative thought. It was the tale of a young man who was two-timing his girlfriend(s). Not an uncommon situation in itself. I don't doubt it still happens now. What made it unusual? The girls *knew* he was two-timing yet both were apparently happy to go along with such an arrangement. I never did learn the long term outcome of that relationship but it fuelled my thinking. Inevitably this speculative pondering led me to ask…trying to love two…was it possibly to do? *Jimmy Mack 1967 Side B* may have the answers…but you'll have to wait and see.

Why not follow me?

**My Website**: johnknightnovelist.wixsite.com/mysite

**Facebook**: John Knight @ Jimmy Mack

**Twitter:** @JKnight_Author

# JIMMY MACK – SOME KIND OF WONDERFUL

The drug fuelled all-night Mod dance scene of the Sixties is the backdrop to a secret love. Soul music the soundtrack to this intense love affair.

You're never too young to fall in love. Some things are just meant to be. A wink outside church one Sunday brings Fiona "Effy" Halloran into James "Mack" MacKinnon's life. It's 1964 in the West Riding of Yorkshire For the two fifteen year olds the next two years will prove a test of their love and devotion to one another.

Growing up is never easy, nor is being young and in love. When Effy's sister Caitlin becomes pregnant by Mack's brother the lives of their families collide. Dealing with a feuding family, itself divided by religious zeal, becomes a serious obstacle for the young lovers. Separated by circumstances can their love for one another survive?

Over time Mack and Effy learn the truth about their respective families because secrets never stay secret forever.

"Jimmy Mack - Some Kind of Wonderful" is the first of a series of novels set in Bradford and Halifax between 1964 and 1969 involving the twosome and their friends. Parallel interweaving novels in the same time period are in the process of being written.

*"...this is a beautiful book. I couldn't wait to finish it and now I'm sad I have as I want more. It is a great journey through teenage life and love that we have all been a part of. I LOVE IT!"*

*"I absolutely love Jimmy Mack. Nostalgia, rite of passage and fashion and music. You covered it all. I am sad I finished it . I cannot wait for the next one."*

**AVAILABLE ONLINE FROM:**

Feed A Read (feedaread.com) and Amazon (amazon.co.uk)

**OR ORDER FROM YOUR LOCAL BOOKSHOP QUOTING:**

    **ISBN-10:** 1788760433
    **ISBN-13:** 978-1788760430

THE BEEFEATER COFFEE BAR

BLACK SWAN PASSAGE

BACK DOOR TO UPPER GEORGE PUBLIC HOUSE.

THE PLEBEIANS (AKA 'THE HALIFAX JAZZ CLUB')

Effy made Mack leave his schoolwork and revising, forcing him to take her out on a ride. They didn't go far. Only to Lister Park and to Cartwright Hall where they'd had their first date over two years earlier. Leaving the Lambretta in North Park Road they walked through the gate leading to the hall. She tried to raise his spirits, her arm tightly in his talking about the first time they'd come here. Stopping in the garden area not far from the main entrance he turned to her. She'd never seen him looking so scared. The young man she knew who never showed fear even when confronted with violence was quiet and seemed terrified.

"You haven't brought me here where we began to tell me it's all over, have you?"

# THE TWISTED WHEEL CLUB

6 WHITWORTH STREET, MANCHESTER 1

Tel. CENtral 1179

*presents*

## Saturday—Forthcoming Attractions

### FEBRUARY

4th **EDWIN STARR**

11th **ZOOT MONEY** BIG ROLL BAND

18th **GENO WASHINGTON** & the RAM JAM BAND

25th **CHRIS FARLOWE** & THE THUNDERBIRDS

### MARCH

4th **LEE DORSEY**

11th **EDWIN STARR**

18th **THE DRIFTERS**

25th **SOLOMON BURKE**

---

### *ADVANCE TICKETS NOW AVAILABLE*

---

POSTAL BOOKINGS ACCEPTABLE (S.A.E.)

No Parking on Whitworth Street, or Minshull
Street South PLEASE

CORPORATION CAR PARK AVAILABLE

Aytoun Street, Every Night (No Charge)

FEBRUARY and MARCH 1967.  (Chapters 23 & 29)

# CROMWELLIAN

## "3 FLOORS OF FUN AMIDST ELEGANT SPLENDOUR IN THE ROYAL BOROUGH OF KENSINGTON"

**Fully Licensed till 2·30am**

England's most famous Discotheque welcomes you

## 3 Cromwell Rd. Sth. Kensington

KNI 7258 for information

CHAPTER 35.

# THE RAMJAM CLUB

## 390 BRIXTON RD., LONDON, S.W.9 Tel. RED 3295

NON-MEMBERS' PRICE INCLUDES 1 YEAR'S MEMBERSHIP

| | |
|---|---|
| THURS., MAR. 23rd 7.30-11.30 p.m. | RAMJAM "HOT 100" DISC NIGHT |
| FRI., MAR. 24th 7.30-11.30 p.m. | JULIAN COVEY & THE MACHINE |
| SAT., MAR. 25th 7.30-11.30 p.m. | JOHN MAYALL'S BLUESBREAKERS |
| SUN., MAR. 26th 3-6 p.m. | RAMJAM "HOT 100" DISCS |
| SUN., MAR. 26th 7.30-11 p.m. | GENO WASHINGTON & THE RAMJAM BAND |
| MON., MAR 27th 7.30-11 p.m. | SPECIAL EASTER MONDAY SESSION THE ALLNIGHT WORKERS |

EASTER SUNDAY, 25th MARCH, 1967. (Chapters 39 & 40)

Lightning Source UK Ltd.
Milton Keynes UK
UKHW042133211118
332741UK00001B/54/P